F

Melindi, whose own hair was covered in a piece of headgear which looked as if she had spent last night busy with the remains of her shower curtain, then put forward her own idea which she had obviously been hatching for weeks. She suggested looking like silent movie stars: retro pin curls, pulling the hair off the face and baring the forehead and temples, waving hair into a thirties bob. There was a deathly hush. For once I felt sorry for Melindi. You could have heard a sequin drop.

'It's a sweet idea, darling,' Ingrid said when Melindi had finished. 'But it just won't do. It's far too old-fashioned.'

'Old-fashioned' is the *primus inter pares* of put downs. Old-fashioned, this magazine is not. We stand for modernity. 'What's new . . .' are the editor's favourite two words. We are thoroughly modern women. We know all about the latest in quick-drying nail-varnish so we can paint our nails in the back of the chauffeur-driven car as we nip off to take over ICI and accept the Booker Prize two days after producing our second gorgeous baby, and fit in time for having our hair cut while preparing our lecture on the latest developments in nuclear fission and teaching the four-year-old to read while not forgetting to run an elderly neighbour to hospital and take the empty Bollingers to the bottle bank.

FAIR SEX

Sarah Foot

Mandarin

A Mandarin Paperback
FAIR SEX

First published in Great Britain 1991
by William Heinemann Ltd
This edition published 1992
Reprinted 1992 (three times)
by Mandarin Paperbacks
Michelin House, 81 Fulham Road, London SW3 6RB

Mandarin is an imprint of Reed Consumer Books Ltd

Copyright © Sarah Foot 1991
The author has asserted her moral rights

A CIP catalogue record for this title
is available from the British Library

ISBN 0 7493 0893 1

Printed and bound in Great Britain
by Cox & Wyman Ltd, Reading, Berks

Fair Sex

1

The Sleek Shall Inherit the Earth

Ingrid, the beauty editor, pulled a prize-size pineapple out of her Hermès bag and started sawing the top off.

'I thought yesterday was your pineapple day,' I said. Normally she only has one pineapple day a week – when she eats nothing but pineapple – and becomes impossible to work with, though not as wretched as I would be sticking to pineapples all day.

'Aren't you overdoing it? You know, with two in a row?'

'Christmas, darling. Christmas – got to save myself.' At sixty-one, Ingrid is a tribute to the power of unremitting self-discipline and incomputable expenditure on collagen injections, haircuts, waxing, Slendertone and pineapples. She speared a chunk. 'Well Eliza, what is it?'

'It's the new colour in make-up article.'

'I thought Rosanna was writing that.'

'She was, but she won't be back until after the weekend now so I'm doing it. And I'm not sure what the new colour is.'

'She should have been back yesterday.'

'I know, but she's ill with food poisoning.'

'Ugh. What sort?'

'Smoked salmon.'

'The worst.'

I have worked for *Circe* magazine for four years. Rosanna and I write all the fashion and beauty articles. Normally we work together but she had taken the beginning of the week off to go to Rome. She was due back yesterday but had phoned from a suite in the Hotel Eden to say she was laid up in bed with smoked salmon food poisoning. Laid up in bed she is, but it is with a man named Xavier, not food poisoning.

'So, Ingrid, what colour is it?'

'Yellow.'

'Yellow? Yellow make-up?'

'Yes, but you mustn't say it's yellow. We're saying it's melon, "The Melon Face", or something like that. Somewhere under here,' she said, rooting around amongst the massed battalions of pots, jars, bottles, tubs and tubes of handcream, nail-varnish remover, cellulite vanisher, tanning lotion and her horde of Chanel earrings which she collects the way other people collect stamps. 'Here we are: "Hot Trotting Ginger Lip Gloss", "Sweet and Golden Honeycomb Foundation", "Shameless Bronze Blusher", you should try some of the blusher, you're looking a bit pale, "Desert Sand Lipstick".'

'Ingrid,' interrupted Melindi, Ingrid's newest assistant. 'Reception say there are two Koala bears downstairs for you.'

'Well go and get them, darling.'

'Are people actually supposed to realise that you're wearing yellow lipstick,' I persisted, 'or is it just to give a natural sheen or gloss or whatever?'

'It's a – '

'Eliza,' shouted Naomi, the editor's secretary. 'Lady Human is on the phone for you.'

'Oh God.' I hate Lady Human. She prides herself on being the busiest woman in Greater London and is featuring in an article on the fifty most beautiful women in Britain. I have to ask her for her beauty tips. 'And in a fearful hurry, she says,' continued Naomi.

'Ingrid, two minutes . . . Lady Human? Hello, this is Eliza Hart. Thank you for getting back to me. As you know, underneath your photo we want to put a couple of lines about your beauty routine. If you exercise, or like a particular make of cream, that sort of thing.'

'Cold baths,' she said grimly.

'Cold baths?'

'Yes. Preferably ice-cold. If you sit in an ice-cold bath for five minutes each morning with the water up to your neck – you have to have it up to your neck otherwise you don't burn off enough calories – you need never exercise or diet as seventy-five per cent of your calories are used up in keeping warm. And aside from the advantage of staying slim, all that cold water tones up your skin.'

'That's, er, unusual,' I said.

'Is that enough for you?'

'Good God, yes. Ample. Thank you. More than enough. Thank you very much. Goodbye. She takes cold baths,' I said to Ingrid, 'to burn off calories.'

'What a brilliant idea. I might try it. Do a feature on it. Or perhaps *you* could try it, for a month or so. Take a cold bath every morning and write about whether it makes any difference.'

'No thanks. But what about the melon face?'

'Well, it's not a true yellow. Not a full-blown golden yellow like, er, like pineapple for instance. ' "Desert sand lipstick",' she quoted from the press release, ' "for lips with a higher intensity".' There you are. Good grief, Melindi!' Melindi had a three-foot high, fluffy toy koala with her.

'There is another one downstairs,' said Melindi.

'It's got a funny smell,' said Ingrid, sniffing. 'What on earth is it?'

'Jasmine, musk, rose,' Melindi read from a press release.

'Oh – it's Stunner.' Stunner was a new perfume from one of the largest beauty houses. 'They've obviously been soaked in it. Dreadful. Well go and get the other one, darling. And Eliza, I don't think I can help you any more as you want the pictures, don't you?'

'Have you got them?'

'No. Persephone has.'

Persephone is the fashion editor and she was puce with rage as she could not hear herself on the phone. Not being able to hear is something we have all had to put up with since a psychologist on sabbatical from Harvard redesigned the offices six months ago. Now it is open plan with white walls, stripped pine floors, plenty of glass and, significantly, a peach ceiling which, the psychologist had shown on experiments with rats, promoted lucid, lively thinking. Previously the office had been divided up into tiny cubbyholes and we had padded around noiselessly on a magenta carpet. It was unremittingly ugly but Persephone had had her own room with a door which shut and a window. It had been a small window but had afforded a view of the Serpentine for those, like the fashion editor, who were over six foot tall. Now she looks out on dripping gutters, the Abbey National manager drinking his tea, a few inches of grey sky above, countless dustbins below and a BMW garage which sends lead-laden petrol fumes wafting straight up through her window and which wreak havoc with her skin.

She was in the throws of trying to persuade the photographer Lord Rainedon, who had already gone to his villa in Positano for Christmas, to return to London to re-photograph the March magazine cover which was a picture of a sixteen-year-old from Norfolk who had won the magazine's competition to discover 'Britain's Unknown Beauty'. In order to win the contest the girl had spent weeks starving herself to photo-thin perfection, but the moment she heard that she had won, she could not be doing with just two lettuce leaves and a carrot a day and had tucked right back into her usual heavy, hearty diet. Lord Rainedon, however, had not taken her picture until a couple of days ago, two months after the competition finals, and during these two months the new touchstone of British beauty had put on twenty pounds. This meant she was too fat for the cover, as for photographs you have to be as thin as a worm otherwise you look all lumpen.

'Rainy, please,' pleaded Persephone. 'It won't be the same if someone else does it . . . No Monday is too soon as she won't have lost enough weight by then . . . Absolutely awful – really jowly, a double chin almost . . . After Christmas is too late . . . Thursday would be best, she'll look better by then and you could fly back that night or stay for the Christmas party and go back Christmas Eve . . . You don't know how I'd appreciate it . . . Please, Rainy . . . Oh Rainy . . . Oh you angel. Thank you, thank you . . . I do appreciate it, very much . . . Darling, thank you. Goodbye.' She beamed. 'Eliza, you want the make-up pictures?'

'Please.'

'Here are the ones for the pink make-up.'

'Pink? I thought it was yellow.'

'No it's yellow and pink. Not worn together on the same face, of course. The point is that there's freedom of choice in this spring's colours. Have you spoken to the editor about it?'

'No.'

'Well, I know she wants a word with you. Naomi should have told you.'

'What about the yellow pictures?'

'Unusable. Quite dreadful in fact. Basil is going to have to re-shoot them on Monday.'

Naomi was cooing down the phone to her boyfriend, Rolo. Roland is a farmer in Dorset and because he won't leave his cattle on their own at night Naomi commutes back and forth to Powerstock every day and this makes her too weary to work.

'Eliza,' she interrupted Rolo. 'I'm sorry. Madam's been wanting to see you for ages. I meant to tell you, but old Max turned up and she had to see him. It's about his wallpaper or something. She won't give him more than ten minutes.'

Max is a brilliant shoe designer. I once described a pair of his strawberry suede slippers as 'cultural icons', whatever that means, and he was so delighted he sent me a twelve-strong bunch of numinous alabaster-white lilies. Now, however, he has started branching out from shoes into interior design.

He walked out of the office, as tanned as a conker and dressed in a jacket printed with the same pattern as his first wallpaper collection: black Baroque squiggles on white, also available in white Baroque squiggles on black.

'Eliza, what a lovely surprise to see you out here.'

'And you, Max. You're looking really well. How are you?'

'Not as well as I look.' He nodded into the office. 'I don't think, in fact I know – I can tell – she didn't like the collection.'

'But we've got your shoes in virtually every other picture in the January issue.'

'No, not my shoe collection. She loves my shoes. She was wearing them herself, the plain lizard-skin stilettos with the extra sharply pointed toe, you know. But I need more than shoes now. I know I make the best shoes in the world but I wanted her to like my fabrics, not just for curtains but sofas, cushions, lampshades too – my wallpapers, all with matching friezes – everything you could want. But she doesn't like them. She just said she would bear them in mind.'

'Hmm. Perhaps you should try someone else.'

'That's what she said.'

'Oh Max, I'm sorry. I'm rather struck with the jacket though – quite remarkable.'

'She said the same, that it was the sort of jacket you couldn't help remarking on.'

'With padded shoulders, too.'

'They're mine.'

'What are?'

'The shoulders. They're mine. They're not padded.'

'Eliza,' bellowed the editor.

Max gave me three pecks on the cheek, turned on his £600-leather brogues with understated tassels and walked off.

The editor's office is full of plants to stop the air getting too dry and ruining her skin. There are orange trees, stephanotis bushes, and pots of jasmine which Naomi has to water with tepid boiled water. Her matt black desk was empty except for some snapdragons flourishing in a chilly white vase. I had to wait six minutes for her to look up from her paper. When I was new it took her nine. In six years' time she should notice me right away.

'Sit down, darling,' she said, taking off her freshly laundered white gloves which she wears to stop the newspaper print making her hands grimy. 'Have you grasped the point of this make-up story?'

'Not exactly. I know there are two main looks – one pink, one yellow – and I've only seen the pink pictures.'

'The melon ones are being re-shot. But the point of both the pink and melon face – that's what I want you to call the story,

6

melon, a honey-dew melon obviously, not a water melon, most definitely not a yellow face, yellow sounds so terribly ugly – is the whole new interest in colour in make-up. It's a definite move away from the restraint of a bland natural look and ties in with a burgeoning femininity. It's about looking womanly and enjoying looking womanly. You no longer have to restrain yourself in your use of make-up, Make-up suggests, even shouts sexuality. But painting your face with strong colours is not about turning yourself into a Sixties doll fit for doing nothing but smiling sweetly at the man driving you in his sports car. Now, women own the sports cars.' She smiled. 'That's the sort of tone I want you to give the piece. In essence, strong use of colour shows how you are in control of your looks and life. All right?'

I blanched. 'Fine. Just fine,' I said, and she picked up her phone which meant I was dismissed.

Dorothy Parker once wrote: 'Brevity is the soul of lingerie,' and that line is held up as something for Rosanna and me to aspire to. And we must also throw in plenty of puns as the editor simply adores them. Pages of banality are excused for a bit of brilliant word play. I couldn't think of any because Melindi, who is named after the town in Africa where she was born, sits within a lipstick's throw of my desk and all the time she was either humming – oh do stop humming Melindi – or phoning her French lover when Ingrid was out the room, or gossiping with the fashion assistants about the billowing bloomers she was wearing and had made at the weekend out of an old shower curtain which she had dyed black.

'Wonderful . . . like modern harem pants,' they were all saying. 'A bit like what Joey was showing at the collections . . . Did you see his collection . . . wonderful . . . so wonderful I cried . . . She's so into her job she cries at all the collections . . . Has she seen these . . .? A shower curtain . . . ? I suppose you could use any sort of curtain.'

And Ingrid kept interrupting to tell me she was having lunch with one of her old schoolfriends. Ingrid's hobby is taking her contemporaries to lunch and coming back to tell us how much wrinklier, greyer and stouter they are than her.

I had just put the monochrome world of make-up through its final, painful death throes and was heralding the advent of the new blazing rainbow of pink and melon faces in heavy-breathing superlatives, when Melindi shouted that there was someone on the phone for me. 'It's personal and he says it's urgent.'

'Oh, put it through, put it through,' I said eagerly, perking up like a Pavlov dog.

'Eliza?' It was The Natterjack Toad.

'Jack. What do you want?' I snapped.

'Were you hoping I was somebody else?'

'Jack, I'm really busy.'

'Why, is there a revolution in suntan lotions going on?'

'Look I'm really tied up.' As far as The Natterjack is concerned I am busier than Lady Human.

'I know you're not. But anyway, Eliza,' he paused, crooning my name as closely as if we had just spent the night together, 'I wondered, please, if you could do me a favour.'

'What is it?'

'Tonight, could you possibly do some babysitting?'

'Babysitting? No, of course not. I'm busy.'

'You're busy tonight as well as now?'

'Yes.'

'How come you're so busy? You never used to be. What is it? A hot date?'

'No. Yes.'

'What do you mean "no, yes"? It is a date and not a hot one or it's – '

'Oh Jack, shut up. Of course I can't babysit. Ring up an agency or wherever people normally find babysitters. Anyway, whose baby is it?'

'I thought you'd ask. Friends', over from New York and we've rung every agency in London but they're all booked up with Christmas parties and we can't get anyone. Look, I'll get Grace to put some food out for you – smoked salmon. I've never known you turn that down.' (Grace is his wife, so lovely she is being featured as one of the fifty most beautiful women in Britain.)

'I've told you, I can't.'

'All right, all right. So you're busy. What are you up to then?'

'We'll probably just stay in,' I said innocently.

'So I could bring the baby round to your place.'

'Of course not. Don't be stupid. Anyway,' I mused, 'I'll be busy making supper.'

'Has your cooking improved, to enable you to win men via their stomachs?'

'No, I've never aimed that high.'

'Oh Eliza,' he laughed. 'Dear old Eliza, you don't change. Well, whatever it is you are doing, I hope you have a good time.'

'I certainly will,' I lied and put the phone down.

Even if I had been going out I would not have got there on time as it took me until nine to finish dredging up the words.

'Now, after understated seasons, colours are seen and not blurred. A new definition comes to the fore. Vividness reveals a strong sense of purpose. Spring seduction demands a new brightness, a new brilliance, a new clarity in make-up. Now women show their true colours . . . lips shining lusciously in sun-kissed melon, the unfathomable allure of eyes hooded in golden topaz . . . eyes defined with deadly nightshade pencil, the temptation of lips like crushed strawberries, lips like raspberry cordials.'

Make-up must be consumed lustfully. What delicious lips you have, my dear. Oh yes! All the better to eat you with. The article should suggest that new make-up assures you of all the food and sex you ever wanted. If only it did. Oh if only it did for I have access to all the make-up I ever wanted as Ingrid had told me to help myself to anything I liked, to Hot Trotting Ginger lips, Marshmallow blushes, Sphinx Amber eyes, whatever. Oh, if only.

2

I'll Give You a Ring

My neighbour's pet, but far from tame, cat leapt out and laddered my tights when I got home. They were my zebra tights too. Although at five foot two I fail the magazine's height test – no one, other than myself, is less than five foot seven which makes them all high enough to be models – I make short work of the slimness test. Even in horizontal black-and-white striped tights, my legs look fashionably spindly, modish etiolated pins of skin and bones. I have a metabolism you don't forget, a man, whose name I have forgotten, once told me. I eat boiled sweets I find on the floor of the car, crusts on sandwiches, sugar lumps after dinner, peanut butter toast, everything. And I never put on weight. I am deeply envied by everyone on the magazine, as they all cultivate the skeletal look.

My zebra tights were ruined. And they were expensive. I had worn them with my fake leopardskin dress, black bear of a coat and my mouse boots which have eyes and whiskers at the toes, so I had looked like some sort of hybrid escaped from the zoo. Clothes are a consuming passion of mine. Indeed, my most enduring love affair has been with the contents of my wardrobe but this is not a state of affairs I like to dwell upon.

It was noisy in my flat. I am in the catchment area of an overcrowded mental hospital which releases less serious cases into the community and particularly into my block of flats. Half of the flats have been sold off to the general public which includes me. The other half are still owned by the council. My left neighbour, who specialises in bondage, was at work, which was why her cat was locked out in the hall. Some of her customers are allergic to its fur. Duncan, who lives below me, was practising his bugle. Duncan is mentally ill and should be in hospital but there is no room for him so he has to be housed in my block of flats and has been given a bugle to keep him occupied. On my right, the ninety-two-year-old colonel, who believes unmarried women living on their own are either witches or whores, was back from hospital and watching a wildlife programme on dogs that whistle, loudly.

My flat was cold too. And so was I. It was a real bruiser of a winter – the worst this century, the newspapers kept gleefully reporting. And my feet were so, so cold. Sometimes I feel I will drown in all the cold. Each day the cold breaks a new record and it just freezes me up. But at least there were three messages on the answering machine. One was from my friend Kate, the second was from Tim St. George, saying we kept missing each other. The reason St. George and I keep missing each other is that I never answer the phone when he rings and I only ring him back when I know he will be out.

It is costing me a fortune keeping St. George at bay. Even though he will inherit a village in Somerset, complete with church, manor house and duck pond, I always have to split the bill when we go out for, however hard I try to like him and overcome my prejudice against his ridiculous name, I cannot work up anything warmer towards him than total indifference.

The third was from Rosanna in Rome apologising profusely for leaving me all her extra work.

Rosanna has been seeing Xavier for the past couple of months, and last weekend he had to go to Rome for business. As her existence is unbearable without him, as she regards life pre-Xavier as worthless, just an interlude before meeting Superman, she persuaded Persephone to let her do a profile on a Roman shoe designer with an atelier near the Spanish Steps. (It takes three people two days working full time to make one pair of his shoes as they are handmade and studded with glass sequins.) And she talked the travel editor into commissioning her to write an article on 'Unknown Rome' – all this so Xavier would not have the presumption to think she was in Rome just because of him.

I replayed the tape. There was no message from Sam. I replayed it again. It said the same thing. Still no message from Sam.

I'm in a critical state about this man Sam. Pitiful, actually. Quite pitiful. I met him in the summer at NASA though he is not an astronaut, thankfully. That would be appalling luck, falling for someone who worked in outer space. Rome is bad enough. Instead, Sam is a doctor and an expert in bones and he was in NASA to discuss the effect of gravity on cell renewal in bones. The reason I too was in NASA of all places was that I had been invited there by one of the top American cosmetic and skincare companies for the launch of a new beauty cream. Ingrid had wanted to go but it had coincided with a major symposium in Jordan on anti-wrinkle creams so I went in her stead. (Beauty organisations can afford to give these sort of trips because even a large tub of anti-wrinkle cream costs peanuts to make. Besides, one line of editorial is worth one page of advertising in black and white or half a page of colour.) A group of beauty editors and I had therefore spent two days touring cosmetic factories and being lectured on moisturisers and the properties of retin-A before the grand finale of the trip: a reception at NASA to meet some astronauts.

So I was at the NASA reception, standing around feeling as I often do at parties – that I am at the wrong one – when I saw Sam put his hands on a huge globe. He was about six foot six, had a nose which had been broken, and he looked as if he might throw the globe out of the window. Then he saw me watching him and walked over and said thank God he had seen me in time, that I had saved him, that he had been about to pitch the globe out the window, that he felt like a weed at a flower show, that he hated these sorts of parties and that if I had one iota of compassion in me would I go to the moon with him? Failing that, would I have a drink with him?

He said something else which I didn't catch for he had a smile which was enough for five and eyes which reduced me to a puddle of lust, so deep a puddle that I abandoned all intentions of going out to the final beauty supper with an after-dinner speech on a new permanent tear-proof mascara, and went and had a drink. And then I went and had dinner.

Never sleep with someone the first time you meet. Never. Ever ever. This is a rule I have. Not even if I can't remember the last time I had a scrap of sex. Not even if he is beside himself with desire. Not even if I am. Never. This is a rule I have and I have never broken it, except I broke it then. Because the night was hot and lust lay heavy on the flower beds and the air had drunk the drowsy smell out of the mimosa. And because I wanted to, very much.

So I went back to his hotel with him. I don't think you ever feel as naked as you do the first night. You break in two and while one half of you acts, the other stands apart, looking at you stripped bare and reproaching, while what you should be doing is enjoying the task in hand. In seconds that delicious antici-pation becomes a tortuous traffic jam of questions: 'What if he hates my cold feet?' 'What if I arouse him in such a way that all he can turn on is *Match of the Day*?' 'What if I go so far as to tempt him to bolt out the door in horrorstruck shock?' This last thought was uppermost in my mind when, with his arms around me to draw me onto the bed, he suddenly pushed me away and leapt up off the bed with a shout rather like a cry of great pain.

'What is it?' I said, marvelling over my effect on men as he scampered about looking for the light switch.

'The bed . . .' he began and started to laugh. With the light on we saw a steady trickle of water coming through the ceiling. The mattress was soaked right through and all cold and clammy. 'Right,' he said, hurling himself into his suit. 'You're not putting up with this.'

(What had happened, explained the manager next morn-ing, was that the man in the room above us liked to bathe in clean running water so he kept the taps running with the plug out. But the water ran into the bath much quicker than it ran out down the plug hole. 'A lot of hotels are having similar problems, especially with their Japanese customers. They like to have a bath but don't like wallowing in dirty water . . .' the manager had gone on.)

13

The only remaining empty room was the bridal suite, and in a heart-shaped bed, with room for six, shrimp-pink sheets, and a six-foot-high red velvet heart for a bedstead, we made love with a delicious, furious, tenderness. But the delight of that warmth and closeness left me with such a sadness. Although we lay wound together we were held tight by nothing but the thinnest thread, for the swooning pleasure of possession is so transitory. That rapturous trance of wanting and being wanted breaks so easily. And as I was grimly wondering why I was pursued by a second-rate Cupid who made me fall for someone an ocean away from London, Sam propped himself up on his elbow and grinned at me warmly.

'I see why it's the wedding bed.'

Wedding bed, I thought with horror. He's married.

But he is not married. Three weeks later, during one of our phone calls, he told me that he was intending getting married last June but that in April the woman he was supposed to marry called it off. With the assistance of her therapist she had decided that long-term relationships were an impossibility. She said that as people were always developing and changing they inevitably grew apart. When I asked Sam if he thought she was right he said he had simply no idea any more.

Next morning in NASA, however, I had to fly to New York to stay with some friends before going home. Three days later Sam too would be in New York for a conference before he flew home to Boston. We would be in New York together for two days during which time we arranged to meet.

The first day neither of us could make dinner as he had to spend the evening at a big conference dinner and my friends were taking me out. So we met for lunch. But lunch is not fit for those for whom you harbour ultra-fond thoughts and should be reserved for business or old friends.

We met the next night and for once I couldn't eat. So we walked back in the direction of his hotel and the moon was high in the sky and the air was soft and warm and we were standing under a tree and the breeze rustling the leaves echoed his laugh and he had his arms tight around me and I

14

was in a decidedly good mood with delicious thoughts of bliss to come. But then I felt this scratching in my throat, and a pressure behind my eyes forcing me to screw them up, and an unbearable tickle in my nose, and in half a second a shock jolted into my head and I sneezed, not an ordinary sneeze but an outrageous sneeze, a sneeze of the gods, so almighty that my nose started bleeding. Bleeding everywhere, simply everywhere, all over my white linen blouse, all over his white shirt, all over my bare feet in their new red suede shoes.

I had been having these nose bleeds every day for the past two weeks and each day they were getting worse. But this was the greatest of them all. I just could not stop it. Sam had a hankerchief but I drenched that in seconds. Blood simply poured forth. Sam ran off to fetch some ice from a man selling Slush Puppies nearby and then packed the ice at the back of my neck and held my nose. He pinched it tightly. How suddenly our circumstances in life can change, I thought miserably as cold melting water dribbled down my back and warm sticky blood congealed on my face.

For ten minutes he stood there, holding the ice and my nose while I sat on a bollard. But still all my blood poured and poured on the pavement. Another five minutes later it still hadn't stopped and he asked me if I had a lot of nosebleeds. I said that over the past couple of weeks I had. Had I had one as bad as that before? he asked. No, I hadn't. He said I'd have to have my nose cauterised. There was no question of it. Being a doctor I suppose he should have known. So he tried to hail a taxi but the first four drove on, worried I might infect them with Aids or spoil their upholstery and in the end he had to flag down a police car and they took me to hospital.

It was three in the morning when a doctor eventually saw me although Sam volunteered to cauterise my nose if they would just provide him with the right equipment. That was not how I had envisaged the evening ending. So we just sat on hard chairs, me as rigid as a coat hanger with my mouth open otherwise I could not breathe and hardly able to talk, and him making a joke out of the whole palaver and telling me how he broke his nose walking into a glass door.

We finally got away about four-thirty a.m. as it took ages filling in all the forms for my insurance and so on. My plane was leaving at eight and he said he would take me to the airport. So we got into a cab. It was an expensive evening for him, driving me around all night as he insisted on paying and I let him. I don't mind men I like being out of pocket on my behalf but I am ready to kick men I dislike in the kidneys if they don't let me pay my way. So we sat in the cab with the meter ticking away in the background and he held my hand and we went to my friend's house where I said a bleary goodbye and collected my suitcases.

By this time, as New York had been boiling all week, it was already getting too hot inside the cab, and outside, when we got to JFK airport, the sun was blinding, glaring harshly as it shone in mirrors of parked cars and the painfully shining metal which was everywhere, reflecting my bloody face. I checked in and in the fifteen minutes before I went through customs Sam kept saying that if he wasn't a tough tower of a man he would cry with the frustration of it all, and the idea of this mad man threatening to cry made me go weak. But our time was up and he gave me a couple of kissess which were very short as I can't hold my breath for long, and a hug, if you can hug a coat hanger – which you can't – and he said he would phone me.

I didn't know if he would. I didn't know if I was just someone he had spent the night with. But he did ring me. Two days later, on a Sunday. And since then I have spoken to him every Sunday. And I speak to him on one of my phones as I have four phones, one in each of my four rooms. (Two years ago I had a four-week aberration with someone in advertising called Ashley – I don't know what came over me, a temporary mental disorder or something – and he was working on the British Telecom account at the time and kept presenting me with phones in new trial colours and designs. I've got a mushroom-shaped phone in the kichen, a hideous mermaid in the bathroom. My old black phone I left in the main room and Executive Steel I put in the bedroom.)

Normally I would not expect a call from Sam on a Thursday

night but last Sunday he said he would ring me during the week. All four began ringing. The wretched things don't ring in unison and the new ones are inordinately shrill so I feel I am living with a barber-shop quartet. I picked up the mushroom.

It was my friend Kate on the line. I have known Kate all my life. There is just a four-week age difference between us, and her parents have lived next door to mine in Hounslow for thirty years. (I would have been called 'Hounslow' if I had had Melindi's parents.)

'Thanks for the message,' I said. 'I was just about to ring you back.'

'I'm at Robert's so I thought I'd better ring you. I've got some news.'

'Yes,' I said, a familiar sinking feeling washing over me.

'I've got engaged.'

'Congratulations,' I enthused. 'That's wonderful. I'm so pleased. Really lovely news.'

'Isn't it? I just wasn't expecting it.'

Wasn't expecting it? *I* was expecting it. Kate is relentless in pursuit, has dauntless spirit of resolution, knows exactly what she wants from life and exactly how to get it.

'No, not at all. It completely surprised me. We were at Mon Plaisir on Tuesday night. We just thought we would go out to dinner.' As Robert is one of the country's top barristers on trade union law and, in her international company of solicitors, Kate is tipped to be the first partner under thirty, going to Mon Plaisir is like popping out for a curry. 'And we had just ordered the coffee when Robert said he had something important to ask me. And I thought, oh no, something is wrong, it's something serious, but then, well then he asked me.'

'How lovely.'

'And he produced this ring.'

'There and then?'

'Yes.'

'God, I hope you like it.' Kate has such fixed ideas of what she likes.

'Oh yes. Though he couldn't really go wrong as he knows I love emeralds and almost everything from Tiffany's. You'll love it. It's beautiful, actually.'

'Lovely,' I raved, repeatedly.

'And Eliza.'

'Yes?'

'I want you to be a bridesmaid.'

'Oh no. No I can't. I really can't. Kate, no, I can't, please.'

'What on earth do you mean? You've got to be a bridesmaid. It's all planned: you and Robert's nieces.' Less than forty-eight hours after getting engaged Kate has the wedding planned. All her life she has known exactly what sort of wedding she wants. At last she can put the plans into action.

'You've got to be. You're my oldest friend. Eliza, you must.'

'But I've never been a bridesmaid before.'

'That doesn't matter. If Robert's nieces, four-year-olds, can do it, you can do it at almost twenty-eight.'

'But I just don't want to start now,' I said.

'Be a matron of honour then.'

'You've got to be married to be a matron of honour.'

'Well, maid of honour? Hold on a minute. Look I've got to go. I'm cooking something. And Robert has just come in. I'm not going to let you get away with this. I'll ring you back. Hello, darling . . . And you're coming round for supper on Tuesday, aren't you?' she continued to me. 'You really must meet this friend of Robert's. It's just going to be you, him, Robert and me. I think you'll really like him.'

'Oh, Kate, no. Not again.' Ever since the NASA fiasco Kate has been holding little dinner parties for me to meet eligible men. The doggily devoted St. George, the man who says he is always missing me, is one of Kate's finds.

'But he's really nice. Robert knows him from Cambridge. I'm sure you'll like him. He's, well, he's umm, he's quite attractive. Not devastating. But nice-looking in a perfectly ordinary sort of way. You know.'

'But, Kate – '

'It's better than moping over what's-his-name, The Bostonian.'

'Sam, and I'm not – '

'Have you spoken to him lately?'

'He said he'd give me a ring tonight.'

'And you're staying in so you don't miss him. Honestly, Eliza. Give Tim a ring. I know he really likes you. He's always asking after you. I've got to go now but speak to Tim. Get him to take you out. And I'll ring you at the weekend. Take care. Bye then.'

'Goodbye,' I said. 'Congratulations to Robert.'

I was with Kate when she met Robert. It was the first really hot day of last summer and we were playing tennis at the Hurlingham Club which Kate had joined more for the other players than the tennis. We were playing doubles with an old friend of Kate's from LSE who was bringing a friend. The friend, of course, turned out to be Robert. The moment he swung himself out of his silver convertible Mercedes Kate gave him that look she always gives new men. She looks at men she is meeting for the first time as other people look at the passengers when collecting someone from an airport. Are they who you are waiting for? Mr Wrong? Mr Not Quite Right? Wrong again. Mr Right?

On meeting Robert, up and down went her eyes, assessing all six foot, all twelve and a half stone of him, his thirty-five years, his black with grey hair, blue eyes, choice of sneakers, socks – shame about the knee-length socks – his legs – bronzed – his car, aluminium racket. Obviously he was all right. Or at least Mr Right Now.

I replaced the mushroom receiver and foraged about for some food. I don't know where all my food goes. I thought I had some. I could only find some cereal but I didn't have any milk, and my bumper box of marzipan strawberries which I had been saving. I ate all twenty-four and then went to bed. But I couldn't sleep because the man two doors along was drilling, fitting in his new do-it-yourself kitchen, the corrugated iron roof on the roadmenders' hut was clanging loose, someone was playing football with fifty-odd beer cans, Duncan was practising 'Silent Night' and I started making a list of all the things wrong in my life.

At midnight the phones rang. I picked up Executive Steel. There was a breathing noise. Oh no, I thought, not dirty phone calls, please. Then a weak woman's voice asked, 'Is that Dolly?'

'No,' I said. 'I'm sorry, you've got the wrong number.'

I hate wrong numbers when it's late, when I'm on my own and especially when I'm hoping for a phone call. A man never rings you when you want him to, when, if he asked you to darn his socks, swing upside down from the shower rail, change his tyre, walk to Peckham with him, wear bright blue eyeshadow, make tea for his football team, dress in crimplene, learn Turkish, or if he asked if he could have you on the back of his motorcycle, by the fish finger freezer in Safeway's, in a bed with dirty sheets, on top of the council rubbish tip, in a draughty garden shed, on a slab of concrete, you would say yes, yes, anything you ask.

I got up and picked the raisins out of the cereal while reading in the paper about the prospect of an electricity workers' strike. My heating runs on electricity. I read the world weather report. It was −10° in Toronto. It could be worse. I could be in Toronto.

3

Model Women

'Absolutely not,' said Bella the travel editor as we were waiting for the lift next morning. Bella is the only woman I know who has worn pure linen on a plane without creasing it. 'You must refuse, Eliza. I advise all my friends over twenty-five never to be bridesmaids. And most definitely not schoolfriends. She'll only put you in some frightful frilly number and you'll have to live with the photos for the rest of your life and you'll have all those other old schoolfriends seeing you look as if you are still seventeen dressed up in all that rampant virginity. No, Eliza. You'll regret it. Just don't. Jasper Conran is much more you.' She sneezed. 'Oh come on.'

We had been waiting for the lift so long that a large puddle had formed at my feet as all the snow from my Victorian boots had melted onto the reception's beige marble floor.

'We're really late,' she grumbled. I am always late when I wear these boots as it takes me ten minutes getting them on, threading and tying all the laces. Not that I am ever in any hurry to get to my desk.

'Come on,' she said crossly and punched the lift button with her French-manicured thumb and off snapped her nail. 'Goodness, that was lucky,' she said picking up the broken end. 'I could have lost it. Ingrid should have some of that stuff for sticking it back on, shouldn't she?'

'Yes – pots.'

'Good morning, ladies,' said the Chairman. *Circe* is just one of the twenty-two magazines he owns. He also owns three Rolls Royces, has four houses and two chins. During the five years since he bought the company he has doubled its already immense profits by buying magazines specialising in cars, racing and royal gossip. He has, maintains Ingrid, lowered the tone of the place irretrievably. 'Yet another cold day freezing ahead of us,' he said pleasantly as Bella started sneezing again. 'Bella, you sound ill.' The lift arrived. 'Perfect timing. After you, ladies. Bella, shouldn't you be at home?'

Bella blew her nose silently. 'It is not as bad as it sounds.' She smiled wanly. The lift is lined with mirrors so unless you keep your eyes on the floor you have a view of yourself from all angles. 'Or as bad as it looks. And my nose . . .' Bella assessed all the many reflecting planes of her nose. 'My nose would make Rudolf jealous.'

The Chairman found this a funny little joke and smiled. Bella smiled too, not wanly this time, but the smile of a woman who knows that she looks good even with a nose Rudolf the red-nosed reindeer would envy. She took another look and beamed some more. Truly, it was a lovely red nose.

'Goodbye then, ladies,' said the Chairman as we got out and he rose up to the eleventh floor. 'Take care of yourself, Bella.'

'Yes,' whispered Bella as if auditioning for Camille.

'*Ma petite,*' Melindi called out crossly before I had got a boot off.

'Yes, Melindi, what is the matter now?' Melindi's meta-morphosis from tea girl – black with lemon, no sugar – into upstart 'fashionette' and member of Ingrid's burgeoning bevy of assistants, has filled me with a mixture of admiration and horror. She began working for the magazine in her summer holiday from her Design School in Paris, which is part, she claims, of the Sorbonne. But when summer was over she would not go back and stayed on here to transform herself into an integral part of the magazine.

'*Ma petite.* You've had hundreds of phone calls.'

'Oh yes,' I said eagerly.

'I began taking messages but then I just got too busy so I had to take the phone off the hook. I really don't – '

'Are these the messages?' Several scraps of paper were splattered with Melindi's great green scrawl. 'Is this all?'

'I really don't have time . . .'

22

Five people had rung: my mother, St. George again, my friend Cassandra, a dress designer called Mr Brook-Barclay, and someone with a Chelsea number named Lucinda Windsor.

I rang Lucinda Windsor first. With a name like that I thought it might be an amazing job offer or an invitation to the Palace but she was a reader who wanted to know what size turkey she needed for twelve. The food and wine editor was away on a gastronomic tour of the Armagnac region. 'Get the biggest you can find,' I said and rang my mother.

She wanted to tell me that someone I knew at primary school was expecting her second baby.

'How nice,' I said.

'Also, Wendy,' she went on. (Wendy is a neighbour's daughter.) 'Wendy thinks her baby will be born on Christmas Day and it's definitely a girl so she thinks she will call it Ivy, or maybe Holly.'

'That's very nice,' I said, making a genuine effort to sound nice myself.

'Also darling, I wanted to ask if you minded sleeping in a sleeping bag over Christmas when the twins come down.'

The twins are my twenty-two-year-old sisters who married another twenty-two-year-old set of boy twins at a joint wedding this summer when they became right old celebrities with their pictures in the *Sunday Express*, the *Hounslow Herald* and *Mail on Sunday*. 'Twinning the Day', 'Twin Sets' and 'Double Act' were the headlines and they are now nesting happily ever after. Their names are Susan and Jane and their husbands are called James and Jonathon and all four of them are interchangeable as they are all doctors, all wear sensible shoes and can all remember what ghastly words like 'peristalsis' and 'haemoglobin' mean.

'I always do sleep in the sleeping bag, Mother.'

'I know darling, but you always make such a fuss about it.'

'That's not – '

'Eliza,' bawled Melindi. 'Countess Want is on the phone for you.'

'Sorry, Mother, I can't chat now.'

'I heard that.'

'What?'

'The Countess. What are you doing talking to Countesses?'

'I've got to ask her her beauty tips.'

'Her what?'

She heard. 'You know. What she puts on her face, does she exercise, that sort of thing.'

'Oh darling. It's so ridiculous. When are you going to get a proper job?'

'Mother, I really must go.'

'Yes, I know, darling – the Countess.'

'Yes, goodbye . . . Hello. Eliza Hart speaking. As you know, in the Fifty British Beauties feature we are running a few lines on people's beauty secrets under the picture.'

'How is the picture?'

'Lovely, very lovely. We are all delighted with it.'

'Oh, I am pleased. But Lord Rainedon is so good. He said it would be in black and white.' In fact I have no idea what the Countess's photo looks like but if it has been shot in black and white the Countess Want's beauty is of the faded variety as you can disguise much more in black and white than in colour. 'Will I be able to have a copy?'

'Yes, of course. But you have to arrange all that with the accounts department, I'm afraid. In the meantime I wondered if you could just fill me in on . . .'

'My beauty secrets?'

'Please.'

'Well, the key, *the* key, to keeping your beauty is to treat all food as medicine.'

'Oh.'

'That's the secret.'

'Oh,' I repeated. 'I'm sorry, I'm not quite with you. How do you mean exactly, "as medicine"?'

'Only eat what is good for you, only food which is actually going to be of benefit to your health and looks.'

'So how does this actually translate into practice? For instance, what did you have for breakfast this morning?

'Four poached eggs. They contain vitamin A for my skin, calcium for my nails. I took the yolks out of course, because of their high cholesterol content. And last night for dinner I started with salmon as the oil is good for the complexion . . .'

I missed what else she had for dinner as heavy footsteps were clomping up behind me. One advantage of these noisy wooden floors is that you can tell in advance who is about to pounce. There is a direct correlation between your importance in the magazine hierarchy and the speed you move. The fashion chicks, for instance, run around like sprinters in training, rushing out for pairs of tights, fetching clothes, doing the ironing. The editor moves at the speed of a horse-drawn hearse, setting down the points of her four-inch stilettos with such precision, you would think she was aerating Buckingham Palace's prize piece of lawn. That leaden step behind me was the unmistakable thud of Tron the features editor, who has the physique and gait of a big-game huntress.

'That should give you a few lines,' continued Countess Want. I turned round.

It was Tron. And she stood intimidatingly close behind me, flicking her long hair, which was all tied up in a bushy fox tail.

'Yes, it should. Thank you,' I said. 'Can I get back to you if I've got any more queries?'

'Yes, but it'll have to be today unless you want to phone me at my hotel in the Maldives.'

'All right, I'll write it up this afternoon. Thank you. Goodbye.'

'Hello, Lize,' said Tron. She abbreviates everyone's names. Her real name is Triona but she likes to be called Tron.

'Hello, Tron,' I said. It's like talking to something out of Flash Gordon.

'That's a very nice top you're wearing,' she said. Oh no. She wants something. When Tron wants something she flatters you. When the new chairman took over the company, he sent select, senior members of staff on assertiveness training courses. Knowing nothing of Tron's character he sent Tron – who is a former head girl, plays a mean game of tennis and was already as assertive as a world-class heavyweight – on a five-day course where they taught her that if you want something from someone, first make them feel good about themselves, i.e. flatter them.

'It's ever so pretty.'

'Thanks.'

'Whose is it?'

'Marks & Spencer's.'

'Really? It's nice. They do some quite good stuff now.'

Tron has not a clue about clothes. I happened also to be wearing a pair of trousers on which I had blown two weeks' salary as they were so well-cut they made me feel like Katharine Hepburn – they have to be brilliantly cut to make me feel like Hepburn – and Tron remarks on a shirt from Marks & Sparks.

'Thanks, thanks very much.'

'And the pink and melon face make-up piece worked out very well. The editor was pleased with it. Especially as we know you're busy at the moment having to do the fifty British Beauties on your own without Rosanna. And write the history of the bra.' She wants something really big. 'Lize.' (Pronounced 'lies'.) 'Lize. I wondered if you would like to go to a health farm?'

Oh no. No. please. Not a health farm. I had to go to a health farm once before. I went to one in April in Spain. There were just acres of beer bellies and gold medallions and I had to have their revolutionary beauty treatment. I stood in the middle of an empty room with no clothes on except for a bath hat and this man in an impossibly small G-string stood there, with a hose, firing water at my flabbier parts. I was in there for hours. And I'm not flabby. And the weather was bad too, all wet with a miserable grizzly rain, and windy.

'A health farm?'

'Yes.'

'Er, when?'

'That's the problem, you see, Lize. I'd got it all fixed up for Lady Tinker to go but now she can't as her children have got measles and it's this weekend. At Chewton Magna Castle. You know, near Ipswich.'

'Oh Tron. I've got a lot on.'

'Yes. I know. I'm sure you have. I'm really sorry about it. Normally we would have postponed it. But we wanted to tie it in with Hermione's health special.'

'Which health special?'

'You know. For March. The one on breasts.'

'What's that got to do with a health farm?'

'Once a month they have a masseuse who trained in Paris under some special doctor. Apparently she's famous in France and said to give the best-ever breast massages.' Oh God. A breast massage – that's the last thing I need. 'She makes a mud mask. It's from Monte Carlo – the mud. Well, I think it is. I'm not sure of the exact details. But she's an authority. Only she doesn't speak very good English so it would be better if someone who spoke French went.'

'Melindi speaks fluent French.'

'I know but it's not a particularly easy thing to write about so I wanted you to do it. Someone with more experience. I thought you would do it rather well.' Flatter, flatter.

'Thank you. But I'm supposed to be going to some parties.' In a magazine where frocks cost so much the prices have to be put in a special section at the back otherwise all the noughts obscure the pictures, social engagements are sacrosanct.

'Lize, I know. I'm really sorry to ask you to do this.'

'Four parties.' A lie. I've got two, both old university friends who, when they got coupled for better or worse, became like cars which go from 0mph to 60mph in five seconds: in the space of a two-week Caribbean honeymoon they accelerated from twenty-five to forty and returned only to splash out on Volvos.

'But I would be very grateful. I would remember this.'

I didn't have much option. 'If no one else can.'

'Thank you.' She spotted some champagne truffles on my desk and took one. 'Umm. These are nice. Where did you get them.'

'Charbonnel & Walker sent them to Ingrid as a Christmas present but she won't eat them so she gave them to me.'

'They are good. Can I have another one?'

'Sure. Help yourself.' She usually does.

'Thanks. I'll take two. It might be an idea to take them with you as I think they put you on a very strict diet at this place.' Off she clomped. And I went through my post, dismally.

There were press releases on a new fabric collection at Liberty's; a new shop for the Rubenesque woman, called The Elegant Elephant; a tin of Weight Watcher's rice pudding with only 130 calories a portion; an invitation to lunch with the shoe marketing board; a mug which sang 'White Christmas' when you picked it up; press releases plus samples of a new body lotion which glittered the more you sweated; a book called *Star Love* telling you with which zodiac signs you are compatible; a fresh date in a box with an invitation saying, 'Make a date in your diary for the launch of the latest in travel irons'. Ironing is not the sort of thing *Circe* readers are expected to be *au fait* with, let alone ironing on holiday. I ate the date and went off to the health and beauty meeting.

Each month we have what we call the H & B meeting to discuss what is going in the next issue. We work so far in advance we were looking at the April issue. Tron was chairing the meeting. What with the March yellow make-up pictures going wrong, and the March cover also going wrong because the unknown beauty had put on all that weight, we were so behind with March the editor did not have time.

Hermione, the health editor was already bellowing forth when I arrived. Disease is her hobby. She talks about the most harrowing subjects in a horrifyingly enthusiastic manner. She had just finished on breast reconstruction and had launched into a couple of short news items. Firstly, if you eat too many carrots you can go orange. I have heard that before. It's not something I have to worry about. Secondly, caviar is one of the purest food stuffs. It is not contaminated with pesticides, hormones and all the rubbish, sewage and nuclear waste in the ocean, because the mother fish's liver absorbs all the junk to keep her eggs wholesome.

Finally, she had a feature on recent advances in foetal medicine and the production of perfect babies. For the past five months we have religiously had to have an article on some variation of pregnancy and childbirth because Hermione is pregnant and finds herself and her baby an inexhaustible source of fascination. Although she behaves as if she is twenty-nine months pregnant with triplets, legs apart, bulge thrust forward, tells you every time it moves and shows round the scans like holiday snaps, it is not due for four more months when it will be delivered in a swimming pool. Tron, who is two years older than Hermione, has no children and is competitive with Hermione on every conceivable level, tires quickly of her lording over everyone as Mother Earth. Flicking her fox tail, she cut Hermione in mid-flow on revolutionary scanning mechanisms.

What, Tron wanted to know from Ingrid, was happening on the beauty front? In particular, what was she going to tell everyone to do with their hair? Ingrid said she had no idea just yet. Tron would have liked her to say: 'Keep it long and natural, loosely swept back for a youthful, healthy look.' Ingrid does say this every eight months or so as this is Tron's favourite look. Tron, with her enviable ability to deny reality, believes that long and natural, loosely swept back for a youthful, healthy look is just how her hair does look. It is true of most women. Their favourite looks are those to which they bear some, albeit insuperably slight, resemblance. Blondes like pictures of blonde models, even though their own tired locks may be as blonde as a lemon and their body shaped like one. Redheads like pictures of redheads and so on.

Hermione, whose hair is short and gamine, suggested Ingrid tell everyone to chop it all off. Tron turned up her straight but considerable nose. Hermione then said she had seen a lot of red hair about recently. This is the only issue on which Hermione and Tron ever agree. 'Yes,' Tron piped up. She too thought she had seen a lot of red hair about. This is because Hermione and Tron both have red hair. Hermione's, however, verges on shocking orange, and Tron's has more mouse and fox highlights. Hermione, of course, politely tells Tron that she wishes her hair was as Titian as hers. And Tron says she wishes hers was more flame. But I know, as they each have told me in confidence, frequently, that they much prefer, indeed are as pleased as punch, with their own red tops. Ingrid said nothing.

Melindi, whose own hair was covered in a piece of headgear which looked as if she had spent last night busy with the remains of her shower curtain, then put forward her own idea which she had obviously been hatching for weeks. She suggested looking like silent movie stars: retro pin curls, pulling the hair off the face and baring the forehead and temples, waving hair into a thirties bob. There was a deathly hush. For once I felt sorry for Melindi. You could have heard a sequin drop.

'It's a sweet idea, darling,' Ingrid said when Melindi had finished. 'But it just won't do. It's far too old-fashioned.'

'Old-fashioned' is the *primus inter pares* of put downs. Old-fashioned, this magazine is not. We stand for modernity. 'What's new . . .' are the editor's favourite two words. We are thoroughly modern women. We know all about the latest in quick-drying nail-varnish so we can paint our nails in the back of the chauffeur-driven car as we nip off to take over ICI and accept the Booker Prize two days after producing our second gorgeous baby, and fit in time for having our hair cut while preparing our lecture on the latest developments in nuclear fission and teaching the four-year-old to read while not forgetting to run an elderly neighbour to hospital and take the empty Bollingers to the bottle bank.

It was then that Ingrid had an idea which was testimony to her forty years' experience and justified her grossly fat salary plus dress allowance. On her desk was a three-dimensional Christmas card of a Christmas tree. Miniature decorations – baubles, tinselled butterflies, glittering angels, trumpets, frolicking Father Christmases, even microscopic pink sugar mice – hung from every available frond. Although only two feet high and made of collapsible cardboard, it was a fine example of how a Christmas tree should be decorated, a tribute to the beauty of brilliant ornamentation, a source of inspiration for Ingrid.

'We'll do a decorated, brilliantly ornamented look. Outrageously ornate and elaborate,' she said. 'You don't go to the hairdresser's for a cut and blow dry any more. Now you go to have your hair dressed, decorated and garnished. Now it's all about looking artificial and contrived for a stunningly strong impression. This is what's new. Hair is pomaded, netted, bouffanted, back-combed, pompadoured and beehived.'

'Brilliant,' said Tron.

'Brilliant,' murmured Hermione.

Indeed it was a brilliant idea. We could follow it through for months. The possibilities were endless. In May, decorate your hair with flowers, in June with ribbons, in July with some seasonal ornament like sea shells, in August with a single, but carefully chosen, fine china figurine. There was scope for special features on back-combing, achieving a spectacularly bouffant finish, the pros and cons of slides as against combs for holding it all in place, a metaphysical look at the very ritual of doing your hair, latest advances in hairspray technology. Truly brilliant. It saved us all from thinking of another idea for ages.

Also the editor would be delighted as it would keep the advertisers happy. There would be all the extra expense of going to the hairdresser every time you wanted to go out for the evening, all the hair decorations you would need to buy, plus the hair curlers, rollers and tongs, the new sprays and mousses for keeping such heady concoctions stuck together, and the cost of false hair pieces for extra-long plaits or outsize buns. It was truly a moment of crowning glory for Ingrid.

Later I rang my friend Cassandra back. Cassandra also works for a women's magazine. Or rather, she works for a men's magazine as it is all about keeping your man, leaving your man, looking good for your man, cooking for your man, loving your man. The magazine is called *Woman's Mail*, and every week Cassandra writes about emotional problems with your man, a subject on which she is singularly well-qualified to write, as I have yet to know her happy in love. Much of her problem is her job. Fifty-two different emotional problems a year is too much for anyone.

John is the latest problem in her life. He is a handsome man aged forty-nine with a wife who no longer sleeps with him and two teenage children. This is according to Cassandra. Because he is married and most of their meetings are on the hop, she cannot let her friends meet and vet him. I reckon he is well past fifty, and show me a roaming married man who says his wife sleeps with him and I will show you a pig who can swim (pigs can't swim as their trotters cut their necks as they paddle).

They met in a first-class British Rail compartment, travelling from Bristol to London. Cassandra had been interviewing the founder of one of the largest marriage guidance councils in the country. At Bristol Temple Meads station she was spotted by an old friend of her family, who asked her to join him and his colleague – John – on the way back to London.

Within two seconds of their meeting, Cassandra had established that John's smile was sexy and so too was his voice; before they had left the station that he was charming; by Bath that he was ravishingly funny; by Chippenham that he was highly successful at ICI; by Swindon that not only his smile and his voice but also his eyes, his mouth, indeed his whole body from his greying hair down to his blessed cotton socks were very, very sexy, that he was politically sound, could recite complete chunks of Shakespeare. By Didcot that he was married. At Reading her parents' friend got off the train as he lived nearby so John and Cassandra travelled the rest of the journey *à deux*.

When they arrived at Paddington they said goodbye but, just as they were about to part, seemingly for ever, Cassandra caught her Louis heel – these have very tiny bases so Cassandra was putting her not inconsiderable weight on an area of less than one square centimetre – on some sort of slippery stuff which had stuck to Paddington Station's floor –

something like a banana but wasn't – and skidded. He caught her as she fell, and it was this bodily contact that cinched it. Arm and waist joined momentarily, eyes met, he handed over his business card and said call him if she felt like lunch some time.

I know the details so minutely because for the next three weeks before she did call him she briefed me on all the intricate particulars, as she agonised over whether she should or whether she should not call him. Had she, she tormented herself, deliberately fallen over on Paddington Station? Perhaps she had. But she had definitely slipped on something, a bit of old fruit or suchlike because she had caught sight of it as she fell and it was easy to slip, especially in those small-based Louis heels. But no one else had slipped. Perhaps she had skidded just so that he would catch her arm. But need he have grabbed her with such gusto? No, he need not. But was it really with all that much gusto? If someone falls over you don't just lift a finger. You grab them good and proper, even if you have never had a hot-blooded thought in your head. But do you give the falling woman your business card and suggest they call you for lunch? Of course not. But if she rang him she would willingly be participating in the break-up of a marriage, destroying his children's lives, destroying his wife's life, and in one lunch becoming a modern Messalina, a twentieth-century Aspasia (not for nothing does she have an MA in classics and a Ph.D. in the role of women in classical literature). And so she went on.

I said no. Married men make a bed of thorns. She should not see him again, even though I did not know how charming, ravishingly funny, politically sound etc. he was and how long it was since she had met someone like him. But, she said, it was only lunch. Nothing could happen at lunch. And she would not make any moves herself, just be really cool and professional because at the moment he caught her in his arms it might suddenly have occurred to him that he needed a journalist to contribute an article for their house magazine.

So they met for lunch at Langan's where he said he had

thought of nothing else for the past twenty days but whether she would call and she said she had thought of nothing else but whether she should call and they both said how glad they were that she had.

The minutiae of other people's happiness is mightily dull but the general upshot of the lunch was that they each discovered that neither had ever met anyone like the other before and that they would see each other two days later at L'Escargot for dinner.

'Typical,' I said when she reported back to me. This is typical of relationships with married men. They move at a pace and with a passion the single man cannot match. Unmarried men won't, before you have had time to decide whether you want the salmon or the hot artichoke salad, have stroked the inside of your wrist while elaborating on the beauty of your smile, entwined their fingers in your hair while waxing lyrical on the colour of your eyes, wondered how much you would like to spend a weekend in a suite at the Royal Crescent and confessed to an irrepressible passion. Single men are scared you might misunderstand them and start enquiring about their favourite china.

Married men, however, know exactly where they stand. They know you know too, and standing around is something they do not have much time to do, so they rush you off down to the Savoy for a torrid night as fast as their would-be Don Juan legs will carry them. Which, of course, is just what John did. And for the past six months Cassandra has been irretrievably smitten, in an incurable catatonic depression, alternately grief- and guilt-stricken.

'I'm so sorry,' Cassandra said on the phone. 'But do you mind if we don't go to that party on Wednesday? You see, John's just rung. His wife is going to see *The Nutcracker* or something at Covent Garden so he'll have time to see me for a few hours then.'

'I thought you really wanted to go to this party,' I said.

'Yes of course, but, well, you know, I'd rather see John and it will be impossible to see him at all over Christmas. I'm really sorry, Eliza, letting you down like this.'

'Don't worry. It doesn't matter.'

'Really?'

'Yes, really.'

'I'm sure you could go to the party on your own if you wanted.'

'No, it's all right, thanks.'

'I do feel bad. But it is a nightmare trying to get a few moments together right now, and it's completely impossible over Christmas.'

'I know, I know. I'm not fussed, honestly.'

'It's just that it's a week since I've seen John.'

'I know. I know,' I said.

'Oh God, I'm really making a mess of things. Aren't I? Letting you down, saying I'd go to the party.'

'You've decided you'll see John, so go and see John and enjoy it.'

'Yes, you're right. But Eliza I just don't know what to do. I ought to stop seeing him, oughtn't I? Tell me I ought to stop seeing him.'

'Stop seeing him.'

'Well, yes, I know you think I should. But right now I can't bear not to see him. Sometimes I think – '

'How's work?' I interrupted. I know all about what Cassandra thinks of John.

'Same as ever.'

'What's this week's problem?'

' "When Prince Charming Turns Into a Frog".'

'But you've just done that.'

'No that was "Wimps in Wolves' Clothing". Will you think about it for me? Perhaps I could interview you.'

'No.' Cassandra is always interviewing me for her problem pages and using my quotes under names she picks out from *The Directory of Headmistresses*. 'Just a minute,' I said.

One of the postboys had appeared at my desk. 'There are some flowers for you,' he said, 'in a basket downstairs. Shall I bring them up?'

'No, no. I'll get them, thanks ... Cassandra, this is

wonderful news. I've got to go. I've got some flowers. In a basket, apparently.'

'Who from?'

'I'm going to find out.'

'Perhaps they're from The Bostonian.'

'Hmm.'

'Has he rung lately?'

'Last Sunday – I rang him.'

'Well let me know if they're from anyone interesting.'

I scurried downstairs. It wasn't a basket of flowers at all. It was a white cabbage. It wasn't an ordinary coleslaw cabbage but it was unmistakably a cabbage in an expensively rustic wicker basket. Bella stopped me as I was lugging it back up to my desk and told me that everyone was sending cabbages this Christmas and that they were terribly chic. As cabbages go, it was chic. Its creamy leaves had curly edges and near the centre it was pure white. Only white flowers and, now, white vegetables are ever sent to the magazine as Cecil Beaton once said that the only chic flowers are white flowers. On Valentine's Day, going to the loo with the sinks full of alabaster-white blooms is so like going into a church, you come out feeling you should be inspired with some good intentions.

Bella then put her head in her hands and sniffed discreetly with her red nose.

'Why don't you go home?' I suggested sympathetically.

'I wish I could but I've got to finish this piece on short breaks in the Seychelles and the phone keeps ringing. Some woman has just rung telling me she is going to Venice for Christmas and wanting to know how many cardigans she should take with her.'

'How many did you say?'

'That if she wore cardigans she shouldn't be going to Venice. It's a nightmare and tonight I've got to go to the Ritz for this dinner and I can't possibly miss it. I feel as sociable as Garbo right now. One good thing though, feeling like this I've lost my appetite.' She opened a packet of Lemsip and poured the powder into her Lalique mug.

'Is that all the lunch you're having?' I asked.

'Yes, last night I was going to have it for dinner but I couldn't manage it then.' And she put her head back in her hands and I returned to my desk where Melindi was sitting in my chair, using my phone.

'I've just done an interview for you,' she said, putting it down.

'One of the fifty beauties?'

'Yes.'

'Oh, thanks, Melindi,' I said more kindly. 'Which one?'

'Lady Grace Gustaad.'

'Oh.' For the past two weeks I had been deliberating whether I did want to speak to Lady Grace myself or whether I did not want to. I have never spoken to her and although I doubt she even knows of my existence my thoughts once revolved upon her like a dentist's drill. For she is The Natterjack's wife.

For nine years The Natterjack was the shining, blinding, white light of my existence, some sort of giant rabbit's paw that I thought I couldn't survive without. He was two years above me at school and we lived together for six years, from when I went to university in London, to three Christmases ago when he rang me on the shortest day of the year to say that he treasured me and I would always be very precious to him – as if I was something out of the Antiques Road Show – but he had fallen in love with another woman and was going to marry her: Grace, or rather Lady Grace, the only daughter of Lord Gustaad, an incomputably wealthy man descended, if there is any truth in the rumour – not much, I suspect – from Charles the Second.

My supreme desolation over their marriage can only have been matched by Grace's father's surprise. But he gave them The Superb Hotel in Brighton as a wedding present and, according to the *Daily Mail*, soon reconciled himself to his daughter's marriage. For Jack is a brilliant (and, at that time, was also an inordinately well-paid) photographer whom *Time* magazine once described as 'the suburban man with an artist's soul'.

The two went to live in New York and I did not expect to see Jack again but we met in my local off-licence in September. I had gone in for peanuts to help me through the last hundred yards home and he was in there buying John Bull bitter. Now we are forever meeting as he and Grace moved back to London in the summer and bought a giant white house a few streets from me with so many pillars it is like a great wedding cake.

Grace actually looks like Grace Kelly with longer legs, and as Jack's favourite film was *Rear Window* – he even bought the video – he must certainly have fancied himself as James Stewart, the worldly, hardened photographer, who has seen it all, endured it all, photographed it all, deriding the perfect Kelly who has never worn the same dress twice: 'Did *you* ever get shot at?' 'Did you ever eat fish heads and rice?' His facts of photo-journalistic life – Eastern Europe with the *Sunday Times*, the Antarctic for *National Geographic*, three months in Ethiopia for the *New York Times*, two books on China – must have bowled Grace, straight out of Wycombe Abbey with three creditable A-levels to her name, right over. Having lived her life on red carpets, fish heads with Jack represented a glamorous entrée into a new world, and I suppose she found him immeasurably lovable. I did.

As Grace is truly beautiful I wish she was stupid as well. But with Jack's photographs, seething with an awesome tenderness I thought he reserved for me, she launched herself into modelling with such success and professional acumen she must now be wealthy beyond even my dreams of avarice, and this summer signed an exclusive modelling contract with Number 10, a British cosmetic company specialising in anti-cellulite creams. Now I cannot pick up a magazine without seeing a picture of her flawless thighs.

'So what,' I asked Melindi, 'does Lady Grace Gustaad do to keep herself so beautiful?'

'You shouldn't say it like that.'

'Say what like what?'

'Gustaad. It's pronounced Gstaad, like the ski resort, Not Gustard so it rhymes with custard.'

I ignored her. 'So what does she do?'

'Nothing.'

'What do you mean, nothing?'

'She says she doesn't do anything.'

'She's got to. She can't say she doesn't do anything.'

'Well she does.'

'But Melindi. She must do something. *"Il faut souffrir pour être belle"*, and *"il faut payer"* too otherwise you'll be out of a job. Oh God. The editor will go berserk if I say she does nothing. She must at least brush her hair. Will you ring her back?'

'I can't.

'Why not?'

'Because I don't know her number as she was at friends', she said, and on her way to the country for Christmas.'

'That'll do.'

'What do you mean?'

'You know. Beauty tip: "Forays out of London grime into the countryside to walk off decadent urban life and fill the lungs with clean air and refresh the complexion," and all that. Can I have my chair back now, please? And my desk,' I said handing her a pot of powder she had spilled over it.

I sat down and reread the note on my white cabbage. It was from Mr Brook-Barclay whom I wrote about last month. He makes ballgowns and hires them out. For an extra £50 on top of the hire fee, however, he will also make a brand new gown to measure. This means that although you don't have a dress to go home with and must return it the next morning, you do have a perfectly fitting gown for the one evening for less than £100 which is nothing for people who frequently frequent balls.

I rang to thank him for the cabbage and he thanked me for the write-up. It had generated so much business he had had to cancel his holiday in Los Angeles but in the New Year when he was less busy he would love to make me a ballgown too. The last thing I want is one of his ball gowns. He only makes them in five styles and all come complete with frills and furbelows and leg o' mutton sleeves of reckless proportions. They are particularly prized by the teenage daughters of the wealthiest families in the country. I thanked him profusely but said I could not possibly accept such a generous gift and the cabbage was more than enough. Later, Naomi said I was mad to have turned him down and that I should have had one made in white so I would always have a wedding dress handy.

4

On the Job

I missed the train to Ipswich because the colonel next door had
fallen over. He falls over frequently and cannot get up again.
He has the end flat and as I am his only neighbour he can only
ask me for help. The woman in the flat below his is stone deaf,
so it is up to me to ring the police and get them to break in and
get him up. I have suggested that he gives me a key to his flat
but he says I am not trustworthy. The man is mad.

Whenever I call the police – which, thanks to the colonel, I
do frequently – my other neighbour likes to know. Dressed in
the erotic discomforts of low leather bustier and high red
strapless shoes, she slumped in the doorway.

'Please can't you ask the police to do something about
Duncan while they're here?' Duncan was bugling 'Silent
Night' as usual.

'I do, every time.'

'But he's gone on all day. It's all right for you. You're out.'

'But so long as he stays in his room, the police don't like to
upset – '

'Christ!' she screamed as he let out a blast and the colonel
bawled 'Help!' 'And what with him too,' she said, doubling up
and coughing.

'Are you all right?'

'No. I've got a cold. Have you?'

'No. Well not yet.'

'You're the only person I know who hasn't. I don't suppose
you've got any of those Lemsips left?'

'Yes,' I said wearily. 'Come on in.'

'Thanks. Actually, I think it must be flu,' she croaked,
installing herself on my sofa and sneezing across the room.

41

By the time I had got rid of her, packed, made tea for the police and got out, it was snowing again. For twenty minutes I waited for a bus, got black slush on my favourite red furry coat, sneezed three times and then caught a cab. If the driver had not been moving in time with Chopin's 'Funeral March' I still might have caught the train.

'Could we possibly go a little faster?' I asked politely. He let two buses and a Mini overtake us. Then he slowed down some more and a pushy Golf started hooting at us. Then a great bully of a BMW.

'Look at those stupid buggers,' he replied. 'Don't they care if they kill themselves, just so long as they get there five minutes earlier than everyone else?'

'Yes,' I said. 'Stupid, aren't they? You're absolutely right. They're mad. But do you think we could possibly go a little faster? It's just that I'm terribly late.'

He changed down a gear and turned round to look at me. We would have gone faster if I had got out and pushed. 'What's it to me if you get there on time?'

'I won't get there on time. I'm already late. I'll miss my train. Please.'

'Listen, love. That's nothing to me. Nothing at all. My brother-in-law was always worrying about being late, and that's why he died. Heart attack. And my father. And that idiot behind us will have one soon too. Believe me.'

The BMW man was going puce. Later I went blue because I missed the train and had to stand around in the cold station watching all the tramps and the drunks as I waited for the next train. Sometimes I feel I am living in one big hospital.

It was eleven-fifteen when my train finally heaved into Ipswich. It was particularly late because we had been held up by frozen points. I was frozen too, and hungry. Most of the time I am cold and hungry but I was particularly so just then. And all I had to read was my brand new copy of *Star Love* which had knocked me down into a great trough of despond. Weighing in at six hundred pages, only fifty were of any relevance, the upshot of which was that I am compatible with

42

Librans and Leos. That's it — two-twelfths of the male population which you have to narrow down to those of the right age, those still unattached, those also attracted to me. Hopeless. Next to me a man was snoring as if he had just had Christmas lunch, the bottom of the man opposite had taken up two seats, and the only other man in the carriage was reading *Your Power and Your Glory: The Politics Of Your Success*. Two-twelfths is possibly optimistic.

Set somewhere in the middle of a bleak Suffolk plain, swept by winds off the North Sea, Chewton Magna boasts of bracing fresh air and rural isolation and a half-hour drive from the station and civilisation. It was a long half-hour because of all the snow and slush, but I slept as it was so warm inside the taxi and the seats were so furry. The driver woke me up saying we had arrived, that I talked in my sleep and did I know? He took my bag out of the boot, dumped it on the ground, gave me a receipt for £20 and drove off.

I was outside two huge gates set in an endless wall topped with spikes. There was a gravel drive, at the end of which I could make out some sort of big building, and trees. It was hard to see exactly — the sky was as black as mud, not a star or the moon in sight, and there were no lights in the building as on health farms everyone has to be tucked up in bed at nine p.m. for their beauty sleep.

I lifted the latch on the gates. They did not move. I lifted the latch again and the gates still did not move. They were padlocked shut. I tried again. I walked the length of the gates, twice, three times. There was just the one latch, the padlocked one. I checked again — still just the one padlocked latch. I shook the gates and kicked them. No movement. No question of it. I was locked out. So I shouted, as loud as I could. Nothing. No lights went on. Again I shouted. Still absolutely nothing. All knocked out on camomile tea.

So I screamed. I had never screamed before and I screamed the scream I want to scream when I am stuck in the Blackwall tunnel, when I am at a dull Christmas party, when I wake up on my own early on a Sunday morning and there is no one to lie in with – that sort of scream. Its noise surprised me a bit and made my head spin and my throat sore. But no one heard. And I screamed again and then I started to cry great fat salty tears that froze on my cheeks.

I didn't know what to do. With a ten-foot wall with spikes, gates twice my size, the place was a paragon of medieval impregnability. I was locked out. Ice cream was coursing through my veins and I could not feel my feet. Snow had infiltrated my boots. And it was so black it was as black as hell, a time when there is no light and no hope, a time people die. And I would die too. And that made me cry all the more wondering whether I would still be alive in the morning, whether I would have frozen to death or, on such a night as this, in such an isolated place as this, whether I would be murdered.

I started walking, slowly. I walked for an hour and came back to the gates as I had walked round in a circle, like Winnie the Pooh. So I screamed again and then, to my everlasting relief, my eternal joy, my good fortune, a police car pulled up. I was going to live. I was going to see morning. Faith was restored. Once again I was a person for whom lights turned green.

A policeman looking less than twenty unwound the car window an inch. He said nothing but raised an eyebrow. I presumed he meant, 'What are you doing here?'

'I'm trying to get in. I got locked out,' I explained. 'I'm supposed to be going to the health farm but my train was so late they must have thought I wasn't coming and locked the gates so I can't get in.' He did not respond. He raised the other eyebrow. 'Would you mind phoning your station and asking them to phone Chewton Magna to let me in? Please.' Still he said nothing. Pure silence. He just moved his eyebrows up and down and glanced at his companion in the driving seat. He did not speak either but moved his jaw up and down as if trying to speak. Still silence. Perhaps they were a mirage. Please no, not a mirage. No.

I opened the door. Warm air gushed out. No mirage.

'Get in,' grunted the driver and he unlocked the back door.

The reason neither of them could talk was that they were eating a packet of extra-hard treacle toffees which stuck their jaws together. I waited patiently for them to finish chewing and then asked again if they would mind getting in touch with their station. The driver looked at me closely and said, 'You look as if you could do with going to a health farm.'

'I know,' I said.

'It's a good job for you that we came by.'

'I know.'

'You could have been out there all night.'

'I know. I'm very glad you did. Would you mind phoning. . . ?'

'How come you can afford to go to a place like that?'

'I can't afford it but I'm writing about the place. I work for a magazine.'

'Which one?'

'*Circe*,' I muttered.

And with that they both laughed, not little ho-ho chortles but hooting great guffaws.

'You don't look like you do – not like that.'

'No way.'

And their laughter became uncontainable. Great raucous side-splitting belly laughs ricocheted around the car. Good God, I was funny. I was hilarious. I was so funny it hurt. Where had I been all this time? The joke of the evening. Were there any more where I came from?

'You really don't.'

'Oh no.'

'You should see yourself.'

I said nothing. 'I wouldn't half mind spending my weekend being pampered in there for free,' said the driver, once his hilarity was under control.

'I'm not getting paid. I have to go in my time off. This is my weekend. I don't want to be here. Not at all. I hate it here. I just want to go home.' And with that I started crying and my tears had the same effect they always have on men. They make

45

them want to get rid of me as quickly as possible. Immediately they rang their station. And they gave me some toffee, and the three of us sat chewing in silence.

'I don't suppose they'll feed you much in there,' said the young one, when he had finished. 'Just rabbit food. Pass the hammer.' And he started cracking up another slab of toffee. He handed over the largest chunk. I was beginning to find him rather sweet. Then he made a noise which, if he hadn't had the toffee in his mouth, would have come out as 'Not 'arf!' For at the gate, dressed in a Barbour and wellingtons, was Miss World.

All blonde hair, blue eyes and large bosoms, distinguishable even under a Barbour, she was vintage health farm stock. Out of the car we tumbled, but none of us could speak – only chew – while this thing of beauty gave us the look only this sort of woman can.

'Good evening,' she said. We said nothing as we had to chew. 'Good evening,' she repeated. 'Or rather good night. We weren't expecting you so very late.' She looked at me from leaking boots and wet red fur to dank hair. I didn't think she liked me. Not that I had taken to her.

'I'm surprised to see you arriving at this hour,' she enunciated slowly as if to three idiots.

'Her train was late, because of the snow,' said the driver, eventually getting his teeth free.

'We'll pass by more often now,' said the young one. 'In case any more guests get locked out.'

'Thank you,' said Miss World. 'But this sort of thing should never happen as we insist that everyone arrives by nine p.m. so as not to disturb the other guests who like to go to bed early.' I sneezed loudly and she stepped back with obvious distaste. 'You'd better come in.'

I squelched behind her up the gravel path and along the Axminster to my room. It was the best room, Miss World said. It was the master bedroom and King George V had once slept in it. My night-time drink was on the table. Someone would wake me up with my breakfast in time for my first treatment at nine. And as it was now two a.m., Miss World was going back to bed.

The night-time drink was a flask of hot water and a weedy camomile tea bag. Disgusting. I got into bed. Either it was damp or I was. I lay there, rigid, looking at a plaster ceiling moulded tortuously into rampant plaster unicorns and fruit. The place was not decorated like a bedroom. A chandelier hung threateningly overhead, armorial stained-glass windows rattled and there was a marble fireplace, ideal for roasting oxen, which let in a gale. I was as cold as death and wanted some more blankets.

I hunted in a great coffin of a wardrobe and found some antlers but no blankets. So I heaved a small carpet off the floor and onto the bed and fell asleep under that.

5

Under Pressure

Like Ursula, wedged in her sarcophagus, I could not move, but someone was shaking the carpet, hard. Then harder still. And off it came. Lying there like a cracked oyster, an unswaddled mummy, I opened my eyes upon another Miss World.

It was evidently morning for she was saying something about not lying in as my first treatment was at nine – oh please go away, Miss World, please – that my robe and slippers were on the chair, that she would get me more blankets and that my timetable for the day was on the table along with my breakfast. Breakfast! I shot up. Wonderful. That was the best news I had heard in a long time. But it was pitiful: a flask of hot water, a slice of lemon, a level teaspoon of honey and five grapefruit segments lost on a large white plate.

I slowly swallowed my grapefruit while watching breakfast television's alternatives to turkey for Christmas lunch – goose, roast beef, venison, extra-large ducks – and an interview with a woman in Dorset who made chestnut stuffing with nuts from her own tree. Then I ate the honey but the lemon looked invincibly unappetising. Lemons are not too bad in sorbets or syllabubs and delicious in lemon curd or lemon meringue pies or on pancakes, but too much on their own. According to the timetable, lunch was four and a half hours away, dinner at six p.m. In the morning I had a massage, the pioneering breast massage, a facial and finally a seaweed cleanse, whatever that was. The rest of the day was free except for tea at four with Lady Chewton, who owned the place.

Dress at Chewton Magna consisted of your own swimming costume – the heating was back on – floppy slippers with the Chewton family's crest on the arch which you were allowed to

48

take home with you, and your own dressing gown. With everyone kerflumping around, dressed as if just out of bed, it was like being in a convalescent home.

I was a bit surprised that Lee, my Swedish masseur, was a man, and not a gay one either. In fact he was about as camp as a pneumatic drill. He gave me a towel, told me to take my clothes off and walked out. I stood there for a minute. It wasn't that it was cold. Oh God. I'm such a wimp about this sort of thing. I took my clothes off, clambered onto the couch, positioned the towels, lay back and stared at the ceiling, which was painted with roses.

On his return, with biceps and triceps working visibly under his tight T-shirt, Lee set to with admirable vim and vigour, first my toes, then working upwards. All six foot six of him, all fourteen plus stone, rubbed, kneaded, slapped and pinched me with an energy normally expended on digging up roads. It hurt. When he was up to mid-thigh, he commented, 'You haven't any cellulite. That's very good.' Then down he pressed, onto my left leg. 'Relax,' he said. And his hands moved further and further up between my legs.

Relax, I told myself. Slowly but firmly he reached the tops of my thighs. Relax, Eliza, relax. For goodness sake, woman. With a good masseur all the sexual implications of what they are doing are lost. Also, if you find it ticklish you are too tense and not relaxing. I was finding it ticklish but painfully unfunny. Dear God, dear God. Please do not let me disgrace myself and laugh. I was as tense as a corpse. I stared at the roses painted on the ceiling and thought miserably of England.

He paused. 'Are you all right?'

'Me? I'm fine. Oh yes. Fine thanks.'

'You should be more relaxed by now. Turn over please.' And he held up the towel at an angle that was supposed to preserve my modesty – huh – and then the kneading, slapping and so on happened all over again.

He put his huge hands around my neck. 'Are you always this tense? Do you have problems relaxing? It is very bad for you,

you know, being this tense. Your feet are unusually cold. Do you have problems with your back?'

'No,' I moaned, to each question.

'Because your shoulders are not straight. When you are older you may get bad backache.'

On every occasion I have a massage I discover something else wrong with me. Last time it was my liver. And the time before that the masseur began by measuring my stress level by attaching a little meter to the palm of my hand. It registered zero which, she said, was the level of relaxation only found in advanced students of transcendental meditation and the dead.

As if locked in battle, Lee finished me off by shooting me back and forth along the couch. It could have been worse. He could have been doing the pioneering breast massage, for instance.

'How do you feel now? You really needed that.'

I said I felt a bit sick.

'That is all the toxins. I have dislodged them for you,' he explained. 'Your circulation cannot cope with them. It is so poor they all just congregate, here, here and here. Now they are all being pumped through your body which is much better for you. But you will have problems when you are older, with all those toxins just sitting together and accumulating in toxic lumps.' And with that parting blow he said goodbye and I sloped off to find the breast masseuse, a bulky woman named Marie-Paul.

When special cones with a little pipe for fixing on to the bathroom tap were invented so women could give their breasts a water jet massage, they sold extremely well in France. French women, Parisiennes particularly, keep themselves well abreast of the latest developments in beauty care and in Paris, breast massages are now the *sine qua non* in body maintenance. Indeed, bookings in Parisian beauty salons giving the full breast massage including cleansing seaweed mask and inert gas toner, outstrip bookings for lymph drainage and algae wraps which were *le dernier cri* treatments last year.

Mention lymph drainage or algae wraps to most British women, however, and they will call in a plumber. As for breast massage, exporting the cones to Britain has yet to prove even the slightest success. And top London beauty salons who bought all the special moisturisers, oils, mud and breast ampoules, and who at huge expense flew over French beauticians to train their staff in the art of breast massage and camouflage of the dropped décolletage, have complained to Ingrid that very few British women actually want the treatment. Business is limited to better-educated tourists, they moan. British women prefer to spend their money on new curtains for the dining room, and regard a breast massage as something which should only be done – if indeed it is done at all – in the privacy of their bedroom by a man whom they know very well indeed. Writing about the treatment in the magazine, as I was doing, would help raise the level of British women's beauty consciousness and their bustlines.

'*Bonjour*,' said Marie-Paul.

'*Bonjour*,' I answered. And she told me to *retirer* my swimming costume. I couldn't think if *retirer* meant pull down or take off. I pulled it down and lay there, exposed. Lying face down is all right, because you have no eyes in the back of your head, but face up you are uncomfortably conscious that you are pointing upwards. Under Marie-Paul's scrutiny I shrank visibly.

'You have small breasts,' she said at a glance. 'I like that. Some women come in here with sacks of potatoes or grape-fuits. Fried eggs like yours are better, in the long run, as they won't droop when you're old. Comfortable?' I nodded. 'They are less hard work for me too.' She pulled my arm. 'This,' she said, pulling my arm another way, 'and this and this and this,' pulling my arm every which way but loose, 'helps support the muscles holding up the breasts. Do you do any exercise?'

Sometimes I roll round the floor trying to find my shoes under the bed. Sometimes I run for a bus. Sometimes I lift heavy bags.

'Yes,' I said. 'But not a great deal.'

'No. I can tell. You should. These arm exercises you can do at home. You should do them every morning, for instance, when you brush your teeth.' She rubbed orange-smelling oil into my shoulders.

'What sort of good does a treatment like this, er, this special massage actually do?'

'Not much,' she said. 'Not much at all. You need to come every two weeks to make a difference. It's more help for the woman with heavier breasts. But for you this is just, well, for you this is just a lesson in breast art.'

So far she had religiously avoided the two crucial areas, just rubbing orange oil into the arms and shoulders. Then rubbing below my neck she worked down to the climax. First little rotary movements with her finger tips while we discussed where we were going to spend Christmas, how we were celebrating New Year, what we would have for Christmas lunch, what we would watch on television over the holiday, that sort of thing. As one does. When we were on to the exorbitant price of crackers in Britain she started a twisting motion, pushing the top half right and the bottom half left and then vice versa and then lots of little tickly, tickly movements.

All in all it was very unrelaxing and like being at the dentist when you fix your eyes on some fascinating part of the ceiling to try and avoid catching his eye. But in Marie-Paul's case, as she worked from behind, leaning her sack of melons figure over your face, it was not her eyes you had to avoid. In the meantime she told me that Thai women actually massage you – or to be exact, they massage men – with their breasts, first covering themselves with soap and no doubt following the massage with other parts of the ritual. It is particularly popular with Western men whose own wives, presumably, will not cover their breasts with soapy bubbles and so on.

She then took a great wad of tissues, removed the orange oil and started fussing about in the corner of the room with something making a bubbling popping noise. It looked like a pot of grey-green slime but it was mud and seaweed from Monte Carlo, pulverised with oil and then heated in a *bain-*

marie. On it went. 'Don't move,' said Marie-Paul, 'otherwise it won't set properly. It will help cleanse and tone you up, just like a face mask. Remember not to move. I'll be back in ten minutes.' And she put on a tape of waves crashing and I lay there while the muddy seaweed congealed and hardened.

Later, when the mask had been sluiced off, she cut open breast ampoules which looked like the little coloured balls that contain bubble bath. These held 'breast serum', a cocktail of placenta, horse-chestnut oil, bovine spleen and other things which I could not understand in French. Udder, possibly. She rubbed it all in.

'Now,' she said, wheeling over a huge piece of silver equipment with cannisters, tubes and what looked like a dentist's drill, 'for a little "spritz".' She directed the rocket at my left breast and sparks shot out as in a van de Graaf generator. Then she went for the other one. After all the namby-pambying massage it was highly acerbic.

Eventually she stood back with hands on hips and admired her handiwork. 'Look,' she said.

I looked down. They were surprisingly pert, in a sit up and beg position.

'Oh. Er. *Merci*,' I said. The effect was rather wasted.

'What have you got next?'

'A facial.'

Marie-Paul put her face close to mine and inspected it. 'Now *that*,' she said with emphasis, 'will do you a lot of good.'

6

Saving Faces

Once a facial gets going you are not in a position to say anything at all. You can't move your jaw with all the steaming, cleansing, toning, exfoliating etc. Miss World was giving it. Miss Worlds always give facials, scrubbing and scraping your face so you have to gaze upon a vision of made-up loveliness while they make your skin look like the surface of the moon.

'Have you had a facial before?' she asked.

'Yes.'

'And you're having a cathiodermie?' (A cathiodermie involves unusual forms of electrical equipment.)

'No, no thank you. Can I just have the normal facial, please?'

'They are very good, you know. Most of the ladies here have cathiodermies.'

'Yes I know they are very good. But I'd rather just have the basic one, please.'

'What do you normally do with your skin?'

'Well I use this special soap – for sensitive skin . . .'

'Everyone thinks they've got sensitive skin.'

'. . . And then I put on a moisturiser for dry skin.'

She took a good close look at my face. 'You could do with a cathiodermie. Why won't you?'

'I had one once and it just didn't seem to suit me.'

'A bad experience?'

'Yes, very bad. I looked awful.'

'That is to be expected, you know.'

I did know. One of the most specious arguments in the beauty business is that in the first couple of days after a facial you should look worse than you do normally. The theory goes that a facial brings all the impurities and junk beneath the skin to the surface and that you have to put up with a few days of spots, red skin and raw ugliness before the benefits are revealed in full glory. After the first couple of days, however, you think a facial has done some good because you are back to normal. And normal is not too bad after your friends have asked you if it is something you have eaten which has brought you out in that rash.

She set to work. On went a tasty, apricot cream. Off it came with white sponges. On went a pale pink liquid – rose smell. Off that came with white tissues.

'You've got a number of tiny spots on your chin,' she said. 'At your age you really shouldn't have any.'

'I haven't got any spots.' I said. I haven't.

'Yes, you have actually. They're all there, under the surface, waiting to erupt.' She covered my eyes with two wads of clammy cotton wool. 'I'm going to steam your face now – keep your mouth closed – to bring all those spots up.' A jet of steam hit my face. 'This opens up the pores.

'You have got sensitive skin, haven't you? It's going quite red. I'm going to put a mask on now to tone your face. It will feel very taut so don't try and talk as you will crack the clay. It's Swiss clay. And you've got a surprising quantity of broken veins for a woman not yet thirty.' She smeared a brown concoction over my face and neck. 'I'm going to have to use a very light mask on your face. Anything stronger and you could end up with more broken capillaries. You really ought to take more care. You can't see them too much now but imagine what they will be like when you are forty. You may have nice skin now but it's so sensitive it will lose its bloom very quickly. Do you ever give yourself a face mask? Just nod, you'll crack the mask if you talk.

'No? Well you should. A gentle moisturising one to nourish the skin. Skin like yours is particularly vulnerable to central heating – it dries the skin out terribly. And of course all the pollution and just going out on a cold windy day can break the capillaries. Some people get them on their nose from drinking their tea too hot – that's really bad for you too. You're not married?

'No, well then, you've got no excuse not to take care of yourself. Of course you can have the red veins removed. I'm qualified to do it myself. You insert a needle under the skin and take out the vein. It helps but of course it never looks as good as it did in the first place. You're lucky you don't have any wrinkles.

'Oh yes, here, I can just see the start of crow's feet. With all the writing and reading I suppose you have to do with your job your eyes will go first. Of course the skin around the eyes is the most delicate anyway but all that close work exacerbates the problem and the moment you walked in I noticed the bags under your eyes.

'Lots of the women here have had collagen treatment – you know, filling out the wrinkles with collagen from cows. That does get rid of the wrinkles but it's only temporary. And so expensive. You keep on having to have the collagen topped up every twelve months or so. But it's cheaper than plastic surgery. You can have bags under the eyes removed with plastic surgery. At your age, you don't need that. You could think about it in five years though. There we are. Now you just lie there and shut your eyes and relax and let the mask do the work. I'll be back in about ten minutes to take it off.'

All facials come with a monologue on how ugly you are going to be, after which you are left on your own to reflect more deeply on the imminent and inevitable destruction of your appearance, the doomed, unhappy destiny of a complexion: a relentless progression from pimples to wrinkles with a mere seven years of clarity from the age of eighteen to twenty-five.

'Oh for God's sake, Eliza,' I said out loud. All the lying about and no food was getting to me. 'Pull yourself together.' I sat up and looked in the mirror. There was mud all over my face. Mud. Ugly, mucky, Swiss, brown mud. At least it wasn't mud from Bognor.

'It's snowing again,' said Miss World, coming in to sluice off the mask and splash on a cucumber lotion.

'This should close up all those open pores. You don't have to worry too much here, what with the air being so clean, but once you get back to London you don't want any more dirt getting in. There, that's better.'

I looked in the mirror. 'I'm a bit pink,' I said. I was puce. I looked like Rambo after a fight.

'That's a sign of how much good it's done you. You needed a good thorough cleanse. And as you never use masks or exfoliate there was a lot of work to be done. The pinkness will go shortly. Just don't be tempted to go and put any make-up on. The great thing about this place is that you don't have to worry about what you look like.'

7

Inside the Walls of Chewton Magna Castle

Seaweed waxes make you feel like one of those monkeys who are always on wildlife programmes having their fleas picked off by another friendly monkey. Intended to leave the skin as smooth and delicious as zabaglione, a beautician gets hold of an emulsion brush and paints you all over with warm wax. Then with a huge plastic sheet rather like clingfilm she wraps you up into a cocoon and leaves you cooking under infra-red lamps for an hour. The heat brings out even more impurities in your skin.

I slept through the whole palaver and woke up with a head feeling like a punch bag. It was hunger and unmet need. 'Satisfaction,' craved my hollow stomach. It was one o'clock. The hour had come. I scurried along to the dining room which was silent except for the rumbling of digestive tracts and the slurping of the Chewton slippers as everyone shuffled to their seats. There were forty of us in there, speechless with anticipation, wondering what the sweet hour might yield. So far, all that was on the tables were discreet but numerous little notices saying: 'If you ask a waitress for more food, she will be dismissed instantly.'

At five past one, the waitresses appeared. On each white plate stood one wedge of water melon and a scallion. And that was it. What there was of the water melon – for it was full of pips – quivered with a pinkish glow and the scallion curled its leaves in shame. I inspected it closely. I almost wept. I almost fainted from weakness. That was lunch, except for hot water with more lemons. No wonder, when a night's board costs even more than an Hermès scarf, that health farms make so much money. What you could quite rightly expect in a place like this, were some hearty bowls of soup, tasty salads, a few souffles, a couple of hefty chunks of carrot cake. It was ten past one. All gone. Time flies when you're having fun. My head throbbed in protest. My stomach roared in protest. Dinner, obviously not something to get excited about, was not till six. The only crumb of comfort was tea at four o'clock with Lady Chewton, three wingless, crawling hours away.

I thought about what to do. 'Love Signs' was finished and a waste of time and in my George V suite. I thought about Sam. I reminded myself that I was trying not to think about Sam. Twenty past one. I considered looking at the tennis courts or inspecting the swimming pool. I passed on both. I thought about Sam again. I could go back to my George V suite but felt too weak to walk up all the stairs, along all the draughty corridors. I sat down on a chaise longue. I wondered if Sam had left a message on my answering machine. I wondered how awful my face looked. I crossed my legs. I uncrossed them. Always imaginative. A paragon of self-sufficiency. Never at a loss amusing myself. I stretched. I stretched a little more, lay back and, shifting the thin cushions found a two-year-old copy of *Woman's Mail*. I looked at Cassandra's article, 'The Dating Game – No Play', inspired by her problem that December of having nowhere to go on New Year's Eve.

That week Cassandra had believed that you get brought up to think that while you are single you will be asked to go out with lots of nice men. 'But now you are not asked out,' she had written. 'Now we do not "date". Such rites of courtship were burnt with bras in the Sixties but courtship, unlike corsetry, has not been reinstated. In the Sixties and Seventies people could have sex whenever they wanted. They can still, of course, but now, both men and women are more wary of making themselves quite so readily available. As a result, you have a situation where not only are you unsure of who makes the first move but you are also unsure of what something as simple as arranging to see a man on his own for a few hours in a restaurant actually means. Are you two androgynes having dinner together? Is this meeting going to be prolonged into the night? Is he supposed to be pursuing and is she supposed to be pursued? The event is pregnant with ill-defined significance. Is he or she worth going through all this for?

'Invariably, you decide he or she is not because, instead of flirting merrily over the melon prosciutto, you have each been launching your long-range plans across the table cloth and by the time the main course is being cleared away, have both decided that you are not 100% compatible, won't marry and have sixteen children together, and are thinking, "Let's not bother with pudding and coffee, let's quit right now and stop wasting each other's time." So you each go home and are back in time to watch *Newsnight* in bed, lying diagonally as there's plenty of room as you both have king-size doubles. And that's allowing for all the time wasted fumbling over who should pay the bill.

'Now, when going to bed has once again been delayed in the "getting to know somebody" process, we are going to have to find some other place and means of spending a few hours alone with a man. Traditional courting rites are going to have to be reinstated. Not, however, for the traditional reason that you need to "date" in order to find out whether you love someone before you can contemplate having sex with them. But because it gets a bit dull spending Saturday night eating Lean Cuisines in front of *Blind Date*.'

I gave up at this point and went and found a mirror to see if my face was looking any better – it wasn't. I knew Cassandra's conclusion anyway. Just before writing the article, she had gone to great expense buying two stalls seats for *La Bohème* at Covent Garden so she could ring up an object of high interest and tell him she had been given two complimentary tickets and ask if he would like one. (She did not want him to have the effrontery to think that she would spend the price of a pair of Chanel earrings just for the pleasure of having three hours sitting next to him.) But the scheme fell flat because the man in question said that he was busy on the night two weeks hence, playing squash. I went in his stead and during the interval Cassandra outlined this dating article and decided that the conclusion had to be that men ought to return to making the first moves 'on the biological grounds that there are certain parts of the male anatomy that are not 100% per cent reliable and therefore make it more expedient for men to set the pace'.

At five to four Miss World announced the most exciting news of the day – that it was time for tea. And she led me to the private wing. Lady Chewton was dressed in Chanel and a hearing aid. Excluding the neat navy pumps, the sheer stockings, all the beads and baubles and, judging by her magnificent bust, upholstery from Rigby & Peller, the holders of the Royal warrant in corsetry, she was walking around in £2,000. I could afford a tub of moisturiser from Chanel but that would clear me out. She asked me how I was.

In truth, I was not well. I could not breathe, and my head ached, and my body hurt and my limbs were weak and I cannot function without nutritional intake and if I had told her everything that was not well in my life I did not think I would finish.

'Yes, thank you. Very well,' I said and sat down in a splodgy pudding of an armchair. It was an extremely flowery, chintzy chair. Indeed, as if to compensate for the weather, the whole room was decorated as if it was a summer garden benefitting from expensive fertiliser. I stared at the wisteria on the wallpaper while Lady Chewton poured the tea. It was ordinary tea, thank God, not an infused herb.

'Black?' she asked.

No. No way.

'With milk please.'

On the table was a plate of biscuits. She did not offer me one or take one herself though it was quite clear she had not acquired her Rubenesque figure from holding back on biscuits. Meanwhile, she made small talk: how Chewton Magna Castle was built in the 19th century after one of her ancestors distinguished himself in the Crimean War and how it was a miniature model of his medieval castle on the Gower coast; how twenty years ago she thought she had made a mistake in converting the castle into a health farm rather than

61

a safari park as the safari parks seemed to be doing so well. Now, however, with the modern interest in health, she felt she had made the right decision as health farms are so much easier to run than safari parks for although you had the problems with staff – no sooner was a beautician any good she went off to London – that was nothing to having coach loads of tourists and lions and monkeys and so on all over the place.

Concentrating on not thinking about the biscuits I didn't catch all she said, and when she paused after half an hour to ask which other health farms I had been to I was still fighting off the biscuits and said, 'Yes please, I'd love one.'

She said something about not having heard of that one, knocked the Chanel earring which hid the hearing aid, and asked if I had enjoyed myself. I said I had had an interesting time there. She hoped I was enjoying Chewton Magna as much. I said I was. She then told me to enjoy the rest of my stay, commented on how relaxed I was looking, invited me to come back again, any time, and wished me goodbye.

And that was that. I lolled about in the drawing room and looked at the ceiling until the dinner gong sounded. All the inmates got to their feet and walked off purposefully, as if late for work. Not everyone, however, seemed to be going in the same direction as me. I am used to going in the wrong direction so I changed course and went down a corridor to a door labelled 'Private Restaurant'. There was plenty of cutlery and crockery suggesting that everyone was going to be better fed. This was more like it. A waitress guarding the door asked my name.

'Eliza Hart.'

She looked at her list of names. 'I'm sorry, but you're in the other restaurant. You're on the light diet.'

'But that's impossible. I'm a journalist. I didn't ask to be on a light diet.'

'Well you are.' She smiled, as at a naughty child.

'I'd really rather not,' I smiled back.

She pointed at one of the signs: 'If you ask a waitress for more food, the waitress will be instantly dismissed.'

'But I have been medically advised to put on weight,' I said, quite truthfully. If I had told her the earth was flat and we were due for a heatwave she could not have looked at me with greater disbelief.

'Madam. You know the rules,' she said and turned away.

'Personally I regard Lee as the alpha and omega of masseurs,' someone was saying in the queue now forming behind. 'He said he would never have thought I was twenty-nine.'

'No?' queried her companion.

'No. But everyone is always saying that I could pass for nineteen.' I turned round. Ingrid would say she looked like a well-travelled suitcase.

'Really?' said her companion, engrossed in assessing her exquisite reflection in the floor-length windows.

'What?' I wanted to say to this miracle of luxurious loveliness as recognition hit me like a box round the ears.

'What?' I wanted to ask of this tormenting vision of perfection with her silk robe crooning the contours of her prototype body, with her pale face framed in a blonde halo, with her blossoming lips and eyes as grey as dusk and as impersonal as the stars.

'Lady Grace,' said the doorkeeper warmly. 'How lovely to see you again. You looked quite wonderful in that exfoliating cream advert.'

'What?' I wanted to cry, as I had visions of her famished thighs consuming The Natterjack like a boa constrictor. 'What, Grace Custard, are your harpooning hips doing at Chewton Magna? You who told Melindi that this face which launched a thousand lipsticks, this face which is the stuff that beauty creams are made of, was nothing but God's handwriting.'

She brushed past me.

'You'd better get a move on or you won't even get the light dinner,' said the doorkeeper.

'Sorry?' I said as someone else said something about me getting out of the way of a trolley piled with cabbage.

'Dinner, madam. You'll miss it.'

I padded back for a bowl of stock which they called soup. Lumps of pack ice started shunting through my body. It certainly was not indigestion. I had not eaten anything. I've had this heartburn before. It was thinking about Grace with The Natterjack. I concentrated on not thinking and ate the main course: a tablespoon of natural yoghurt topped with three sultanas. It was not as bad as some of the things I have eaten. The soup, for instance. I passed on the lemon water and went to bed.

It was twenty-five past six. I switched on the television. I imagined I was made of brass or rhinoceros hide, whichever is the tougher. It was cold. I looked at the television. It is appalling how much eating goes on on television. Every ten minutes or so, be it on an advert or an integral part of the programme's plot, someone pops something into their mouth – chocolate especially, as it contains a substance that the body produces of its own accord only when it is blissfully happy or in the throes of passionate lovemaking. Right now I can't live without it. Yorkie bars for everyday days, and on days when my soul is severely tried, bitter chocolate truffles oozing inside with a white chocolate cream as light as a sigh. White Toblerone appeared on the screen in close up. It was too much. The cold sealed up my heart and knocked out my brain. I switched off and went to sleep.

8

In Sickness and In Wealth

First thing Sunday morning I called a taxi, went straight to the station's Traveller's Fare, bought two jumbo coffees with cream, a huge hunk of extra-fruity cake, a raunchy read, and started tucking in. By King's Cross I was back to normal.

At home, three of the messages on the answering machine were variations on the theme that Bella had fallen over at the Ritz and was in St. Hilda's hospital after breaking one of her Max shoes and her ankle. There was also a message from Tim St. George and one from my sister Jane.

When Bella is in hospital you do not trouble yourself as you usually do when friends are ill. You do not worry whether she will want to be seen looking awful, ailing and prostrate in a great cast-iron bed. It does not occur to you that she may be feeling poorly and prefer to rest in peace. And it never even crosses your mind that she will not be receiving visitors. With Bella, you get round there as fast as a cab can take you. Except there were no free taxis as it was a sodden, rain-soaked Sunday lunchtime and the wind was hell-bent on becoming a typhoon.

I know St. Hilda's well because a year ago Bella fell over skiing and broke her knee. She was also in residence in the summer, after stepping on an unusual, worm-like creature in Egypt which started burrowing its way up her leg and had to be extracted under general anaesthetic. If the worm had picked on anyone else, me for instance, people would have backed off thinking, 'My God, she's got a rare worm nesting inside her.' But Bella felt the worm gave her a unique charm and she lay in court with her exquisitely manicured toes peeping out from under the bandages in Go-Getting-Red

65

varnish. The worm has been preserved in a pickle jar for research purposes.

I cannot abide hospitals but St. Hilda's makes the Ritz look like the Stockpot. Dress is formal, and gifts to patients lavish. Because of the wind and the rain, because of flooding on the Circle line and because only a qualified orienteer can find a bus on a Sunday, I swam across London on foot and arrived at the sunglass temple to St. Hilda, with its green-tinted windows stretching from floor to ceiling and up to the sky, looking like a drowned fox as I was still in my red fur coat. I don't know what made me put it on. I should have gone in a plastic bag. It would never dry at home. And the only flowers I had been able to buy were four scraggy pink carnations and three yellow ones, as the shop had run out of white flowers. They were as pretty as old dishmops and all wrapped up in crinkly, crackling silver paper.

The doors eased open automatically, the floors were marbled, the lift stopped at the seventh floor with a discreet ping. There were no signs and arrows to Casualty, Plastic Surgery, Gynaecology and similar horrors as in your everyday hospital where my sisters and brothers-in-law work. There were no hard plastic orange chairs, grey tiles. There was no one camping out in the waiting room reading year-old copies of *Woman's Own*. There was no smell or sign of ghastly bits of boiled metal, and the individual rooms were an ideal size for small cocktail parties.

'Darling, I do believe that's my drink you've got,' Bella's sister was saying as I walked in. We had met at St. Hilda's before. Steam began curling off my coat as the room was so hot. I wished I was back home with a sandwich. 'Eliza, how sweet of you to come. Peregrine,' she called to her husband who was mixing kirs, 'a drink for Eliza, please.' Peregrine gave me a drink and said I looked as if I had swum there. Ignoring him, I squeezed through the packed room. At the back, a few miles away, I spotted Bella in a state of perfect languor, propped up on snowy white pillows.

Her hair billowed around her, framing her pale face but

highlighting her lips painted in the new Hot Trotting Ginger lipstick. Dressing in an ivory shift in the sort of silk that is as soft and light as soap bubbles but hangs as if weighted with lead, she looked as if she were cruising on an ocean liner. Last winter, after her skiing accident, she plumped for peach rather than cream silk. I spotted other bits of silk peeping out the wardrobe, which was stuffed so full the door couldn't shut. Whenever she travels, even if it is just to hospital, Bella likes to be prepared for all eventualities, drinks at Buckingham Palace, whatever.

'Eliza darling, come over here,' she called. I negotiated some handsome devotees standing over her bed. Behind her were great stands of every out-of-season flower imaginable, including some fancy cabbages. They were all white. 'How sweet of you. My favourite flowers.' All flowers are her favourite.

'You poor thing,' I said. 'How did it happen?'

She lowered her eyelids, slowly.

'She's been through it so many times,' said a man trying to position a stephanotis bush so she would not have to move her head too much to look at it. She opened her eyes again, wearily. 'Her heel caught on the carpet and she tripped and fell awkwardly.' Behind me, some braying barristers were arguing her chances if she sued the Ritz. 'And her ankle broke.'

'And my shoe,' interrupted Bella, perking up. 'One of my Max Blarney's. You know, the silver suede, scalloped-edge courts. The heel snapped right off.'

'Perhaps he can make you up another one to match,' I suggested.

'Do you think so? Do you think he would do just the one? It might be difficult. They were last season's. Though I'm a good enough customer. It would be wonderful if he could. I didn't think this winter's collection had anything in it to match. Would you ask him? I know how much he likes you. And you're always writing nice things about him.'

'All right,' I said. 'I'll ring him first thing tomorrow. Your cold seems much better.'

'Yes. All the painkillers seemed to shift it,' she sniffed. 'But you don't look too well yourself.'

'I had a facial.'

'Oh dear . . . How lovely.' A nervy young man in a bow tie had just walked in with seven three-foot-long white lilies. Where do these people buy such flowers on Sundays? 'My favourite flowers.'

There were no vases left for mine so I held them as they wilted in shame. A nurse came in to raise Bella's bed one-quarter of an inch and I talked to Hermione who will be having her baby in St. Hilda's.

'In the special swimming pool they have in the basement,' she said.

'Marvellous,' I said for the millionth time in connection with her baby's aquatic delivery, but with obviously less conviction than usual as she laughed, 'You're so funny Eliza, the way you're so squeamish. What with your sisters being doctors.'

'And my brothers-in-law.'

'Really?'

Yes, I thought miserably. How typical. How typical that even I too have fallen for a doctor – though unlike the Twin Sets, Sam does not look as if he relishes the burden of it all. For doctors are Hounslow heroes, intelligent but considerate fantasy figures who will care for you, provide for you, look after you. Not that my sisters, who are as self-possessed as Bengal tigers, need much looking after.

'Well I can't see a doctor marrying you. But Eliza,' she hesitated, peering at my facial-battered face. 'Your skin . . .'

'Should I try and marry a dermatologist?'

'No. But I wondered if you were allergic to something.'

'No.' I began to explain wearily when Bella's sister joined us.

'Hermione, I hear that you're going to be working right up until the baby is born.'

'Of course. I'm not going to subscribe to the male myth that you have to give your life up to the cause of reproduction, like some women. Yesterday I saw a friend of mine who had a terribly good job at Kensington Palace which her husband persuaded her to stop five months before the baby was due.

And now she does nothing all day but arrange flowers and even that she does ineffectually.'

'I know. So many women become dead meat the moment they have children. But what sort of help are you going to get?'

'My cleaning lady will do full time. Other than that we're going to try and restrict ourselves to just the one nanny.'

'Well do make sure you register for one right away. When I had my first I left it till she was born and was suddenly so desperate I had to take this girl from our local Knightsbridge Nannies who in just six weeks got engaged to a shepherd and I had a nightmare of a time finding a replacement.'

Meanwhile, someone behind me was debating whether a case of vintage port made a good present for a baby's first Christmas and eventually decided it did. Someone else was saying that they drew the line at getting baby's clothes dry cleaned but in the case of white lace they made an exception.

A second nurse came in to check that Bella was still all right and a third took her lunch away.

'Didn't you want it?' the nurse asked. It was a prawn cocktail with two prawns removed.

'I couldn't manage it,' said Bella feebly.

'Are you eating enough?' chorused the men.

'Oh yes, yes thank you,' she said even more feebly. Going to hospital presents Bella with a consummate opportunity for losing weight. Far from her own kitchen she is out of temptation's way. Also, she never eats much when observed, and as going to hospital means she is forever in company she has no opportunity for heartily tucking in.

Just then, four men who had been playing indoor tennis at Hampton Court squeezed into the room, plus another of Bella's sisters with her three overactive children.

'Take these for me,' Bella whispered as I said goodbye. She handed me two pounds of designer chocolates in a box double-glazed with thick velvet and done up with three yards of scarlet ribbon, a gift from some misguided devotee.

9

Out in the Cold

Home at last. I looked in the fridge. It takes an Einstein to shop for more than one meal in advance. All I possessed was butter, the tin of Weight Watcher's rice pudding, plus a packet of Ryvitas, cereal with all the raisins picked out and Bella's chocolates. I thought about eating my chic white cabbage but it was going brown at the edges.

I paddled out into the rain again to the corner shop. All the winos, weirdos and madmen in the neighbourhood were there too. I don't know how they can afford to shop in open-all-hours shops. I discovered a tin of tuna costing more than a tub of caviar and for the next twenty minutes walked up and down the aisles trying to find something more exciting and less expensive and couldn't.

I stood at the end of a long queue behind everyone else buying twenty Marlboro and Winalot. Outside, a sleek silver Jaguar was stallioning itself in front of the shop. Out got The Natterjack.

'I might have guessed I'd meet you here,' he said, muscling his way in. He has always walked as if he was born in Brixton and his face looks ten years older than it is. He picked up two John Bull bitter four-packs. 'Can I join you?'

'No,' answered a voice behind me. It belonged to a tattooed ten-ton Tarzan. 'Get to the back.' We did as he said.

'So, sweetheart, how are you? How was your hot date?'

'Very nice, thank you,' I said politely. 'Did you find a babysitter?'

'No. We didn't go in the end.'

'Oh what a shame for you all. That was pity. So you stayed in too?'

'That's right, my darling. We stayed in. And, dear God, Eliza,' he said with disgust, looking at the three tins of tuna I had picked up, 'you're still eating as if you're permanently pregnant. I hope you didn't feed Mr Hot Date that stuff. But you're not, are you? Pregnant?' I ignored him. 'You look . . .' he paused and looked me up and down. If I had had tyres he would have kicked me. 'It's hard to tell in that coat but you still look pretty skinny to me. Would you like one of these?' He picked up a large white Toblerone.

'No,' I said. 'Actually, yes, on second thoughts. Please.'

'Thought so, I can always depend on you to be hungry,' he laughed smugly. 'I'll treat you to two if you like.'

'One's enough. How's Grace?' I asked sharply, wanting to know why she was at Chewton Magna while The Natterjack was here in London drinking John Bull, when the old woman behind me suddenly hissed, 'I know your game.'

I ignored her.

'So, Grace, how is she?'

'I know your game,' she cackled louder and then shot forward and prodded me with her filthy finger.

'Ugh,' I cried, moving away for she smells of generations of grime.

'Hey. Leave her alone,' said The Natterjack, coming on all protective and standing between us as the woman gave out a great laugh like a buzzard who's just got a good joke. Rather Jack than me, I thought, for I have encountered this mad woman before and she is prone to spit.

'Ignore her,' I warned. 'She's always attacking me.'

'What do you mean, "always attacking you"?' he said, backing away from her as she started dribbling and muttering I don't know what.

'Get on with it, love,' interrupted the man on the till. 'Are these all yours?'

'Come on, I'll take you home,' said Jack outside.

'I'm fine. I'll walk.'

'Don't be daft, Eliza. It's pissing down.'

'I need the exercise.'

71

'You hate exercise. Get in,' he said, opening the door of the snarling, silver machine. So I got in and we accelerated off proudly with a deep-bellied roar.

'Do you always go for such horny cars these days?' I asked him.

'This is Grace's.'

It would be. You can feel the power of a car like this in the loins.

'What have *you* got then? No, don't tell me: a Range Rover with black leather seats, four-wheel drive and all that?'

'Spot on.'

'Really?' I said, delighted I could still assess him so well. He was laughing. 'Really?'

'Yes. Really.'

'But which has never been anywhere more rural than Sloane Square?' I continued. 'Unless Grace has made you take up hunting and shooting so you actually need that four wheel drive to negotiate fields sodden with dead duck.' He said nothing. Not surprisingly.

'So how is Grace?'

'Fine.'

'Her career is doing really well at the moment.'

'Uh-huh.'

'Getting that job at Number 10 gave her great publicity.'

'Yes.'

'She's in the fifty most beautiful women piece we're running in March.'

'Yes.'

'Rainedon did the pictures.'

'Uh-huh.'

'Does she enjoy the modelling?'

'Yes.'

'She's been up for some film role, hasn't she?' I persisted. It would have been easier extracting his wisdom teeth.

'Yes.'

'Which one?' I persevered.

'She's keeping all that quiet at the moment.'

'Is the John Bull for her as well?'

'Eliza.' He looked at me and grinned. 'Give over, will you?' and he pulled up outside my block.

'Thanks.' It's like doing breast stroke getting out of a car that low. 'Bye.'

'Hold on,' he said, retrieving his beer and locking up. 'I'll see you in.'

'There's no need.'

'I want to see you in safely.'

'No, you don't.'

'I do.'

'You want to see what my flat looks like.'

'That too. Do you still keep those pink basket shoes on the mantelpiece?'

I said nothing. The strawberry pink basket shoes were designed by Max and were the most exquisite shoes imaginable, the ones I had described as 'cultural icons' but no one would buy them so Max gave me a pair. But the first time I wore them the heel fell off the left foot.

'Are you hiding something, Eliza?'

'No. I'm just busy.'

'Busy? You're a thunderingly bad liar you know,' he said, brushing the rain from his forehead. 'You've never busy. You're the most slothful woman I have ever known.'

'I was only slothful because I lived with you, Jack. You needed a balance.'

'Can we talk inside? You already look like you've been stuck in an automatic car wash but I'm still quite dry.'

'Only if you don't stay long as I'm going out.'

'Yes, I know. You're busy.'

'Do you want a drink, some tea or something?' I said when we got in.

'I'll have one of these if you don't mind,' he said, opening a can of his beer.

'Do you want a glass?'

'No,' he mumbled, taking a swig. Kate always said he was a thug, though Rosanna with her unsurpassable ability for calling a spade a silver spoon found him 'disintegratingly masculine'.

'Good God, what is that?' he said, looking at the mushroom as I hunted around the kitchen.

'A phone.'

'But it's hideous.'

'I know but I was given it.'

'And that one,' he said looking in the bathroom. 'A mermaid?'

'Stop nosing around and get in there,' I said pointing to the sitting room.

'Wait, wait. Let me look. What have you got in here?' he said going into the bedroom. 'You've still got those mouse boots, I see. But where's the phone? Oh that's a disappointment. Very dull. A steely grey one. Gun metal. Interesting choice.' He looked at the bed. Its sheets and covers are pure white as they were given to me and, like all my freebies, be they flowers or sheets or cabbages, cannot be tainted with colour.

'That silly smirk, Jack,' I said, 'never became you. Now, out, please.'

'Seriously, I like it. The way you've done the flat, I mean.'

He was bound to like it as, except for my free white sheets, the place is a riot of colour. Living in the flat we shared was like being resident in a kaleidoscope as his artist friends were always coming round and painting on the walls. Once he started making all his money he kept commissioning his friends, and he liked fooling around with colour. So one year we had Italian frescos, another Egyptian friezes, Fragonard in the bathroom, Redouté roses in the hall. It was wonderful. It really was, except for the smell of the paints. My place is not wonderful as I do not have Jack's eye but it is much better than my *Circe* friends' homes, who all live in interior designers' interpretation of *nouvelle cuisine*: everything is pure white except for one or two reputedly extraordinary pieces of furniture which stand out against the white walls in the same way as a petit pois or a carved baby carrot is said to do against a white plate. I feel the same way about their white walls as I do about their black clothes. One reminds me of funerals, the other of hospitals.

'So who's the hot date tonight?' he asked.

'Well . . .' I began, when the phones rang.

'Hello,' I said, relieved that they had rung and did not look as if they were purely for show.

'Hello, Eliza, it's Cassandra.'

'Hello, Jeremy,' I said loudly.

'Eliza, it's me, Cassandra.'

'I know,' I said sweetly.

'Have you got someone with you?'

'Yes,' I continued as if I were a barley sugar.

'What are you playing at?'

'Can I ring you back?'

'I think you'd better. I want to know what you're up to. Bye then.'

'Goodbye.'

I replaced the phone when, to my surprise, they all rang again.

It was Ashley, the advertising man who gave me the wretched phones in the first place.

'Ashley!' I said delightedly, though I know he only rings when he wants something. 'How good to hear you.' I never even liked him that much. He was the first man I saw after The Natterjack and the man with whom I learned that you can spend the whole night in bed with a man with no invasion of your solipsistic universe. You can do the deed, fall asleep holding each other tight, wake up closely entwined with your breaths mingling, with no abatement in your solitude, still as lonely as ever.

'You too, Eliza,' he went on, making choice compliments until he came to the purpose of his call. 'I wondered actually if you could possibly do me a favour?'

'I'd love to,' I said, as if he had just asked me on a free trip round the Maldives. The Natterjack looked up.

'You see, I've just taken over a new account for men's

beauty products and I wondered if you could possibly put them into the magazine. The range is called "Shogun" – do you think that's a good name?'

'Brilliant.'

'Yes, so do I. I thought of it. And the point is, we're not actually going to call them beauty products. No. This is the key, Eliza. They're not beautifiers. As I see it, the problem with men's products is that they're still marketed too much like women's beauty products so men are wary of them. Moisturising your skin is seen as effeminate. It all sounds too much like wearing make-up. You know.'

'Yes,' I said, watching Jack rub his eyes.

'It's too cosmetic. Instead, Shogun – and this is what makes it so exciting – is a survival aid. It fights wind-battered, office-stressed skin, battles mightily against masculine exhaustion, combats the ravages of a virile life.' He paused. 'And the complete range is based on ocean products, the idea being that men must enlist the power of the great seas, so we have a genuine sea mud soap, a seaweed toner . . .'

'I'd love to hear more,' I said as if Bogart was whispering sweet nothings down the phone. It turns my stomach to think this man earns in one month what I earn in a year. 'Could I ring you tomorrow?'

'Sure, Eliza. Sure. Look forward to it. Bye.'

'You're certainly in demand,' said The Natterjack.

'I thought I'd stop looking for one man and settle with many,' I said, giving him my Mona Lisa smile – men are but moments in a woman's life.

'All right, I've got the message. I'll see you around then,' he said.

'Yes.'

'Watch out for old ladies.'

'Yes.'

'Goodbye then.' He took a step towards me. I moved back. I didn't want him touching me.

'Goodbye,' I said. And he let himself out.

10

Phoney Talk

'So who was with you?' asked Cassandra later, when I returned her call on the mermaid.

'St. George,' I lied. If I had told her it was The Natterjack she would have wanted all the details so she could have used them for a piece on 'Meeting Your Ex'.

'Are you egging him on?'

'Of course I'm not egging him on. He just keeps ringing me.'

'Hmm. I think I might do a piece on it.'

'On what?'

'Modern St. Georges, I'll call it. The men that women keep at the end of a lead. Whom they ring up if they want to go out to dinner, whom they use as an escort . . .'

'I do not use him. He rings me, we split the bill and I leap right into a taxi the moment I leave the restaurant.'

'You don't see it the way I see it. You still see yourself as Anne of Green Gables even when in four-inch heels or wearing your Crimson Joy dress.'

'And you see everything as another piece for your problem page,' I said crossly. 'I wouldn't mind it so much if you paid me a consultation fee. Anyway what did you ring for in the first place? Are you all right?'

'No, I'm in a pretty bad way actually.'

'Oh, yes,' I said unsympathetically.

'Yes, I've got this awful spot. Well I haven't actually got it yet. I can just sense it starting.'

'Well I had a facial yesterday so I've got loads, if it's any consolation.'

'But is there anything I can do about it?'

'No.'

'You're suppose to know about this sort of thing.'

'I do and there's nothing you can do about it.'

'I haven't eaten chocolate in days.'

'According to my sisters it doesn't matter what you eat.'

'I don't trust your sisters.'

'Nor do I. But there's no point in depriving yourself unnecessarily.'

'I keep going to the bathroom to put antiseptic on it. It's getting red and inflamed and horribly . . .'

'Cassandra, please.'

'But it hurts when I laugh. Not that I've got much to laugh about.'

'Oh go and write your St. George article.'

'Don't rush me. The Bostonian should ring tonight, shouldn't he?'

'That's right.'

'So you're sitting about waiting for him to ring.'

'No. I'm having a bath.'

'Wallowing about then.'

'No.'

'Going over what you said last time he rang, wondering whether, if you had said something different, you wouldn't be on your own in the bath?'

'No.'

'Imagining what you will wear if you see him again?'

'No.'

'I don't believe you. What's he doing at Christmas?'

'Going to his sister's in Vermont, skiing.'

'Skiing? What are doing with a man who likes skiing? You hate people who ski.'

'Look, Cassandra, I've got to go but I'll see you soon.'

'Do you want me to get off the phone just in case he's trying to get through?'

'No, but goodbye,' I said and put the phone down.

Half an hour later they rang again.

'Hello dear. It's Madge here.'

'Oh hello, Madge.' Madge is Kate's mother.

'You answered that quickly. Were you expecting a call?'

'No. It's just that I've got a phone by the bath. Isn't it lovely news about Kate?'

'Isn't it? He is such a lovely boy. We all like him so much. Of course you have met him lots of times, haven't you?'

'Oh yes, he's terribly nice, yes, very nice, very.'

'We're all delighted. But what about you though, dear?'

'Me? I'm fine. Yes I'm really well, really well, er, thank you.'

'Well let's hope this time next year it'll be your turn. A lovely girl like you. I'm sure your day is not too far away, dear.'

'Hmm, whatever, Kate didn't tell me when the wedding was.'

'May Day. May 1st.'

'Very romantic.'

'Isn't it? Now dear, what I want to talk to you about is the bridesmaid dresses.'

'Oh yes. I know everything about wedding and bridesmaid dresses. Fabrics, designers, latest fashions, whatever you need. I can fill you in on it all.'

'Yes I'm sure you can, dear, what with your job. But Kate knows exactly what she wants. And I wondered when you would be free for a fitting, since you're chief bridesmaid.'

'Well – '

'There'll be seven of you, four big ones – though of course you're not very big – and three little ones, all under five. And I know how you're always so busy so I thought I'd better let you know about the dress as soon as possible what with there only being four and half months to organise everything – more like only four months as you can't do anything over Christmas.'

'No, I suppose not.'

'So I thought I'd just give you the address of the designer and you can make the appointment yourself.'

I didn't say anything.

'Is that all right, dear?'

Kate has such a fixed view of what she wants and does not want, combined with such a reservoir of formidable determination, that in a short round I am no match for her. When she used to say you will play Monopoly with me, I did. Now, when she says you will be my bridesmaid, I am.

'Yes. Fine.'

'It's a woman called Lady Cutlet.'

'Lady Cutlet?' Lady Cutlet has designed the wedding dresses for about a third of the women in Debrett's. 'She's in Holland Park. I know her.'

'Well, that's most convenient then, dear. Now I can rely upon you to get everything organised. And I'll be seeing you at Christmas, won't I? I bumped into your mother yesterday and she told me you'll be at home for the holiday. Kate and Robert are spending Christmas with his family then on Boxing Day they're driving up from Somerset to us. It's quite a long drive but Kate says that in Robert's Ferrari and with the roads being empty it should take less than two hours. Where are the twins going to be?'

'I'm not sure exactly. I don't think they know what their timetables are.'

'And of course they have got their husbands to fit in with now too. Are they all well?'

Oh, Madge, please get off the phone. Please. Right now. Sam must be trying to ring me. I know it.

'Well, dear, I'll say goodbye.'

I put down the phone. The cold tap dripped. The colonel's television was on. The woman next door was shouting – others elsewhere are having problems with love. I ran some more water. Lying in hot baths is bad for your skin, Ingrid is always saying. Duncan was bugling away. Five minutes later the phones rang again.

'Hello,' I said. I knew who it would be.

'You've got such a sexy telephone voice, Eliza.'

'Oh, hello, Kate.'

'You really have. You sound amazing on the phone.'

'Kate – ' I began.

'I know, I know. My mother just rang. I really appreciate this, Eliza. There's no one I'd rather have as my chief bridesmaid than you. You don't mind, do you?'

'No,' I lied.

'Thank you. Thank you. You're brilliant, you know, Eliza. I'm so happy and I really can't wait to see you. I've got so much to tell you. And you really must meet Robert's friend Paul on Tuesday – at dinner. You haven't forgotten, have you?'

'No, but Kate, I hate this blind date business you keep getting me into.'

'It's not a blind date.'

'But have you told him you're setting him up with me?'

'Not in so many words.'

'It's really kind of you, but . . . ' At Kate's little soirées – this will be her third dinner on my behalf – I sit there grimacing at the gravadlax, working myself up into an aggressive frenzy, asking myself: does this man think I'm some sort of clot, an ugly clot too, a sort of hideous clot who could not possibly find a man on her own and needs her friends to give her a hand? And then I worry he is asking himself: how could Kate imagine I could possibly like such an ugly clot? And once I start thinking that I then start behaving like a clot and go into militant overdrive.

'I've said eighty-thirty,' interrupted Kate. 'But can you come round early so I can have a proper talk with you? And come in one of your nicer outfits.'

'What do you mean? All my clothes are extremely nice – exceptionally so.'

'I know, but sometimes you look like a spilt paint box.'

'Who says? Robert?'

'Yes, no. I'm just saying this because I want you and Paul to like each other so you stop wasting your time with Sam. I want you to be as happy as me. But I'd better go as I've got to ring Robert's sisters about their bridesmaid dresses. So goodbye and thanks again, Eliza.'

The phones rang immediately after I put the mermaid's top back on her fish's tail.

'Hello,' I answered in my sexy telephone voice.

'Are you all right?' It was Jane, my sister.

'Yes,' I said.

'You sound really funny on the phone. Horribly husky and phlegmy.'

'Oh.'

'I thought you might have a cold.'

'No.'

'Had you taken the phones off the hook?'

'No.'

'Well they've been engaged.'

'People have been ringing me, that's why.'

'Oh, I thought you were in one of your anti-social moods or something. Anyway, I was just ringing because I wanted you to bring, if you don't mind, that salad bowl of yours.'

'Bring it where?'

'To the party, of course.'

'Well, yes of course. It's not for another two weeks though, is it?' The Twin Sets are having a joint New Year's Eve party to which I am supposed to be going.

'No, but we just wanted to check.'

'Well I'm not doing anything else with my salad bowl that night. But it's huge you know. It's pretty difficult to move.' I own the world's biggest but ugliest salad bowl. It is more of a trough. Last year, the Twin Sets, all four of them, clubbed together to buy it for me as a joint Christmas and birthday present. My birthday is at the beginning of January and they always fob me off with a joint present. And I don't eat salads if I can avoid it.

'I know it's big, that's why we need it.'

'All right. But what about Christmas? Are you going to be able to come home or have you got to work?'

'It depends. James's hours keep changing so we might have to. I suppose you've got the whole time off?'

'No. I've got to go in those days in between Christmas and New Year but I've got the week after New Year off, so I might decorate the bathroom. Possibly not. I can always go and see Colette, that friend of mine in Paris.'

'The one that works for that fashion designer?'

'Karl Lagerfeld. Yes. Anyway I'll see. I don't know yet. But there are all these tidal marks over the bathroom walls.'

'I know, when we had a burst pipe . . .' And I had to let her go on, uninterrupted, as between them, my sisters have the monopoly on suffering.

Sam rang when I was in bed. Every time he rings I think he's the nicest, funniest, kindest, sexiest man I've met in a long, long time. He sings too. He sings on the phone. He sings and changes all the names to Eliza but I don't really listen to the words because he sings in such a way that makes you think that if the tune is sung right, life is full of sex and fun, and still more fun and sex.

But the conversation goes nowhere. It is all in the area of suggestion and unspoken possibilities. We just flirt on the phone. And because we have the Atlantic between us, the flirting is of the highest order. There is the potential for further intimacy, but with three thousand miles between us as we speak, there is no guarantee. We can lead each other on brilliantly, but only so far, only to the point that we heavily suggest that things should go further without actually having to commit ourselves to doing anything about it.

In the Sixties, I suppose you knew where you stood after sleeping with a man. You just stepped right on to the next man. Pre-Sixties, I suppose you didn't do anything in the first place, and if you did, then you did not know where you stood, poor you. But now? Where are you? At the finale of a fun fling? At the start of a relationship? Are you inviting him for family Christmas lunch? Are you ever seeing him again?

I don't know and it is all deeply dissatisfying. I put the phone down and am disconnected once more, left in suspense until the next phone call. Also, when the connection is bad it takes time for the person at the other end to hear what you have just said so you have these long awkward silences. Sometimes I wish I could just forget Sam and have a relationship with the phone – especially with four to choose from.

11

Altar Ego

When I got in to work Monday morning, two more prize white cabbages were on my desk alongside a perfect specimen of a cauliflower sprouting in a wicker basket and a note from Naomi saying two bears had arrived for me and were in the cupboard. They were white bears wearing bobble hats and with 'Happy Christmas from Sellcookers' embroidered on their right paws. Sellcookers is a large department store. The cabbages were from Number 10, the cosmetic company for whom Grace models. The cauliflower came from Cole, an environmentally sound jewellery designer who makes accessories out of rubbish.

The week before Christmas it is impossible to do any work with all the distraction of presents arriving, paper being torn open and everyone trying to find out what everyone else has been given and comparing it with their own presents. There were six Sellcookers polar bears on Ingrid's desk, all different sizes to make up a family – father, mother, children, toddler, baby and so on – and a crate of champagne. She was on the phone to her housekeeper, Peggy, who, at fifteen years Ingrid's senior, is seventy-six. Neither of them have a hundred per cent hearing.

'I'll just have smoked salmon and some of those cherry tomatoes.' Today is not a pineapple day. 'The cherry ones. Not those squelchy tasteless jobs . . . What . . . ? Marks & Sparks, probably. And make sure they are English too. Not Jersey. And you can give Raffles the rest of that *château boeuf Wellington*, but take the pastry off as he's eating too much.' Raffles is her white Scottie dog. 'And there are some frozen sausages which need eating up – for you. They're in the top part of the freezer,

I think. All right? . . . Don't forget the tomatoes . . . Just a minute. Melindi, what time am I having that new facial with beeswax?'

'Five-thirty,' said Melindi.

'Seven-thirty to eight, so long as I'm not kept too long . . . Bye.

'Hello, darling,' Ingrid said to me. 'You look dreadful. Didn't you go to the health farm?'

'Yes, but – '

'Have you seen all these bears? I don't know why they have to send me bears every year.' She sat two in her black silk lap. 'It was bears last year, brown ones. Why can't they send me a nice hamper round from their food hall? Or just do what Number 10 do? Something simple, like champagne. What did they give you, darling? It should have been something nice after all that work you did on the cellulite special.'

I told her about the vegetables.

'Well, they're terribly expensive, you know. It's not like being given an ordinary cabbage. But champagne is so much more useful. I'm terribly sorry. Look, have a bear.' She gave me the largest bear.

'Thank you. But aren't you saving them for the god-children?'

'They had bears last year and I've got all those "Free as a Bird" flamingos they can have.' To publicise the launch of a new 'Free as a Bird' make-up range, she had been sent a five-strong flock of pink flamingos, 'Good God, who's that for?' said Ingrid in alarm.

Two of the postboys were going into the editor's office with a crate of the company's very own personal supply of Veuve Clicquot. Champagne from the company cellar was most definitely not a Christmas present. The company donates a crate of champagne whenever a member of staff gets the sack or engaged. Be it a marriage or a firing, the company like to send you off in style.

'Naomi,' called Ingrid. 'The champagne?' she mouthed in a stage whisper. 'Who's it for?'

'I don't know,' said Naomi, worriedly.

Hermione, spotting the champagne, came bounding up. 'Who is it?' she asked.

I did not know.

Persephone and her entourage of assistants sidled out of the fashion room. 'Who?' she asked suspiciously.

'Don't know,' said Ingrid. 'Naomi, is anyone in with the editor?'

'I'm not sure. I'm sorry.'

'Naomi, you're hopeless,' said Ingrid. Naomi looked more worried – with reason.

Engagement celebrations occur slightly more frequently than sacking wakes but none of us could think of anyone about to get engaged.

'Oh dear. Bad news pending for someone, I'm afraid,' said Hermione, with the same glee that she reports on a new disease she can write about. Naomi sat down. Hermione started humming: 'The outlook was decidedly blue,' when the editor's greenhouse doors swung open and Rosanna, obviously back from Rome and recovered from her smoked salmon food poisoning, sporting a diamond so large her other ringless fingers looked underdressed, bowled out.

'Rosanna!' cried everyone with relief. And congratulations and compliments gushed upon her with the full force of Niagara.

Who? When? Where? Everyone wanted to know.

'Is it Cartier?' Ingrid asked about the ring. It was Cartier. Apparently Xavier's godfather was on their board.

'Is he French then?' said Melindi. His father was French but his mother was English and he had spent five years at Harrow.

'Is he a French *comte* or something?' Tron wanted to know, as she always falls in love with a title. When she herself got engaged three years ago she waxed lyrical for five minutes on the joys of commitment to eternal love then said that the really best thing about her husband-to-be was that he was an honourable too. As for Xavier, his father was a *comte* which meant that ultimately Rosanna would be a *comtesse*.

'And what does he do?' demanded Ingrid. He was in the French Foreign Office. Ingrid and Tron nodded approvingly.

'How old is he?' asked Naomi. He is forty-one. 'Old enough to be her father,' Naomi whispered to me later. Girls of Naomi's age frequently make this mistake, thinking anyone topping forty is old enough to be your father. Naomi, along with all her contemporaries and my younger sisters, is an arch traditionalist and does not hold with age differences of more than two years between husbands and wives – the man, of course, being the older. 'It just makes so much more sense,' she says with a pragmatism, prudence and dispassion that horrifies me.

I am shocked at Rosanna's news. Kate's engagement came with the absolute and predestined certainty as the further falls of snow this morning. But Rosanna's? No. I never expected it. In the three years I have known her she has never sustained a relationship for longer than eight weeks and three days. That she now intends to spend the rest of her life with this man has stunned me. It is not that Rosanna had never wanted to get married. Nor that she did not have everything going for her in the race for a mate. Quite the reverse. She is the extremely beautiful daughter of an extremely wealthy businessman. She uses *Who's Who* as her address book and can play the piano, flute, cello and medieval recorder. The third landing of her parent's stucco-fronted home with a view of Regent's Park is lined with her watercolours. She plays a fair game of squash and was runner-up in Kent's under-sixteen tennis champion-ships and has been skiing brilliantly since the age of five. She played Portia in her first year at Oxford and Sarah in *Guys and Dolls* in her final, when she also got a first-class degree in English. She can knock up an impromptu dinner for twelve, knows the Latin names for most species of butterfly and can drive a tractor. For twelve years she had ballet lessons, and more recently has learnt jazz, tap, and a selection of Scottish reels. She is also the author of innumerable brilliant puns and can invent a page of faultless fashion froth in a morning.

Despite these advantages, however, Rosanna was

perpetually dissatisfied. She left university with her brilliant expectations, hoping life would be full of Byronic gestures and opportunities to act heroically like Portia. Finding that she spent most of her days just plodding along, getting depressed and deciding to cheer herself up again, was gnawingly disappointing. Having this sudden, passionate, tempestuous, escapist romance must be the nearest she has ever been able to get towards satisfying her desires and living with the sense of occasion she feels her life deserves. She certainly can't behave like Portia all the time. If she did she would be locked up or given a bugle like my Duncan.

'Eliza, darling,' she said, taking me aside. 'I'm sorry I couldn't tell you myself. I tried to ring you last night but you were engaged all the time. And we flew in at seven this morning so I got in before you and as old Madam was in, I spoke to her right away as − I haven't told the others yet, so don't say anything about it as she's got to speak to different people etc. etc. − I want to stop work now.'

'Now? Right now?'

'Xavier starts a new job in Washington on March 2nd, you see, and we want to get it all over and done with, the marriage and everything, so I can go out there with him. And I don't want to hang about here any longer than I have to. But I have to have a proper talk with you. Not here. So I can tell you all about it.'

'Oh Rosanna,' I said miserably. 'It's brilliant news. I'm really happy for you. But I'm going to miss you so much.' I really am going to miss her.

'Rosanna,' called the editor. 'Can you come in here, please.'

I sat at my desk. I am delighted that Rosanna is so happy. Of course I am. I do want my friends to be happy. Of course I do. It is just that their happiness makes me look more closely at my own and sometimes I find it wanting. And I'll miss the sanity of her company at work. One of Persephone's assistants was talking about some coats which were so beautiful they brought tears to her eyes; Persephone herself was moaning that she had put on four ounces over the weekend − she weighs herself as if she were as precious as a lump of gold; Hermione had just announced that her baby – which now seems to be bouncing around like Tigger – had moved; and Tron was telling Zenith, *Circe*'s astrologer to 'beef up' the horoscopes.

'I mean, what's this on Taurus?' asked Tron. (Tron is a Taurus.) ' "Your love life and finances should see some improvement." I need something better than that. What about, "Lightning strikes, sparks leap and an explosive Full Moon brings all your romantic desires to fulfilment and rockets your finances up to the Heavens"? Yes, that's more like it. Now Leo . . .'

'It's all right,' said Rosanna returning to my desk after the editor had finished with her, 'I just have to do that thing on men's shoes then I can go. And,' she whispered, 'I'm having a celebratory dinner party on Wednesday and whatever you are doing you must cancel it as you simply must meet him. There'll be about a hundred at dinner so I won't really have a chance to chat, so can we have lunch some time? I wish we could have it today but I've got to run now as I've got to speak to my mother. She, thank God, is arranging it all.'

A celebratory dinner party for a hundred and a full-panoplied wedding – all within the next six weeks – will present no problem to a woman like Rosanna's mother who, during her tenure as Lord Mayor of London, mustered such formidable organisational skills she banished as many as five thousand illegal stall holders selling vegetables and fold-up Japanese umbrellas from the streets of her capital, something no Lord Mayor had managed to do before.

'Thursday,' Rosanna went on, 'is best for me for lunch because I'll come in then with the shoe piece before we go to Lady Cutlet's show. Are you all right?'

'Yes. I'm fine.'

'It's just that your face is really red.'

'I had a facial.'

'You should eat a raw egg.'

'Yes.' (Ever since a Chinese woman she met on a bus in

America in New Orleans told Rosanna it was the best possible thing for the skin, she has eaten a raw egg every day.)

'Any developments with The Bostonian?'

'No. Except it looks as if he'll be out of a job by the end of the year. He's having this row with the man he works under, so he might have to go. You know, on a point of principle.'

'Oh, darling. Perhaps you should go over and comfort him. Oh, I really want to speak to you properly about it all. But I can't see when. And I'm so going to miss you – '

'Let's talk about it Thursday,' I interrupted. And slipping into her floor length Jean Muir coat, Rosanna ran off.

When she had left the room, Naomi said to Ingrid, 'At her age, I thought it was time she got married.'

Oh Naomi, shut up.

'And what's this I hear about you being a bridesmaid?' Ingrid asked me. 'Are you really?'

'Yes,' I said, 'though I don't feel like it.'

'It's not how you feel, it's how you look. Talking of looks, why don't you borrow some make-up? You really look as if you could do with it.'

'Ingrid, please, I've got to work.' And work I did.

12

Face Values

Jobs and frocks may not feed the soul but they sure pass the time. It took me all Monday and all Tuesday, to write interestingly about Britain's fifty most beautiful women. It is a task I am singularly unqualified to do for I could not give a toss about one of them. In the past, Shakespeare, Keats and co. had the job of glorifying beautiful women, but now poets are too preoccupied with inner-city deprivation and the imminence of nuclear annihilation.

Bella has paroxysms over the very concept of the country's fifty most beautiful women because she believes any such list is incomplete without her crowning it. At Oxford she was so assured of her own beauty, she held a Valentine's Day party to which she invited a hundred men and no women other than herself. Everyone had the most marvellous time, she says.

I find it such a depressing job even though virtually any woman in Britain can be made to look beautiful in a photograph, given the right conditions. A good hairdresser and make-up artist, for starters. Next, a photographer who knows just what sort of camera, lens, film, filter, and lights will show you off to maximum advantage and then takes about a hundred different pictures from which to choose just one perfect photograph. And finally an art department to 'touch up' the picture – painting over wrinkles, for instance, or cutting off offensive hips. (In last month's magazine there was a photograph of a glossy soap actress, which was the virtual creation of the art department. The photographer – it was discovered too late – hated the actress because she had had an affair with his ex-wife so he took her picture with her sitting at a table on which he had lain a sheet of silver foil. Silver foil reflects the light and it amplified her every wrinkle and face-lift scar. The art department then had to cover them up to turn her face into a flawless mask.)

Looking at all those perfect faces makes you feel decidedly inadequate. Reading about them makes you feel you've gone on a romp through the Thesaurus as these women – all of whom are mentioned in Debrett's – have to be described in language more flowery than a Colefax and Fowler settee. There is Lady Sophie Fitzgibbon-Wolf, for instance, the creature of generations of loveliness, privileged to have inherited cheekbones which soar up to eyes so misty they could tame a dragon and have been spellbinding unlucky gentlemen through centuries.

Then Countess Claudia Coletta Cole whose limpid, lambent, lilac eyes slant like almonds in a face with all the innocence of Alice in Wonderland but which occasionally breaks into a rare smile suggesting a wanton but endearing depravity.

India is as exotic as her name. Always dressed in skintight black as if she has been dipped in treacle to reveal her exquisitely tuned feline body. Those who have felt the brunt of her wrath – rather than her wit – wonder if she is indeed half cat.

And Lady Grace Gustaad, of course. She is an etiolated beauty with legs as impossibly slender as the racehorses she owns, skin finer than anemone petals, eyes of grey and all the grace of a twentieth-century Titania.

It makes me feel quite sick and I have to keep eating to get me through it all, with Persephone and her assistants moaning in the background that they can't remember the last time they ate a flapjack, an egg sandwich, a Mars bar, a doughnut, non-diet Coke, toffees or whatever I'm wolfing down. Their problem is that they have the typical eating habits of the unobserved female. Persephone will go to Le Caprice and order scrambled egg made with one egg and no butter or just nibble on smoked salmon. But when she has an evening in on her own, she eats. She gets in about eight p.m. and starts off with some main meal substitute like a couple of leaves of radicchio with half a tub of low-fat cottage cheesé, perhaps followed by a plain yoghurt. At nine, she will have a few handfuls of Special K; at ten she will eat up the rest of the cottage cheese, sultanas, and crumble Ryvitas in milk. And at eleven she will investigate the freezer, eat a Lean Cuisine and finish off the left-over vat of lemon sorbet from her last dinner party.

As for the fifty most beautiful women's beauty tips, they fall into two categories. The first, like Lady Human or the Countess Want, take the whole business absolutely seriously and, immune from embarrassment, readily divulge their offbeat beauty tactics: they roll around on green plastic balls they bought in Denmark; drink a glass of hot water with a spoon of honey from their father's beehive last thing at night; buy £50-tubs of royal jelly; go on champagne-only diets.

The second group are like Grace Gustaad. They go all coy and say: 'I don't do anything. I really don't. No. Honestly,' as they do not want lesser mortals reading about what they get up to in their own bathrooms. These women try my soul particularly sorely as they have to be pressed into saying something.

'Do you at least wash your face?' I ask.

'Oh yes, of course I wash my face.'

'What do you wash it with?'

'What do I wash it with? Heavens what a funny question. I've never been asked that before. Ha, ha.'

'Well, do you wash it with soap, do you use a cleanser, do you use one of those special detergent-free cleansing bars, baby soap, a soap for dry skin, splash your face with cold water . . . ?' It is like conducting a multiple-choice test.

'Actually I use soap. Baby soap. But I've never bought a cream in my life. Not in my life. Can't see the point.'

'What about exercise?'

'Oh no. Can't abide it. I always skipped games at school. Can't think why people want to get all hot and sweaty. Never run or anything. Except, ha ha, to catch a bus.'

I don't believe a word of it. These sort of women, generally the wife or daughter of a man who could afford to kit out the entire female population with royal jelly and plastic Danish balls, would not get up from their chaise longues to run for a bus. A cab perhaps, but never a bus. Being blindingly beautiful – they would rather you believed – just comes naturally. But although very few are blindingly beautiful, they all, even those who are blindingly ugly, are brilliant at presentation. They know how to make sure that you see what they want you to see, be it glamour, wit, talent, humanity – and they know what to hold in check.

13

Blind Date

Tuesday night, after unremitting slog, I finished off the beauties. It had been dark since four as it was the shortest day of the year. It was also the coldest. Yesterday had been the coldest as well but the weather keeps getting worse so each day it breaks another record. It could be worse. It was seven degrees colder in Boston and twenty colder in Moscow. It could be worse – the electricians could have gone on strike – much, much worse I told myself as the snow froze in my hair, gelid air reddened my nose and melting ice seeped through my boots as I trekked from the tube to Kate's flat in Pimlico Square.

Being her law firm's highest-achieving woman for her age, coupled her with becoming their youngest-ever partner, could, Kate feared, be construed as unattractively un-womanly. Her flat, at the top floor of a great converted Victorian mansion, was therefore lavishly decked out as a tribute to her femininity.

In the hall was a mural of cherubs peeping out from behind rose bushes and a large rococo mirror. Immediate impressions were of an idyllic pastoral scene. The whole flat certainly smelt of one, for everywhere you encountered great flowery chamber pots full of heavily scented potpourri. Her bed was an antique wooden four-poster. Gauzy muslin curtains hung from its brass rails and white lace pillows were carelessly strewn over the white lace counterpane. Items of silk lingerie and the turquoise-and-peach dressing gown she had bought on receiving her first month's salary, hung over a spindly gold chair. On the dressing table, inlaid with mother-of-pearl, stood serried ranks of perfume bottles, some decanted into cut glass flacons, others, like her Penhaligon's collection, allowed to stand in their little glass bottles with stoppers and coloured bows – blue for bluebell, peach for orange blossom.

In the bathroom –'sometimes it was a bit awkward getting into the bathroom – was a virgin forest of dried lavender trees which were all made for her by Robert's sister who gave dried-flower arranging courses. Her kitchen was well equipped with sugar shakers, a silver muffin stand, a Devon Violet china tea service and an antique cake slice.

Despite her formidable abilities (she had the second-best first class degree in maths in her year at LSE and had been encouraged to stay on to do a Ph.D. on the nature of infinity) Kate always intended putting her sense of worth in the man she married. She would deny it, but I think the reason she worked so hard to achieve so much was to ensure she found a first-class-degree husband. Which she has. If she had set out with a list of commodities she wanted to find in a man, she could not have done better than Robert. He is just the sort of man she felt she should marry.

He is intelligent, and because his intellect is of a different sort to hers, Kate finds him doubly intelligent. He is attractive, politically sound, as far as Kate is concerned, owns a two-bathroomed flat with a conservatory in a part of Notting Hill he calls Kensington, has recently bought a château in Normandy, earns £100,000 a year, not counting what he makes from freelance journalism, commenting on trade union and legal matters for the quality newspapers. (He does the writing, he says, because sometimes he feels the need to do something more creative. Although anyone on £100,000 a year is in the Pulitzer league, to my mind.) Most importantly, he will inherit a fifty-one per cent share of one of the finest Palladian mansions in Somerset. (Kate, being an only child, will inherit the entire estate of a three-bedroomed semi, complete with armies of frilly standard lamps, wall-to-wall carpets and singing doorbell.)

By not building an extension at the back of their house and going without holidays abroad, Kate's parents could afford the fees of a very good girls' private school. At eighteen, the sixthformers were lectured on interview technique and dress sense, and advised by the headmistress not to look too attractive otherwise their good looks would detract from the good sense of what they were saying. Kate, however, only took advice she wanted. When I arrived at her flat, she was dressed in her office gear: a plain black, curve-enhancing suit nipped tightly at the waist and just covering her knees. Her black stockings were seamed and at the 'V' of her jacket you could glimpse a whisper of her soft-as-a-soap-bubble silk camisole. Her long black curly hair was tamed into a bun which might have looked severe it Kate did not arrange for one stray ringlet, carefully curled into a perfect corkscrew, to fall loose accidently.

She was unlike the models on the magazine, who are either a minimum of five foot eight, a maximum of eight and a half stone and possess an outstanding feature like gap teeth or an odd mole, or are six foot two, with endlessly lean and muscular legs; but on the books of a good agency all Kate's rampant next-doorness would have commanded £150 a day for saying, 'Well, I never knew my washing could be as white as this,' and modelling in Angel Delight adverts. Men were attracted to her like bees to honey.

'I'm so glad you're here early,' she said, 'because I want to make that mussel and pasta dish you cook and I'm not sure how to do it. I've got all the mussels and the tomatoes and basil and things. And onions. There are onions in it, aren't there?'

'I don't know,' I said. 'I've never made that sauce. I just get it in jars.'

'But you always have mussels in shells on the top of it.'

'I know but they're just a few mussels I buy specially for scattering around so people think I've made it.'

'Oh God, I thought you made it. You always used to make things properly. I was convinced you did. So what do you do with real mussels then?'

'Scrub them.'

'Do you know how to?'

'What, scrub them?'

'Yes.'

'I suppose you scrub them in the same way you would scrub anything else.'

'Could you do it? Please.' I took off my coat. 'Thanks, Eliza. You're brilliant the way you know these thing. Do you think you could do the whole sauce?'

I thought I could and started scrubbing while Kate described her wedding dress. I have known what it would be like since I was ten.

'It's going to be white. As you know, I don't hold with this vogue for cream wedding dresses, and besides, cream washes me out. It will be a soft white, not a dazzling satin white but white lace, and I might go to Brussels to get it, take the day off or something. And I'm having it low, as I've always said. Here.' She pointed to halfway down her chest. 'Well perhaps not that low, but quite low and off the shoulder, and then really fitted down to the hips and then really full again, and – there's no point in having short measures in things like this – a long, very long train. The trouble is, though, finding a style to suit both you and all the big bridesmaids – Robert's sisters and his step-sister – and all the little ones. The fabric – I've already bought the fabric – is a very pale-pink damask. I'm not sure what to have done with it, though. What do you think?'

I thought of Kate swishing down the aisle in her long lace carapace embracing a torrent of numinous roses, followed by the other bridesmaids and myself in something like table-cloths.

'Something plain and simple would probably be best,' I suggested.

'That's what I think. Look,' she said, rooting around for her photo album. 'These are Robert's sisters and these ones the step-sisters.'

'They all look the same.'

'I know. It's his mother. They all take after her.'

All four, with large hips and large bosoms, were dead ringers for a fertility rite.

'Very English-looking, aren't they?'

'That's why I was thinking in terms of something very traditional, you know, fitted bodice, sweetheart neckline and full skirt.' I looked at her in horror. 'It's not really your style, I know,' she said assessing the traffic light red-and-green lycra number I had on, 'nor your colour. But I think that something like that is the best idea. And have everyone in ballet shoes.'

'Oh Kate. I can't wear ballet shoes.'

'Why not?'

'Not at my height. Not flat shoes. Please. I'll be muddled up with the five-year-olds, especially with all those big sisters of Robert's.'

'Of course you won't. You'll look lovely. Like a ballet dancer. Petite and graceful. You used to do ballet anyway. You were quite good at it.'

'But I'll be dwarfed. I always wear heels.' Even my mouse boots have high heels.

'But you won't be able to get them in the right sort of pink.'

'I will. I know a place that dyes shoes to the exact colour you want. I've got an old pair of cream courts I can have done.'

'You've really got a hang-up about your height.'

'I haven't.'

'It's the magazine. It gives you the wrong perspective on life. Not every woman is five foot ten. You're just, what? Five foot one?'

'Two.'

'That's only two or three inches below average. Possibly four. There's nothing abnormal in that.'

'I know. I'm just thinking about the, er, composition of it all. Bouncing ideas around.'

'Don't you think it will be all right?'

'Of course it will be all right.' It could not be more spectacular if Spielberg directed it.

'You will wear the ballet shoes then?'

'Whatever you want.'

'You don't sound very certain about it all. Are you *sure* it will all be all right?'

'Quite sure,' I said sharply. 'Listen, Kate,' I continued more kindly, 'it will be a simply beautiful wedding and you'll look heavenly in that dress. The mussels are finished.'

'Oh, thanks.'

'And I'll mention it to Tron. See if she'll put it on the "Who's Who" pages.' Kate is scared that Robert's friends and relations will not think her wedding up to the scratch of their Bach and Bollinger affairs and a mention on *Circe*'s social pages is a seal of approval. 'Robert's friends are the sort of people who'd know Tron.'

'Would you?' she said delightedly. 'Oh Eliza, it would be marvellous if you could.'

'I'll see what I can do. She owes me a favour.'

'Oh thanks. You're wonderful. Now come and sit down because I've got something to tell you. I met someone you know yesterday. Well I didn't meet her exactly and you don't really know her and she certainly does not know you. Lady Grace Gustaad.'

'Oh yes,' I said blandly.

'I saw her going in to see Ambrose Fraser-Bell. He's one of the partners. One of the best. He gives the firm a social profile and deals with old families, you know.'

'And?'

'I thought you'd be interested.'

'Why should I be?'

'Well, you know. Her having to see a solicitor.'

'So what? She probably had to see him about her money. Maybe she's come into some trust fund or inherited something, or whatever these people do for their money.'

'She's unlikely to have seen Ambrose for that.' She paused. 'I was just surprised. You know. It seemed an odd thing for her to do. And I thought they were both in New York.'

'No, they came back in the summer.'

'How do you know?'

'The Natterjack told me.'

'My God, Eliza. Why didn't you tell me? I thought you said you would never see him again.'

'I did. I hadn't spoken to him since just before their wedding.'

'So why are you seeing him?'

'I'm not seeing him. I just bumped into him.'

'What do you mean, "bumped into him"?'

'I met him by chance in the corner shop.'

'Which corner shop?'

'The one round the corner from me.'

'What was he doing in there?'

'They live nearby,' I said wearily. No wonder she is such a good lawyer. 'In Windsor Crescent.'

'Honestly, Eliza. You should have told me. How long has this been going on?'

'Nothing is going on.'

'No wonder his marriage is on the rocks.'

'It's not on the rocks. What are you talking about?'

'It wouldn't surprise me if it is. This is a prime time for a divorce. Her career is taking off, suddenly eclipsing his, and it looks as if she might end up in Hollywood. No way will The Natterjack be able to compete, even if he is a brilliant photographer. Not that I ever thought he was that brilliant and I can't think why else she had a meeting with Ambrose.'

'Because he's her solicitor, of course. People like her always have solicitors to visit. I'd visit a solicitor too if I could afford it and get him to do something about Duncan's bugling.'

'But Ambrose only does family law.'

'I thought your firm only did moneyed stuff.'

'With families like the Gustaads, it is moneyed stuff. So are you still seeing him?'

'I am not seeing him.' Kate spells seeing with an extra 'l' and a 'p'. 'I see him on the rare occasions when I run out of food at the same time he runs out of beer. That's all.'

'He still thinks he's one of the lads then?'

'I don't know what he thinks he is. I haven't said more than ten words to him for three years.'

'He hasn't been to your flat then?'

'No,' I lied.

'Look, Eliza, I'm only saying this for your own good. But if he's about to get a divorce – '

'He is NOT about to get a divorce. You've got an imagination like a bloody toad, leaping all over the place like this.'

'Eliza, Jack is the toad and if she is seeing Fraser-Bell – who loves a good divorce – I can see you getting hurt if you get involved again. Believe me, I never could understand what you saw in him. Grace yes, falling for the glam, photographer act, but you've been wild about him since he was a nobody, unless you count being Hounslow High's football captain.'

'Kate, please stop it.'

'All right. I'll say no more. But I worry about you.'

'On this score, I promise you there is no need. But have you got anything I can eat this minute? I'm starving – it's the cold.'

'It's your appetite, not the cold,' she said, opening a packet of pistachios. 'I really hope you like Paul. I'm sure you will.'

'Hmm,' I said dubiously.

'He might at least take your mind off The Bostonian,' she persisted. I said nothing. 'I mean, what's so special about him?'

'His mind,' I said after some deliberation.

'His mind? Come off it, Eliza. You don't spend a most nuptial night with someone and then say it's their mind you like.'

'But I've spoken to him for ages every week since then. And I do like his mind. It's like Clapham Junction.'

'Clapham Junction is a horrible place. And,' she said with emphasis, 'unreliable.'

'What's that supposed to mean?'

'Well it's not fair of him to say he'll ring you and then not bother.'

'Men don't think like that,' I said wearily. 'They don't read magazines like Cassandra's *Woman's Mail* and get so obsessed with who should ring who and when.'

'But did he actually ring on Sunday night?'

'Yes.'

'And did he say why he didn't ring on Thursday?'

'Yes, because of his sister.'

'I thought his job was the problem, not his sister.'

'That too. But his sister – '

'The one in Vermont?'

'No, *she's* all right. But he's got another sister who's a bit mad.'

'What, seriously mad?'

'No, just normally mad. But she gets involved with the wrong men – she's forty-two – and she is forever setting up new businesses or whatever and she gets bored and they go wrong and he always bails her out and she started this handmade knitwear company – she got into designing sweaters in a big way – but they have gone bankrupt so she hasn't any money and she thinks her life is a mess as she's forty-two and doesn't know where she's going so she turns to Sam for support and he has to pay her rent otherwise he thinks she'll try and move in with him . . .'

'Eliza,' she interrupted, 'you do not need this man. Forget him. Find someone who has a job, has a sister who is not deranged, has a home this side of the Atlantic . . .'

'I can't just say I want a man who has x, y and z. You can't say x, y and z will make me happy so that is what I will look for. It doesn't work like that . . .'

'It does, Eliza. Believe me. You can.' And as if to prove her point, the key turned in the lock and Robert walked in carrying four bottles of red wine.

Robert was in excellent form and enthusing about a picture he had just bought from Sotheby's. It was an oil painting by someone with whom he had been at Cambridge. Kate thought it sounded an excellent buy and asked if I wanted to go round with her to Robert's one night to view it.

'Yes,' I said, meaning no. I have frequently been to Robert's flat and already admired everything from his Aubusson rugs to his Victorian whatnot. The place looks like the world according to Harrods, with Tiffany lamps and marble chopping blocks and Dartington champagne glasses and copper saucepans and a string of onions hanging from the kitchen ceiling and a wooden rack full of French red wines and a six-foot-long bevelled mirror and chrome bath taps and bottles of Moët and mahogany loo seats and bookshelves filled with new hardback books and a table with lions' paws feet and a hatstand. Besides, one person in love can be interesting, but an evening in the exclusive company of two together bores me like snooker.

Paul, Kate's intended for me, arrived while the three of us were on the second bottle of Robert's wine and I was concentrating on fighting the temptation to polish off the pistachios. Meeting Paul did nothing to dim the attraction of the pistachios. He was dressed in about £2,000, a very pale taupe Armani jacket, a mushroom suede side-zipped gilet, a white cotton shirt, Havana-brown wool trousers, chocolate suede loafers and cream cashmere scarf. He looked like a melting choc-ice, utterly and incalculably casual, the product of an account at Simpson's and two hours spent trying on his clothes all evening. Any more casual and he would collapse.

Kate had given the wrong impression of his looks. He was extremely good-looking. Well, he would have been if he had been six inches taller, for he was a shortened version of the male models at work with their beautiful but bland faces like Harrods' shop windows. I felt as much chemistry towards him as I do towards a tube of copper sulphate.

At dinner the four of us exchanged our uniform opinions of life: how short-sighted we all found the prime minister, how delicious we all found the mussel dish, how cold we all found the weather, how good we all found Robert's red wine which he had discovered on his Christie's wine course, how expensive we all found our mortgages, how worrying we all found the prospect of an electrician's strike. I found the prospect of an electrician's strike particularly worrying as my central heating is electric, but Robert gave us a less subjective opinion, talking for twenty-seven minutes without interruption on the matter. When I first heard him give one of his highly articulate, intelligent monologues, I was excessively impressed because at the time I did not realise that he was just rehearsing his ideas for his next newspaper article, which I could read in full the following Sunday.

Robert's commentary sparked Paul off into saying that he

too would not mind doing a bit of freelance financial journalism. (When he was not being a choc-ice, Paul was something fabulously pin-striped in the city.) Robert then explained how he thought Paul should go about getting something published. Then he suggested that I might have a few ideas on the matter. I began saying that financial jouralism was not really my field but Robert interrupted to make a joke: that given the price of the frocks I write about, I was underestimating myself. I said that writing for newspapers was very lucrative as they certainly paid well. Paul said he was not interested in the money aspect and that he had just had a two hundred per cent salary rise. After that we had coffee and Paul drove me home in his car, which was coloured and shaped like a carrot.

14

Material World

I overslept next morning and by the time I had stopped off to buy a book, *Josephine Butler: the Authorised Study* for my father's Christmas present – he never reads except for biographies of the dead – tried on a cashmere sweater which, even if Persephone can get me a discount, will set me back more then £100, got to the office, removed my boots and most of my wet clothes, broke free from the man who signs my expenses and who trapped me in the corridor to say I was taking too many taxis and should take more buses, had been accosted by a typewriter repairer who couldn't find the woman with the broken-down machine and sent him off to Ingrid who is always spilling powder down the back of hers, it was ten-fifteen when I sat at my desk.

'I marked you down as being in at nine,' Naomi whispered to me. She had had to take a register that morning. She always has to take a register to see who is at their desks when the magazine is running late or the editor is in a bad mood, or both. By now the magazine was running exceptionally late because of having to reshoot the yellow make-up pictures, and the difficulty of getting decent pictures of the beauty talent contest winner, and the hard time the art room was having in making her look worthy of being called 'Britain's Undiscovered Beauty'. But, Naomi told me, the editor was also in a major fury because of a problem with the January issue.

The January issue appeared on the newsstands last night. It is always nerve-racking when the new issues appear, in case you discover you have made some ghastly mistake which will have everyone coming down on you like a ton of lipsticks and complaining for all they are worth. The dress designer John Ledeen was complaining because of something we had not written about him.

As a typical New Year January piece we had compiled a list of Britain's top ten fashion designers and we had not included Ledeen. He had phoned the editor at home at ten-thirty last night and whinged unremittingly for three-quarters of an hour and had called in to see her in the office at nine o'clock that morning. He had only just left. Normally the editor would not spend her time appeasing peeved designers but Ledeen had, yesterday, just hours before he learned that we did not include him among the top ten British designers, been commissioned by the Duchess of York to design her wardrobe for her six-week visit to America in the summer; the whole wardrobe, Ledeen had emphasised, from suits to swimsuits to evening dresses. It was outrageous that he should have been left off, especially when we had included that fellow Chitts who hadn't produced an outfit Ledeen would feed chickens in.

Ledeen actually kept chickens in his Kensington garden and his style of design suggested as much. They were the sort of clothes in which Marie Antionette might have gone romping around, and he was very fond of extravagantly flowering cotton prints. He would have a field day with the Duchess.

To run a piece on the top designers and to have excluded the man who was going to be in the news when the Duchess's choice was made public – January 5th – was going to be embarrassing for the magazine. But as nothing could be done about it the editor promised him they would photograph one of his dresses on the cover of the May issue.

Not much more than bad luck had kept Ledeen off the top ten list. In September, when we were preparing the January issue, a memo had circulated telling everyone to come up with ten possible candidates. A week later we all met in the editor's office to decide and the discussion had gone like this.

'How about Tom Cotton?' someone would say.

'Too boring.'

'How, exactly, are we defining "top"? Most innovative? Most influential? Most . . . ?'

'We're defining it as top.'

'Shouldn't we have Mary Silk?'

'Too old.'

'If we've got Pins we can't leave off Needles.'

'There's not room for both.'

'We can't have one without the other.'

'What about Aurelia Wooler?'

'Not enough stature.'

'Ought we to include Brad Bare?'

'He's gone off a bit this year.'

'Does "top British" include British people who manufacture abroad or non-Britons who manufacture over here?'

'Like who?'

'Jay O.'

'Not after the way she behaved, getting all upset, when we got the tailor to shorten her suits for that piece in June.'

'Oh yes. Definitely can't have her.'

'Are we forgetting Ledeen?'

'Too boring.'

'Too boring,' delivered as if it was the death sentence, had been Persephone's verdict. Now, stomping around like the Duchess herself, she was puce with fury at having to do a cover she didn't want to do and moaning that if he was the Duchess's first choice he should be our last.

She is fortunate, however, that it is the May issue. In May, you can do a soft, grainy, out-of-focus picture – suggesting lazy, hazy days of summer – in which it will be easy to camouflage his clothes. You can put the model in a huge, wide-brimmed hat, close up on her face. What is more, if the fashion editor chooses an off-the-shoulder dress – which she undoubtedly will – the whole front page will be taken up with the hat, model's face, neck and shoulders. Ledeen will be lucky if as much as two per cent of his dress gets on to the newsstands.

I made some coffee. I can only look at the new magazines after mental and physical fortification as I cannot stomach the fear of spotting some monumental error. It was an archetypal

January issue with lists of who was who in the past year and who would be who in the coming one, extensive fashion forecasts and turgid beauty predictions. My piece was on the Paris couture collections.

It wasn't until I started writing about 'couture' that I found out what the word actually meant. Saying something is a 'couture' outfit does not just mean it costs what I earn in six months, nor that it is the inspired creation of a famous designer. It means that the dress has been specially made to fit your shape. It does not mean that the design of the dress will be unique. You still run the risk of running into someone in the same dress – if you run in couture circles – but your dress will be a unique shape as it will have been made to fit your unique body.

You do not do anything so banal as 'shop' for a couture dress. Instead you either choose the outfit at the designer's show – to which you received an engraved invitation – or you take your pick when you have a moment to visit the designer's atelier on your next trip to Paris or Milan.

Measurements and fittings come next. Remembering to dress in your best underwear and squirt yourself generously with the designer's latest perfume, you pop back to the atelier where the designer's underlings busy themselves with tape measures. (Regular clients save themselves from the fitting bother by having dummies made of themselves.) Couture collections are therefore different from the ready-to-wear collections, as at the ready-to-wear, designers show clothes they want to sell to the shops and which customers then buy off the peg.

No way am I important enough to go to the Paris couture collections. Attendance costs the magazine a fortune as they are an orgy of keeping up appearances. You have to stay in the best rooms in the best hotels, eat at the most expensive restaurants – or be seen in them as everyone is too thin to eat – take taxis rather than walk two hundred yards. Instead, I just stay in the office and describe the clothes from the photographs.

109

In the autumn I had written about bronze breastplates in starched lace, studded with gold buttons, and fringed with tassels; maroon velvet gowns trimmed with golden passementerie, inspired by the curtains at Covent Garden; a slip covered in appliquéd silk red cabbage roses like a prize bush and topped by a cartwheel hat piled high with more red roses; a pale-pink ostrich feather slip worn with an oriflamme of feathers in bright pink; a candy-striped taffeta outfit like a big sweet waiting to be unwrapped by its sugar daddy; a matador outfit in blood-red worn with a pancake beret skewered with a gold pencil; a dead ringer for *Come Dancing* in lobster taffeta; a damask dress trimmed in mink worn with a beaded purse with a gnarled gold twig handle; a black-and-white milkmaid ensemble in duchesse satin.

One designer, who didn't know when to stop, had shown a series of evening gowns with trains which grew and grew and grew. Firstly two feet long and finally dragging twenty feet of silk chiffon along the pavement. If you wondered how much it cost to dry-clean a mile of chiffon, you were looking at the wrong dress. And if it occurred to anyone to wonder whether it might be uncomfortable wearing a dress with all that chiffon billowing out the back, they should return right away to the draughty changing rooms at Top Shop. Saying something is 'wearable' is the kiss of death at the Paris couture.

Particularly unwearable hits this year included a dress which inhibited walking as it was gathered into a thick tight band at the knees; a transparent mini which put paid to any ideas of leaving the house, as it revealed your knickers; a blouse with a starched collar like a stovepipe and a rim under the chin which stopped you from eating; a black rubber catsuit all done up with gold bauble decorations which made going to the loo a half-hour procedure.

Biggest hit of all was the great train dress, which cost £20,000 with a plain train and £50,000 if you had a train embroidered by fifty seamstresses working flat out for a fortnight. Very popular too was the £15,000 baubled rubber catsuit – an extra £10,000 if you had it made up with real gold-plated baubles –

and the £20,000 rose bush. Just because you have £20,000 to spend on looking like a rose bush with legs does not mean you are any better off when it comes to taste.

Designers adore the couture collections because they provide the opportunity to scorn the obvious, abjure the commonplace and give their creativity full rein. And what a mess it can look. In the magazine, however, you cannot just write: 'Sorry, there aren't any very nice clothes about this season, so just make do with what you bought last year and wait till the next collections when, let's hope, something better will crop up.' Instead you have to make the best of a bad job and write about the 'armoured elegance' of the bronze, buttoned, tasselled breastplate; the 'aloof severity' of the stovepipe neckline; the 'jaunty sophistication' of the pancake beret; the 'medieval romance' of the gnarled twig handbag. And at the same time the clothes must be all things to all women. Young, but also sophisticated. New, but also classical. Racy, but not immodest. Original, but not outrageous.

The fashion editors speak of Paris couture as if it were a re-run of the Battle of Waterloo with the Americans, Japanese, Italians and Germans in there too. They carry hard-hitting handbags, dress in heavy metal chains, get speared by razor-sharp stilettos, perch their bony derrières on rickety gilt seats, get frisked by a hundred policemen and go down with headaches from Chanel No. 5 fumes.

Half the wives of the French government are there, so security is tighter than a corset and the show rooms are like Saturday afternoon in Miss Selfridge. Everyone has to watch more than twenty shows in less than five days, strategically located at opposite ends of Paris in Louis XV ballrooms, ateliers up ten picturesque flights of stairs, and nightclub basements. They must not shove anyone over when trying to get to their seat nor be seen to sweat. They must remember what all the clothes look like, go to lots of little luncheon parties and compete for invitations to select and sophisticated soirées. They must appear to be on kissing terms with everyone they meet, punching little kisses onto both cheeks or, if their friend is on the opposite side of the room and obscured by giant sunglasses, smooch the air in the appropriate direction. All this in the company of about five hundred women who are, of course, impeccably dressed.

Customers whose day dresses decend from £10,000 and whose evening gowns rise from £10,000, attend the collections in the suit they bought at the previous collection. The press all don black, not just because they are feeling so mournful that they cannot afford a £10,000 suit, but because fashion editors, regardless of what fantasies they write about or photograph, believe that the black is the *ne plus ultra* in chic. Also, black is the most slimming colour. En masse they look like a flock of starving crows.

I couldn't find any mistakes in my piece so that was another month I had managed to pull it off. I opened my post. There were no invitations to Paris, no head hunters hoping to poach me, no letter announcing I had won any money. There was nothing worth opening. Most had spelled my name wrong anyway.

I tried to read the rest of the magazine but I already knew what it would say. I still had to do the history of the bra but listened to Melindi on the phone instead. She was obviously speaking to Ashley for I caught words like 'ocean', 'survival', 'seaweed' and an entire alphabet of superlatives: amazing, brilliant, cool, divine. She was up to 'splendid' when one of the Twin Sets rang asking me to bring some chocolate mousses to their New Year's Eve party.

'All right,' I said. 'How many do you want?'

'Three,' said Susan. 'No, make it four and if there are any left over we'll eat them. Right, that's all then. Oh, are you well?'

'Fine, thanks.'

'That's good. Jane told me she thought you had a stinking cold and that you were off somewhere tropical after Christmas.'

'No. I might go to Paris, that's all. Or I might just stay at home and paint my bathroom and,' I added without thinking, 'spend the money on a cashmere sweater.'

'A cashmere sweater? Honestly, Eliza, you have no understanding of the meaning of money.'

'Of course I do.'

'If you saw the people I see every day you'd think otherwise. How much are they?'

'About £70,' I said reducing their cost by two-thirds.

'You could get three sweaters for that price.'

'But I'd rather have one really good one than three mediocres.'

'But you've already got millions of sweaters.'

'I've hardly got any – well, any that I wear.'

'You've got more clothes than anyone I know. You even have to have two wardrobes.' It's true, I do have two wardrobes and they are both full of clothes but I only wear those from one wardrobe as the other houses my mistakes. 'You ought to be giving clothes away not buying more,' she went on, but not for long as she had to be in hospital by twelve.

Then I listened to Naomi on the phone to Rolo, her boyfriend farmer. She was telling him that on Christmas Eve he would come and collect her from the office at about twelve and that they would drive straight to her parents' where they would spend Christmas Day – the Saturday – and Boxing Day – the Sunday – with her parents on Exmoor; that he was to wrap up the presents in the Harvey Nichols bag in the bedroom in the gold Christmas-tree wrapping paper he would find on top of the dishwasher; that they would drive to his parents' after breakfast on the Monday morning and spend the Monday and Tuesday bank holidays with them and fly to Paris on Wednesday, staying at the Hotel Lotti and flying back to Gatwick first thing Monday 3rd and she would go straight into work and he would drive his car back home. If I was Rolo I would have bolted long ago, Naomi bosses him about so much. But I am as certain as I am that the weather will be bad tomorrow that she will marry him.

Although dazzlingly unambitious at work Naomi is determined to take what she wants from life. She wants Rolo. She wants to get married at twenty-two. She wants to start a family at twenty-five. This is what she tells me. She also tells me that her contemporaries want much the same. It is much the same as what my sisters wanted too. If you get all the marriage business out of the way at an early age, she maintains, you are less at risk of Aids, heartbreak, insecurity, and loneliness. Less at risk of everything. Naomi is a prodigy of reason. Even, she says, if the person you are marrying is not especially special, getting married will ensure you of an intimate relationship, just by virtue of the number of years you will have to spend together, of having children together, of sharing a house together.

Cassandra rang when Naomi was telling Rolo where he could find the angel she had bought that summer when they were in Berlin and which she wanted to take up to her parents to put on top of the Christmas tree.

'Can you talk?' she asked.

'Yes.'

'What are you doing New Year's Eve?'

'I've got my sisters' party.'

'Oh.'

'Have you got anything to do?'

'No.' Naomi may be right. Cassandra is thirty-two.

'You can always come to my sisters' party,' I said.

'Hmm. Thanks,' she said, 'but no.'

'I don't blame you.'

'I hate New Year's Eve.'

'Me too – sometimes,' I said.

'I've had the best of times and also the worst of times.'

'I know,' I said.

'Hardly anyone, except for people your sisters' age, have parties any more. Most of my friends are staying at home for a cosy night in together. I might just stay in as well.'

'What's the "homo maritus" up to?' I asked.

'With his in-laws. That's what I'll do, I think, just forget about it being New Year and stay in and work.'

'What's the problem this week?'

" 'Out of a Date." You know, wanting to go out but not

114

having anyone to go out with. How you get brought up to believe – '

'But Cassandra, you did that one a couple of years ago. I came across an old issue at Chewton Magna.'

'I know, but I'm doing it from a different angle this time. I'm saying that men and women don't go out with each other just for a fun flirt, as they don't find each other attractive any more.'

'I find some men really attractive.'

'Yes, but hardly any, and think of the number of times you ring me up and say that you've got nothing to do but go out with one of your St. Georges when what you really want is an evening of stimulating flirtation.'

'I never say that.'

'Don't delude youself. You do. Anyway, the problem is that now men and women are expected to be the same and to want the same things – to be airline pilots and look after the children – so we're leading parallel lives with less chance of our lives ever meeting. Women don't know how to behave like women and men aren't sure how to behave like men. I was reading in a magazine the other day – your magazine, actually – about an American invention, a lump which men can holster onto themselves to get an idea of what it's like being pregnant. What are we supposed to make of that?'

'That was just Hermione and one of her mad ideas.'

'But it makes the point. Roles have got confused. If women cannot sack their subordinates without an emotional qualm, and lift bricks at the same time, they worry that they will be sent back giggling to the kitchen. And if men are not doing their best to have the baby for you and coming to grips with the finer points of the menstrual cycle, they think they'll be branded male chauvinist pigs. So he sits there being terribly understanding and worrying that if he opens the door for you, you'll give him one of your self-defence karate kicks for being sexist. And you, Ms. Bossy-Busy-Body, sit there thinking how unmasculine he is. I mean, if you're doubled up with period pains do you want a man to faff around with the Paracetamols, saying. "There, there, I know how you feel"?'

'No.'

'Exactly. You'd rather he said. "Let's have sex." You've got friends like me to get the painkillers. Intellectually, of course, feminism is great. I know I am a modern, liberated woman, fully aware of women's sexual, emotional, intellectual and economic oppression, and that we have to be eternally vigilant against male imperialism and all that. I don't want to be in a kitchen right now, barefoot and pregnant. But the New Man and New Woman feminism conceived just haven't got much sex appeal. I know that no one has a good word for sex these days. I know dirty weekends at the Royal Crescent don't last a lifetime. I know sex isn't the most important thing in a relationship, though I wish I knew what is. But when men and women are becoming so alike they're not attracted to each other in the first place, it's no wonder that all my single female friends say they don't know any nice men and all my single male friends say they don't know any nice women. The problem is that we are all turning into hermaphrodites.'

'I'm not,' I interrupted. 'It's hard enough being a woman without having to be a man as well. I don't have the energy.'

'But look at you and St. George. You told me that next time he went. "Poor you", "Mmm, you're right", or looked sheepishly at your shoes, you'd string him up or shoot him.'

'He doesn't know I'm going to do that.'

'But you think he's a wimp because that oestrogen-packed sensitivity and deference doesn't turn you on.'

'New Manism has just sanctioned wimpdom. I'd never have liked him.'

'Maybe. But with men behaving as women were expected to behave, and women behaving as men were expected to behave, the signalling has gone all wrong. Even asking for your telephone number might look too wolfish, be a bit gross and steamy or in bad taste. Now, when you meet someone, you hardly ever get that sense of him thinking, "You're a woman, I'm a man and what's the obvious next step?" '

'You're going to get loads of nutcases writing in if you say this,' I said, 'all maintaining that what you want is to be Scarlett O'Hara and have rampant Rhett Butler whisk you upstairs.'

'That's the problem. Some of the things that we associate with masculinity and which I am not now supposed to find attractive, I do. I mean, I do not want to have to do the pursuing and ring him first. I do not want to take the lead in bed and of course I like flowers. And I like confidence as it's infectious. And when you've got the prospect of staying in with the TV on New Year's Eve, a bit of protectiveness or possessiveness seems highly desirable.'

'Cassandra,' I said, 'do you really believe all this or are you just getting in your combative mode before you sit down and write the piece?'

'Of course I believe it.'

'It's not always true. You're seeing John tonight.'

'Yes. But that's a stalemate if ever there was and depressing me beyond belief. At least my skin's better. How's yours?'

'Back to normal.'

'Good. And I've been meaning to ask you, what are you going to do for your birthday?'

'Let me get through New Year's Eve first.'

'But it's right after.'

'The sixth.'

'Twelfth Night?'

'Yes.'

'The day you take the decorations down.'

'That's right.'

'Thought so. Oh, did Sam ring?'

'Yes. On Sunday.'

'Anything else to report?'

'No.'

'Do you really think I should end it with John?' I said nothing. 'You're right I know but – '

'Look, do you want to meet me for lunch?' I interrupted. 'You sound fed up.'

'No. I've got to get this date thing done by tonight.'

'Well just ring me if you change your mind. I'm not doing anything.'

I rang Kate to thank her for dinner last night. I said, quite honestly, what a delicious meal it was, how pleased I was to see her and then, less honestly, that it had been nice to meet Paul.

'Did you like him?' she asked.

'Yes,' I said.

'Oh,' she said. 'Did you really like him?'

'Well, quite.'

'Oh. Robert just rang me and he'd been speaking to Paul and Robert didn't think he sounded too keen on you. I'm sorry, Eliza.'

'Don't worry. I can bear it.'

'Good. Anyway, I've just spoken to the florist. She's got the most wonderful idea for the church. Over the aisles she's going to create a canopy of apple blossom by fixing apple trees – small ones – onto the ends of the pews and covering them with more blossom. And I'm going to wear my hair loose with a crown of wild roses, though, as it'll be May, they'll be hot-house wild roses. And she suggested weaving in a few wild strawberries. She said it would make my hair look more black. She also thought she should put strawberries in the bridesmaids' posies and in their hair, but I'm not so sure about that. What do you think?'

'Well,' I said not very enthusiastically. 'It might be a bit much.'

'Oh. I thought it was quite a good idea actually. I rather liked it.'

'Well have them then. It's your wedding.'

'You're not being very enthusiastic, Eliza.'

'I am. I'm really enthusiastic.'

'You're a bit anti the whole idea, aren't you?'

'What idea?'

'Weddings, marriage. I mean, just as a matter of interest, do you actually believe in marriage?'

'All I was questioning was whether I should have strawberries in my hair, not the institution of marriage.'

'I know, but do you? Even if you don't, I still want you to be chief bridesmaid. So, do you?'

Sometimes I do. Sometimes I don't. Sometimes I think people get married because marriage is the richest, deepest, most intimate relationship you could wish for, and sometimes I think people get married because their dread of loneliness is greater than their dread of being tied down. Sometimes I think marriage is the most natural thing in the world, and the human way of choosing a mate, and sometimes I think that expecting people to choose just one person with whom to spend the rest of their lives is impossible. Sometimes I think people get married because they love each other and sometimes I think people get married because they are just tired of going it alone, because they are simply exhausted with having to appear to relish their freedom and be twice as strong as everyone else, because they cannot put up with that guilt and shame of not being part of the social duo, a married couple, head of a family, society's foundation stone, any longer. Sometimes I look at my married friends and I envy them, but sometimes I look at them and think that marriage only looks great from a distance and that it is only the idea of marriage, the fiction and romance of it, the happy ever after, that is so seductive. Sometimes I think marriage must be the best thing ever because it assures you of security, companionship and sex, and sometimes I think marriage must be the best thing in the world because unmarried you waste too much time worrying that no one will ever want to marry a toad like you and finding something to do on New Year's Eve.

'Of course I do,' I said. 'But I've got to go,' I lied. 'Tron's clip-clopping around. Bye.'

Tim St. George rang me the moment I put the phone down. Sometimes I wonder if there is a life beyond my phone, and I wonder whether I could conduct my whole life without ever moving or ever doing anything, and just live on the phone.

Tim said he had been trying to get hold of me for days and he wanted to check that I had not forgotten that we were meeting for lunch. I had. 'No, of course not,' I said. 'But can we make it quite a quick one? I'm really sorry, but I'm totally snowed under right now. Actually, could we just make it a drink?'

'Of course,' he said. 'Anything you say.'

Later, as I was debating whether Cassandra would count a drink with a man you did not want to see as a date, Hermione bounded in, and started bellowing, as if addressing a thrill-hungry mob of television children with ear damage, about her interview with a friend of Ingrid's who had just had liposuction on her thighs.

Liposuction – the removal of fat from thighs and other unwanted places – is like cutting the crackling off a lump of pork. It is one of the most popular cosmetic operations in America, and a rapidly increasing number of British women are undergoing it as well.

'It was fascinating,' began Hermione. 'Absolutely fascinating. But also so, so *horrifying*,' she said emphasising her favourite word. 'Simply horrifying. You should have seen her tonnage to start with. She showed me these pictures the surgeon had taken – they send you off to a photgrapher who takes Polaroids of your thighs from all angles – so he could see where the worst of the fat lay. She was seriously whale-like. Positively blubbery. And she had to see a liposuction counsellor to ensure that she had done all that was humanly possible to lose weight.'

(Womanly possible is more like it. What man would have liposuction on his thighs or beer belly?)

'The surgeon grabbed hold of her thighs in his two hands, drew red felt-tip pen lines to mark the areas of fat he had to extract. Then he made small cuts, little nicks in the areas to be trimmed – she had been put to sleep by this stage – in which he injected an enzyme which liquefied the fat and then he sucked it out with a sort of modified vacuum cleaner.

'She woke up in the most dreadful frenzy, in agonising pain, shaking uncontrollably, encased in a waist-to-knee corset, and had to be drugged all night. And going to the loo – forget it.

She couldn't put any weight on her legs. Though not being able to stand up is quite normal, because of the pain.

'Anyway, they sent her home and a week later she went back to have the stitches taken out. The corset was removed and then, if you think it's been ghastly so far, listen to this. It was so horrifying, she fainted, for her legs were black: not just bruised in blue, but pitch-black. As black as if she had been dipped in ink, though you could still faintly see the red felt-tip pen marks.

'But they expect your legs to go black and the surgeon was very pleased with her progress and told her that every morning she was to massage a tub of cream into her thighs for a quarter of an hour to get rid of the lumps and set the circulation going again and in six months' time she would have the thighs of a new woman.'

'Does she?' murmured one of Hermione's assistants.

'Take a look,' said Hermione, pulling out some more photographs. I went to look as well. They were of a woman of about sixty in a size small bikini cut as high as her waist, with abnormally tight thighs and pert bottom.

'She does, doesn't she? She's lost all those globs of cellulite on her legs and her bottom is as round as a peach. After about a month she took off the corset for good and most of the lumps and swelling had gone. It wasn't sore any more and she had lost five-inches round her thighs – all for a bill of £2,500, which her husband paid as a fifty-ninth birthday present. Worth it, don't you think?' Hermione asked her assistants.

'Oh yes. Remarkable. Money well spent. I'd never have guessed. You really can't tell. Worth the pain,' I heard them saying with varying degrees of conviction as I went out for lunch and to collect the Twin Sets' Christmas presents.

15

Out to Lunch

Outside, the pavements were six deep with shoppers slurping through melting snow. I ploughed through tinsel and bauble stands, a lot of people playing trumpets badly and the Salvation Army, to John Lewis where I had ordered the Twin Sets' bird tables. The last thing I would want for Christmas is a bird table but between the four of them they have everything else and both Sets have garden flats in Clapham and keep packets of Swoop by the back door.

I had spotted them in an advert and they were much bigger than I remembered, with little houses on top. And they were also twice the price.

'I thought they were only £20,' I said to the shop assistant.

'That was the special-offer one. You have got the de luxe bird table.'

'De luxe one? What do you mean de luxe one?'

'The de luxe one is supported by a smooth metal pole to stop cats climbing up and has a house on top. The standard one has a wooden pole and only a perch instead of a house.'

'I didn't know that.' The woman said nothing. 'I wasn't told I was buying a de luxe one.'

'When you ordered it were you asked which sort of pole you wanted?'

'Yes, and I asked for the metal one. Everyone must have asked for the metal pole rather than the wooden one. No one would buy one with a pole which cats can climb up.'

'Not at all, madam. The special offer was extremely popular and, being one of our limited editions, had sold out by November. And you ordered yours, let me see, only last week. Yes, you left it very late so you wouldn't have been in the running for the cheaper one anyway.'

'Well I don't want them, thank you.'

'You've already paid for them, madam – over the phone by credit card.'

'But I would never have bought them at that price. I thought it was £40 for the two, not £40 each.'

'You obviously didn't listen when you placed your order.'

Didn't listen. I'd heard that one before. Oh God. If I didn't get them bird tables I couldn't think what else to give my sisters. They weren't like other sisters who would like a nice sweater or some perfume or goodies from Ingrid's beauty cupboard. My sisters are so puritanical in their tastes and wise with their money that they always head straight for the 'reduced' trolley at Sainsbury's. They think they are living dangerously if they buy a tin of fruit which hasn't got a dent in it. I carted the bird tables out with me.

They were very heavy and there was a little bell in each of the houses which rang as I walked. After spending £80 on bird tables I wasn't going to get a taxi. I hoped my sisters appreciated them. After ten minutes, I had moved a hundred yards, a pushchair had rammed into my ankles, a Father Christmas on a bicycle had sworn at me for getting in his way, someone in DMs had stood on my right foot. I stopped a cab.

'What you want is one of the new cabs,' said the driver, as we couldn't fit the tables in, even with their ends sticking out the window. 'They're that little bit bigger. I've got a bird table just like this. Made it from a piece of scaffolding with a bit of wood on top. I didn't make a house, though. It's quite a nice touch having the house, with the bell.' Some dirty rain started to grizzle down. The Twin Sets had better have bought me something nice. After fifteen minutes, while the rain worked itself up into a proper downpour, an empty modern taxi stopped.

The traffic was so jammed I was late getting to The Ritz where I was meeting St. George for our quick drink. The place was packed full of mercilessly chic women looking like Christmas trees with piles of presents at their feet, and businessmen setting fire to fat cigars. St. George looked up the

123

moment I walked in. In fact most people looked up. In the street I had not realised how loud the bird tables' bells were.

'Can we put those in the cloakroom for you, madam?' asked a waiter, rocketing to my side.

'Yes, please,' I said before he offered to put me in the cloakroom too.

'Eliza, how lovely to see you,' said St. George, walking over. He put his arm around my shoulders and let it stay there. It must be an inviolable biological trait. There is nothing you can do about it. But if you do not find someone attractive you cannot make yourself. No way. No possible way, I thought, with St. George's Armani-clad arm still sitting there.

'And you, Tim,' I said awkwardly, shrugging myself out of his grip. He wears Armani aftershave too.

'You're looking lovely.'

'Thank you.'

'You really are.'

'Thank you,' I said again and then again to the waiter as he took my emerald coat with scarlet lining in which I remind myself of a holly bush.

'You always wear such wonderful clothes,' said Tim.

'Thank you, Tim,' I said.

'No other woman I know,' continued St. George, 'dresses like you.'

'Thank you.'

'I read your article in *Circe* – the one about the clothes in Paris.' The man had done some homework. 'It was very good.' Not many men will wade through three pages of description of clothes. What, Tim, do you want? I thought.

'What do you want, Eliza?' he asked.

'A tomato juice, please.'

'Two tomato juices,' he said to the waiter as I ferreted in a bowl for some brazil nuts. The great thing about the Ritz is that they have a good selection of nuts. 'They were quite spectacular bird tables you had with you.'

'Yes, and very heavy ones too. And loud.' I never know what to say to Tim. 'So what have you been up to?'

'Oh not much,' he said meekly. Why Tim always comes across as so pathetic I do not know, because he can't be pathetic – not to do his job. Among criminal barristers he is up and coming, according to Robert, though heavens knows what I would make of him if I was a murderer. 'Tell me about you.' I think he read somewhere – in Cassandra's magazine probably – that men talk too much about themselves so he lets women do the talking.

'I've been to a health farm for work,' I answered.

'That's what I could do with.'

'Not this health farm you couldn't. It was painfully cold, there was nothing to do and only lemons to eat.'

'Lemons?'

'Yes, raw ones. The heating did not work, my bed was damp, I had to put the carpet on the bed as there were no blankets and I found a dead deer in the wardrobe.'

'No!'

'Well, its antlers. There were cataracts of ice on the windows, a blood-frosting gale down the chimney. Plus I got locked out in the middle of the night, all alone in the ice-bellied depths of some part of the country thinking I was going to be murdered or freeze.'

'My God, how frightening,' he exclaimed, going to put his hand on mine.

'Yes it was,' I said bravely, moving my hand away.

'So what on earth did you do?'

'Eventually – about four in the morning, maybe even later – I managed to find this place in the wall where there was a tree growing nearby and I climbed up that and then sort of leapt onto the wall – which was twelve feet high with spear heads on top – and managed somehow to get over that way. I didn't have any option because I'd have died of cold otherwise, it was so bitter.' I paused, for Tim was looking so terrifically concerned he must have found it a strain. 'According to the radio it had been minus 20°C – as cold as Siberia, colder in fact.'

'My God, how frightening,' he repeated. 'You poor, poor thing. I'd have been terrified too, on my own like that.'

'I'm sure you would. But that's not all, for when I jumped down from the wall I hurt my ankle so badly I could barely walk – though it's much better now – and although I knew I was in the grounds, it was so dark I wasn't sure where Chewton Magna was exactly and – '

'Not Lady Chewton's place?' he interrupted. I nodded. 'She's my aunt and my sister's godmother, well, one of them.'

'Oh,' I backtracked rapidly. 'I'm exaggerating a little . . .'

'But I know just how you must have felt. She's a frightful woman and when I stay at her castle in Wales it's as cold as that and I got lost once there, walking in the mountains, only for a couple of hours mind you, and it was daylight and the middle of August but I know how dreadful it is being on your own, lost in some uncharted part of the country.'

'Yes. Are you going away for Christmas?' I asked to change the subject from his aunt.

'I'll be in Wales, in fact, at my aunt's, with the rest of the family. But are you sure you're all right and that your ankle's all right?'

'Yes, yes I'm fine,' I snapped.

'I'll have to tell my aunt what happened.'

'No, no don't, please. Really. I don't want to talk about it.'

'All right then,' he said tenderly. 'So what are your plans for Christmas?'

'I'm going to my family, then I might go to Paris the week after.'

'Who with?'

'On my own,' I answered without thinking as my mind had gone on to whether the waiter would bring more nuts soon. Eliza, I thought, you idiot. Tim leant forward. I fell for that one. He brought his face, with its excellent patrician-pink complexion, close to mine. Any minute now, I thought with horror, I'm going to get embarrassed. He put his hand on mine which was suspended midway between what was left of the nuts and my mouth. Oh my God, really embarrassed.

'Why don't we go to Paris together?' he said softly. 'I'm tired of just meeting you like this. Come to Paris with me. My

Christmas present to you.' He brought his boyish face close to mine. His skin is so smooth he could advertise Ashley's ocean-based range of Shogun. 'There's a hotel near the Place des Vosges where . . .'

That's the problem, I thought. It's not just that he treats me with the reverence and seriousness I would accord a nuclear bomb about to go off. It's his skin. And his naive eyes. And his kittenish face. Women can wear innocence and vulnerability but it unmans men. It is as if they had slipped on a little black silk dress and were forever asking you to zip up the back. And besides, I never trust niceness, and in such large quantities it brings out the worst in me. On a farm I would have been the one chosen to drown excess kittens.

'Oh no,' I said. 'Thank you, er thank you. God, I'm immensely flattered, but believe me I'd drive you mad in just minutes. Believe me. I'm like that. And you're just far too nice for me. Really. Too nice. But thank you so much for asking. But no. And I'd better get back to the office because it will take me longer than usual as I've got those bird tables,' I blundered on. 'I wish now I hadn't bought them but my sisters love that sort of thing. They were always finding dead birds when we were young and looking after them. Not dead ones, I mean baby birds. You know, which had been deserted though they were dead soon enough after my sisters had been looking after them. I had to hunt for worms for them to eat and bugs and flies and . . .' I dried up. 'So goodbye and thank you for the tomato juice and have a lovely Christmas,' I said and rushed off.

I felt a bit sick after all that. If someone had told me I was too nice for them I would have bashed them with my bird tables, and trying to get them through the crowds packing the streets I did bash a few people.

Back at the office, standing in reception being talked at by Melindi, was The Natterjack. One of the reasons he takes such good portraits of women is that he looks at them as if he has

127

never seen anything more beautiful. The only photographs I have ever liked of myself are the ones taken by him. Melindi was gazing at him adoringly, saying something about how she thought the pictures of New York in his latest book were the best she had ever seen.

'Eliza,' he called as I tried to slip by unnoticed. 'I wondered who on earth it was, making all that ringing. What are you doing with those things?'

'They're the twins' Christmas presents.'

Melindi, so impressed that I knew Jack, looked at me if she had found a pearl in an oyster.

'Jack and I once worked together,' I said in explanation. 'And I've got to dash as I'm really behind on something. So, nice to see you again, Jack, and 'bye.'

'Wait. What are you so busy with?'

I couldn't think.

'The history of the bra,' piped up Melindi.

'Really? I hate to take you from that but could it wait five minutes?' He turned to Melindi. 'I'll say goodbye, Melindi. It was lovely to meet you and I'll see you tomorrow.'

'The history of the bra, Eliza?' he said when Melindi had managed to draw herself away from him. 'What a way to spend your day.'

'What's wrong with it?'

'Haven't you got something more important to do?'

'Important? If more people appreciated the importance of the unimportant,' I said angrily, 'if fewer narrow-minded bigots did not let their lofty ideals lure them from frivolity, the pleasure of a hot bath, a silk dress and a good cup of coffee, there would be a lot more happiness, believe me.'

'All right, all right. I believe you.' he said wearily. 'But do you want one of those good cups of coffee? You sound as if you need one. Just leave those ridiculous things here. No wonder you and your sisters never get on if you give each other presents like that.

How are the Twin Sets?' he asked when we were sitting in a café no one from *Circe* would visit as they only serve complex

128

carbohydrates. 'I was sent, thanks to my mother, a great big picture of them in wedding tackle, cut out from the *Hounslow Herald*.'

'They're all right.'

'And Kate's getting married too, I hear.'

'Your mother keeps you well informed, doesn't she?'

'A weekly bulletin. What's he like? Kate's husband-to-be?'

'Extremely nice, actually.'

He laughed. 'No he's not. At least you don't think so.' He is right. I think Robert is horrible. 'You don't like him one bit.' Sometimes, when Jack was lying next to me, I thought we could read each other's mind and understand each other's thoughts so perfectly that we were as close as you ever could be to another being. 'What's wrong with him?'

'Nothing.'

'Has he got a stately home so Kate can play lady of the manor? Eliza? Speak to me, Eliza.' I said nothing. 'Thought so. Kate would not feel he was good enough for her otherwise.'

'That's not fair,' I said, turning on him bitterly. 'If men can regard women as objects, assess the length of their legs, evaluate the blondness of their hair, and,' I added resentfully, thinking of Grace, 'select ones with daddies who own race-horses, the best hotels in the country, and have Charles II as an ancestor, women can too. Kate's just played men at their own game and beaten them.'

'I hope the victory makes her happy.'

'I'm sure it will.'

'Well that's Kate settled then. And your sisters. How nice for them all.'

'And you're settled, Jack.'

'Yes. Do you want one of those doughnuts?' I nodded. 'Two doughnuts, please,' he called to the waitress.

'Make it three. I want two.'

'They're both for you.'

'Aren't you having one?'

'No.'

'They're very good.'

'I know. I just don't want one. And, Eliza, are *you* settled?'

'As settled as I want to be, thanks.'

'How nice for you, too.'

'Isn't it just,' I crowed, after which we both sat there in silence.

'So why are you seeing Melindi tomorrow?' I asked eventually.

'I'm doing some work for Ingrid.'

'How come?'

'She rang me.'

'But why?'

'She'd heard I was back and wondered if I would do a piece on hair sculptures, whatever they are. Apparently everyone is going to go around looking like Marie Antoinette this summer, or with their hair like whacking great beehives.' He leaned over and lifted my hair up. I had forgotten how warm his hands were. An old, thawing sense of arousal kindled confusing messages in the farthest depths of my memory. I earthed them right away and took a bite of doughnut. 'You're prettier with it loose.' I concentrated on the doughnuts. I look the way I look and it's my business. He paused. 'You're looking very beautiful at the moment.'

'I've got to go,' I said, turning my head from him sharply.

'You're busy?'

'That's right.'

'With the history of the bra?'

'Yes,' I snapped.

'Honestly, Eliza. You're made for something better than all that trivia.'

'Stop getting at me,' I cried. 'What's wrong with trivia? I can't live without it. It's all right for you. You've got a talent and you married out of it but without trivia and fantasy what else is there to take people away from Hounslow, squabbling kids, bullying by the boss, late nights of ironing, endlessly exhausting routines and the dullness of it all when hopes of anything better were hoovered up long ago?'

He was looking at me with alarm.

'There's nothing,' I answered for him. 'Absolutely nothing else.' And I walked out, like a carping fishwife, my heavy head full of old grievances.

16

Present Imperfect

'Darling, what are you doing with them?' shrieked Ingrid, looking up from a plate of beansprouts as I walked into the office with the bird tables. 'Have you turned into one of those . . . ? Oh, what do you call them? Those people who go round ringing bells.'

'Hari Krishnas,' said Melindi.

I ignored her and picked up my phone which was ringing too.

'Eliza?'

'Oh hello, Jane,' I said.

'I haven't got long as I'm on duty at four but when you come to the party can you bring the salad bowl full of salad?'

'Full? Who are you inviting? The Flopsy bunnies or something? The rotten thing's huge. It holds about ten lettuces.'

'Oh God. You're not in one of your moods, are you? What's the matter?'

'Nothing's the matter with me.'

'You're being terribly touchy, going off alarming when all I asked was for you to make a bit of salad. For a party to which you are invited, please note. And can you not just put in lettuce but use plenty of avocados and that red lettuce stuff.'

'Radicchio.'

'That's it, and lots of coriander as I love coriander. Just make sure the bowl is full as there's going to be about forty of us. You've met most of them, Jim and Kathryn, David and Jill, Mary and Michael, John and Sally, Hugh and Anna . . .'

I'm going to love this party. It will be like going to Noah's Ark on my own. Two by two, male with female. Jane went on, but I stopped listening as I was rather embarrassed at the way Tron and the editor were talking and looking over at me sitting between the bird tables. If I had known they were this big I would have collected them after work. Since the office was redesigned everyone has become terribly precious about upsetting the tone of the place. It was not as if they were designer bird tables. These had John Lewis, suburban back garden stamped all over them.

'Just one moment, please,' I said to Jane as though to a business colleague as the editor stepped slowly over and positioned herself by my desk.

'You don't intend keeping those here for long, do you?' she said.

'No, of course not,' I said demurely. As if I'd try and feed the bloody birds in the office.

'But Susan said you were,' said Jane.

'Were what?' I'd lost track of what she was saying.

'Going to get a cashmere sweater.'

'Jane. Give over please. I've got more than enough problems right now without you two getting at me.'

'You don't know what problems are. You should see what I have to do this afternoon.' And she went off to relieve the sick. I displayed the history of the bra all over my desk and stared blankly at the peach ceiling. I was feeling pretty sick with misery myself.

'It's taking you ages, that bra piece, isn't it?' said Melindi, hovering round my desk.

'It needs a lot of thought,' I said. 'How come', I continued casually, 'Jack is working for us?'

'He rang up this morning. Right out of the blue.'

'He rang Ingrid?'

'Yes. Ingrid didn't think he was interested in our sort of stuff but I think it must be Grace's influence. He's married to Grace Gustaad, you know.'

'Yes.'

'But why's it taking you so long to do that piece?'

'Melindi, go back to your own desk, please, and leave me alone.'

133

I hadn't even found out when the wretched bra was invented, let alone started writing – not that anyone, even someone used to composing copy in the middle of a war zone, could have written a word with all the commotion going on in the fashion room. For the latest batch of Christmas presents had just been delivered.

Chanel had sent Persephone a two-foot-long, black-quilted leather bag with unmistakable Chanel clasp and heavy metal link chain which was exactly what she wanted. It was exactly what the executive fashion editor and managing fashion editors wanted too, but theirs were in brown, an inferior colour to those in the know – and we all did know.

The four junior fashion editors were given scarves with the Chanel logo discreetly monogrammed in magenta. Expecting, not a two-foot-handbag, but at least a quilted purse, they were all disappointed, loathed the scarves and decided to give them to their mothers. I didn't think they were too bad – better than the pungent perfume Rosanna and I are always given. My mother, however, would regard a scarf with Chanel written all over it, as she does Sainsbury's plastic bags. Chanel should pay *her* to wear it, for advertising their name all over her head, and if Mr Sainsbury is going to use her as a walking billboard she insists that the plastic bags should be free, otherwise she turns the bags inside out.

The fashion chicks had all been given weighty earrings with the date of the year inscribed in black on a great white pearl in a gilt setting. Last January they would have cost about £75. Now, with only ten days of the year left, no one would buy them and they wouldn't go in the sale. Everyone – except for Persephone who was clacketting around merrily on the pine floor, viewing the hang of the bag from her left, then right shoulders – felt somewhat miffed.

Tron had also just been sent a present and she came in to use the fashion room mirror to look at herself in a dress which should never have been allowed to leave the cutting room. It was in camouflage khaki suede and made from about two medium-size cows. It was obviously the creation of Cowleys,

London's most expensive, most exclusive and most awful leather shop.

'The big game huntress look,' said one of the up-and-coming fashion chicks.

'Or Annie Get Your Gun,' said a student who is working here in her holidays from Cambridge and terrifying in her enthusiasm for a full-time job.

'Hmm,' pondered Tron. 'I think . . . ' She flicked her horse tail of hair to help her think.

'It's wonderful,' persisted the student.

'Is it Cowleys'?' asked Persephone, losing interest in her new bag.

'Yes, a present.'

'Hmm. It shows,' said Persephone. 'But their suede's always good.' The skirt, cut in a complete circle with just two seams, emphasised Tron's resolute hips.

'The skirt really is wonderful, you're right, quite wonderful,' mused Tron. The woman's blindness is astonishing. 'And I know what you mean about the huntress look, but it's not so much big game as Wiltshire.' Tron owns three horses named after Roman emperors.

Naomi's spindly heels came running up behind me.

'Eliza, have you got a moment?'

She looked as if she had put on melon foundation.

'What's the matter? You look really odd. Are you all right?'

'You know that – '

Ingrid laid down her chopsticks and stopped munching her bean sprouts. 'Naomi!' she called.

'Yes.'

'Where have you been?' It was obvious where Naomi had been as she was still in her coat and had Harrods bags hanging all over her arms.

'Shopping,' said Naomi.

'I should have been lunching at Orso's.'

'Oh,' said Naomi blankly. And then: 'Oh God, Ingrid, I'm so sorry. Oh God. Was she waiting there?' Ingrid nodded. 'How long?'

'Half an hour.'

'What did she do? Did she come back?'

'She rang through from the restaurant. We said we'd postpone it. We wouldn't have time. I've got to go at three.'

'Oh Ingrid. I'm so sorry. What am I going to say to her?'

'Naomi.' That was the editor calling Naomi, loudly. Something unfortunate happens to the names of the editor's secretaries. Before Naomi there was Helen and before that Emma, two of my favourite names. Now they remind me of the noises you might bellow calling a taxi in an unlit street. 'Naomi,' bawled the editor. Or a battle cry. Naomi went into the green house.

'What's happened?' I asked Ingrid.

'She was told to book a table for Madam and me at Orso's but she forgot to tell me anything about it so Madam turned up and had to sit there waiting for half an hour at a table on her own.'

'Poor Naomi,' I said. 'And she's still not been forgiven for getting those tickets muddled.'

Last week the editor told Naomi to book three tickets for Saturday's performance at the National Theatre of the new Alan Bennett play to which she could take some American magnate and his wife. But Naomi had got muddled reading the programme and booked tickets for the Olivier rather than the Lyttleton, where they were playing a modern but epic rendering of the Bible, complete with heads on plates, cripples on trolleys, and a real-life little donkey. As they had first-class seats in the middle of a row they had to sit through an hour and a half, all the way up to Herod.

'She's so tired. That's why she keeps making all these stupid mistakes,' I said to Ingrid.

'Tired? Huh, she's having too much sex – in Dorset.' Ingrid slung the remainder of her beansprouts in the bin. 'Phone Peggy, will you, Melindi, and tell her I'll have new potatoes as well tonight. Too much sex. Plus having to commute for it. And tell Peggy not to stint on the numbers this time. She's driving back and forth to Dorset morning and night. Melindi, I won't be back until tomorrow as I'm off to try that salmon egg hair massage that Knightsbridge Top Knots are doing.'

Later that afternoon I found Naomi at the back of the library as I was rooting around some fashion history books, trying to find out when the bra was invented. Naomi had a raw chicken with her.

'Eliza, please,' she said, 'don't let Madam know you've seen me. I wasn't able to get her chicken.'

'What's that then?'

'It's from Marks & Spencer. But not the sort she likes. She'll only eat them from Partridges – you know, free range, free from salmonella and so on. The man who owns their farm is a friend of hers. She likes to know exactly what happens to her chickens. Normally I get them to reserve her one but I forgot and they had run out so I had to get one from Marks & Spencer. Oh God.'

Naomi had taken the Marks & Spencer chicken out of its plastic bag and was trying to wrap it up in brown paper. 'I just can't do it the way they do. Partridges always tie them up in brown paper and string. They sort of fold it at the end. Oh God. It just won't go right. And I couldn't get the right sort of string. They use that thick hairy stuff. Do you think she'll notice? It is a fresh chicken.'

'Did you take the giblets out?'

'Yes. I shouldn't think she has the giblets, would you? She's not the sort of person you'd expect to want giblets.'

'Do you want me to have a go?'

'Oh, please. I hate this sort of thing, raw meat and all that.'

'I thought you wanted to spend the rest of your days with a beef farmer.'

'Eliza, please. Don't *you* get at me as well.'

'All right. But I think we need some more paper. This has gone too clammy now. It's all wet and horrible. Can you get some more?'

'Can't you make do? It's just that Madam told me I'm not allowed to leave my desk without her permission. And I've already been gone ages.'

'Where does she think you are now?'

'I asked if I could go to the loo. The postroom have got tons of it,' she said pleadingly.

'All right. I'll do it.' And I went and found some paper in the postroom, wrapped up the chicken, stuck it surreptiously in the editor's fridge and then went home to get ready for Rosanna's celebratory engagement party.

17

To the Manner Born

Rosanna's party was at her parents' pile of three-storey stucco just off Regent's Park. Having monopolised the market in barbed wire, her grandfather had bought this little mansion in 1922, and in 1960, Rosanna's father, who inherited the business, moved in and installed a lift to the roof where he built a glass dome terrace and now grows miniature orange trees. Rosanna's mother is descended from an ancient line of Scottish chieftains.

I know her parents well because they only live a fifteen-minute walk from me and they often ask me to dinner and I always accept because I like her father enormously and I like sampling and looking at their life although it is not my life at all, not one bit.

The entrance hall is like a mini-Versailles, with Louis chairs and spindly ankled escritoires, gilt chandeliers and banks of perfumed flowers. When I arrived, it took two men dressed like footmen to remove my coat and a third to hang it up. It wasn't a particularly good coat and it would have been less embarrassing for all of us if they had just bunged it under the stairs. A fourth asked if I would prefer champagne or kir royale, a fifth asked my name, a sixth announced it as I entered the drawing room and a seventh offered me a platter of smoked salmon rolls and obese prawns. At the end of the room, half a mile off, stood Rosanna encased in black chiffon from the bosom downwards. I sallied forth past acres of lamé and taffeta, miles of black ties, endless strings of pearls, troops of Max's shoes, tons of heavily beaded bags.

'You're wearing that dress, Eliza,' said Rosanna. I was in my Crimson Joy dress. For three weeks in November I had contemplated its purchase. It was in a shop window near work and after about ten days of making detours to look at it longingly and lustfully, I went in and asked how much it was. It was too expensive. Far, far too expensive.

I left it, but didn't forget it. Lying in bed or waiting for the bus or writing something for the magazine or trying to find my shoes or hearing my sisters' tales of unparalleled suffering or talking to Tron, I would imagine myself in this dress and think how wonderful I'd look and how it would fill all the gaps in my life. And ultimately I went back, out of curiosity, to try it on.

It was a tribute to what a well-cut dress in a fine fabric can do for you. It made a marked improvement. I asked the price and it was the same as it had been three days ago – too expensive. So I left it again. But from then on my existence depended on my owning this dress. In this clinging scarlet slip of the most delicious feel-appeal velvet, I would have a new face, new hair, a new shape. Everything about my life would be quite stunning. Absolutely everything. So I bought it. And very glad I am too, although this is only the third time I have worn it – two times more often than many of the flops in my second wardrobe.

'It's perfect,' continued Rosanna. 'I knew you were right to buy it. And this velvet. So soft and sensuous. How short is it when you sit down?'

'Very.'

'Perfect. A thing of brevity is a joy for ever. Just the right combination of demureness and depravity.'

Demureness had never struck me as characteristic of this dress but standing next to Rosanna, whose golden-tan breasts were rather in evidence, perhaps it was.

'Thanks,' I said. 'Yours is rather wonderful too. Is it a Cutlet?' (It is Lady Cutlet who will be designing Kate's wedding dress and my Chief Bridesmaid uniform.)

'Yes,' she whispered. 'And she's going to do my wedding dress.'

'How lovely. So where's Xavier?'

'Over there,' she said, 'with his back to us, doing his duty talking to my aunt, the one dressed like a canary in that yellow thing, but stay there, don't move and I'll get him away.'

Amongst all the other young men, who looked the sorts you see playing doubles at Queen's Tennis Club – tallish, wellish-built, blondish, blandish – Xavier stood out like a string of onions. He had the sort of looks that make Anglo-Saxons anti the Common Market: he looked French, emphatically so. He had the gaunt face and loose lips which the French need for talking French with a decent French accent, and the languid shoulders for shrugging *peut-être*. He spoke as if he breakfasted on Gauloises and from what you could surmise from his hands and face, his body was as brown as toast.

'I'm so pleased to meet you, Eliza. Rosanna speaks so warmly of you,' he began, kissing me at the same time. He looked as if he had just got out of bed and wanted to get back in there – with you. No wonder Rosanna liked him. A number of men I know would also find him attractive. 'And I hope you're going to come to Washington and stay with us as soon as possible.'

'Thank you,' I mumbled. I was a bit taken aback. But Xavier did the talking in flawless English, holding my eye as he spoke, touching my arm to emphasis a point he was making – something about the dangers of travelling on the London Underground, I think. He was just in the throes of saying how he really admired the way Rosanna and I managed to write (it seemed to him) exactly the same thing each month but made it sound different in each issue of the magazine, when one of Rosanna's uncles – Rosanna has more relations than the population of Hounslow – interrupted. The uncle had some new data on the European reaction to the Channel Tunnel in which he thought Xavier would be interested. Xavier grimaced at me and said he would give 'of his utmost' to have a word with me later on.

Right away Rosanna sashayed up to my side and raised her eyebrows questioningly. 'I really like him,' I said truthfully. I did like him.

'Really?'

'Yes, I do. He's charming. Handsome. Diplomatic – he said

he liked our stuff in the magazine. He asked me to Washington.' I turned round to look at him again. 'Terribly handsome actually.'

'Do you really think so?'

'Yes I think he's . . .'

'Rosanna,' called out another of Rosanna's aunts, dressed like a male parrot showing off.

'I'd better go,' said Rosanna. 'But I'll introduce you to Mungo. Mungo,' she called to a short young man of about twenty-one.

'What a wonderful name,' I ventured, feeling terribly sorry for him.

'Yes it is,' he said without hesitation. 'It is Lord Mungo actually, Lord Mungo of Bankengine. Bankengine is derived from Enginé, which is a French village at the base of the Pyrenees where my ancestors originated. And when they came over to England – my grandfather says it was with William the Conqueror but I think that may be wishful thinking and it was more likely a couple of centuries later – they were given the greater part of Lincolnshire – for killing hordes of Anglo-Saxons no doubt – and built a castle on the banks of a river. Hence, Bankengine, with no accent now, of course. I didn't catch your surname.'

'Hart.'

'Heart like this,' he said, hitting his chest, 'or like the male deer?'

'The deer.'

'Gamekeeper, probably. Many gamekeepers were called Hart. What are these?' he asked, turning to a waitress with a plate of miniature pastry things.

'Bombay baskets.'

'And these?'

'Marchioness's Treats.'

He took both. 'But what do you do now?'

'I work with Rosanna on *Circe*. And you?'

Lord Mungo of Bankengine looked at me as if he had just found half a worm in his Bombay basket.

'I am a Lord,' he said slowly and deliberately, as if explaining quantum physics to an idiot. 'That's what I do. Cleopatra!' He waved to a girl with flowers in her hair. And that would have been the end of our conversation if he had not at that moment bitten into his Marchioness's Treat. Instead of putting it in his mouth all in one go as I had done with mine, he bit it in half and squirted the taramasalata stuffing plonk on top of my hair and on my cleavage – or what cleavage was left to me after my breast massage.

'I'm awfully sorry, I really am,' he blustered, whipping out a white silk monogrammed handkerchief and alternately dabbing my dress and my head.

'It's all right. It doesn't matter,' I said as he went on rubbing my hair. 'Please stop. Really. It's all right. There's a hair salon in Knightsbridge where people pay £50 to have their scalp rubbed with fish eggs. It doesn't matter. Though they're salmon eggs, not cod's eggs. Please let me do it. Don't worry. I'll go and rinse it out myself.'

En route upstairs – the lift was full – I met Rosanna's mother bearing down upon me like a galleon in full sail. She stopped midway and said, 'You do look smart, terribly smart, Eliza.'

'Thank you,' I said. This dress wasn't smart. I didn't think I looked smart one bit. 'How are you?'

'How am I?' she laughed and, smoothing down her crackling Black Watch tartan taffeta dress and adjusting her tiara, she told me how she had already got the wedding plans well underway, that the service would be at St. George's Church in Hanover Square, that she had employed an extra secretary to take care of the arrangements, and another temp for the Christmas week to wrap up all her Christmas presents – all of which she had bought from Harrods' catalogue. She asked what I had bought my family and when I said 'bird tables' she told me how she always used old dinner gongs as bird tables, and she wondered whether I would write a report for her on how I found the street lighting in my area for her 'See the Street Light' campaign, and told me that I could use

143

her bathroom, through her bedroom, for washing the taramasalata out of my smart dress.

There was a wet stain on the front of my red dress by the time I had finished removing the cod's roe. I didn't really want to go back to the party, especially smelling of fish. Amongst the Lord Mungos and Lady Cleopatras I felt I blended in like a horned rattlesnake. I didn't want to leave the beautiful bathroom. I would rather have had a bath. It was the sort of bath I aspire to, a magnificent marble cocoon, thigh deep and long enough for easing myself into at full stretch and lying totally immersed and shielded from the cold with steaming water furling deliciously about me. I sat on the edge of it. My bath at home is not the same as it is so small and the hard narrow sides snub my body and it is such a practical little tub that it induces visions of Ingrid going on about how long, hot, soaking baths are so bad for your skin they make you look like a dried-out old beetroot before it's been put in vinegar. The underfloor heating curled through my toes and up my legs. In a bath lie this, Ingrid and other women would be the last thing in my head.

I walked out. Rosanna's father was in the bedroom tying his bow tie.

'Oh I'm sorry. I should have knocked,' I blustered. 'Your wife told me to use your bathroom.'

'Eliza, what a treat to see you emerge. You're looking so lovely.' He kissed me. 'Quite beautiful. Sit down, sit down, my darling.' This man is as handsome as a Michelangelo statue but more worn and worldly. I find him deeply attractive. I would rather not. 'I'm appallingly late – for my own party too, thanks to my wretched secretary. Why does the woman have no common sense?' Sometimes, to my shame again, I find male chauvinism a turn-on. 'So sit down, my dearest, do. And cheer me up, please, before I go and meet all those people.'

I sat on the edge of the bed and watched him tie his tie. I think it has something to do with the stretch of the neck and because it is peculiarly masculine, but I like watching men tie their ties. He untied it and re-knotted it. He did it deliberately.

For every million miles of barbed wire he has sold he has had to tie hundreds of bow ties. He could knot them in seconds in his sleep. He got it wrong again and in the meantime I talked to him.

He is such a consummate flirt that he quite outruns me. All that titillation and repartee, being locked in verbal battle with an untouchable, exhausts me. It's the mental equivalent of a sleepless night. Thoughts not tongues must meet. Half the skill is in making your partner think that the two of you together are the funniest duo since Laurel and Hardy, and for the next fifteen minutes I sat thinking I was the wittiest woman north of Regent's Park.

Once he had finished polishing his gleaming shoes we went back to the party where Rosanna was standing at the bottom of the stairs with four young women who looked as though they had once played a ferocious game of netball.

'Daddy,' she called out and put her arm round him. 'You remember Cecilia, Emily-Jane, Viviana, and Bambi, don't you?' Of course her father remembered them – though they all looked the same to me. He greeted them charmingly and I went off to find Mungo the Lord to give him back his fishy silk handkerchief.

At dinner I was seated between a boisterous young bond dealer called Peregrine and an equally boisterous but not so young exiled Polish Catholic Count named Stan. Patrick, one of Rosanna's cousins, sat opposite, between Bambi and a woman looking like Thumper in a bunny-rabbit dress with heavy white netting under the back of its short black skirt.

As we wolfed down a great *millefeuille* filled with spinach and a fishy mousse which quivered with a pinkish hue, Peregrine filled me in on how much money he had made for his company last Monday; how many points he scored in rugby on Saturday; how he had been to Harrow, Oxford and Harvard and could make a very good pasta dish with sun-dried tomatoes and was able to make the pasta himself with his pasta machine; how last summer he had moved into a mews house in SW1 and had just got rid of the plasterers who had been installing a new cornice; how, at birth, he had been put down for a Morgan which his grandfather had bought him for his seventeenth birthday and in which he would have given me a lift home if it hadn't blown its chief gasket; how a couple of months ago he had received a letter from the royal representative at Ascot saying he was no longer on the list for Royal Ascot as he had not accepted their invitation for tickets for the past three years but his mother had written an apologetic letter to the Queen or someone like that and this very morning he had received a note saying he was back on the list and eligible for tickets once more; how on Christmas Eve he was going down to his family's estate in Devon where some relations from Texas would join them so forty in all would be sitting down to Christmas lunch; how he was going skiing at Klosters in the first week of January; how tomorrow night he was going to a Christmas dinner at Harrow for Old Boys.

Males like Peregrine progress from schoolboy to Old Boy with no man in between. It is because of all the rugby they play (Peregrine had been a blue at Oxford) and having to spend all that time running about in shorts.

While Peregrine was explaining that he had learnt to ski in Canada where conditions are more favourable to beginners, and scallops and peas in their pods were being served onto my Wedgwood plate, a tubby hand began to squeeze my right elbow.

'You mustn't let that young man command all your attention,' said Stan the Count, in a deep-throated sort of way. 'Are you a sportswoman yourself?' he asked as the waiter asked if I would like a fennel sauce on my scallops.

'Yes,' I said to the waiter, and 'No,' to Stan, who had severe eye-level problems and it wasn't the taramasalata stain that was interesting him.

Stan was surprised that I was not a sportswoman. I looked as if I might be. He looked down on me some more. I looked down at my scallops. Sport is not a subject for leches. Most subjects aren't.

'Was your mother a Countess?' I asked.

She had been a Countess, but an exiled one, and he talked about her Roman Catholic dynastic family until the arrival of the pudding when he started upon his autobiography. His was a story of brilliant success in the face of unrivalled deprivation, of setting up a multi-national, multi-million company with outlets in America, Australia and on the continent, manufacturing exotic mustards and horseradishes, after a quite unimaginably appalling childhood spent moving from one European capital to another, staying with other exiles.

As I attacked a scroll of glazed meringue and some blackberries which you can pick for free in the summer but which are almost unobtainable and very expensive at Christmas time, Stan the Count's chubby left forefinger arrived on my right kneecap and made irregular circular movements. Needless to say it sent me into transports of erotic ecstasy. I moved the knee away and turned to ask Peregrine to explain one of the rules of rugby which had always confused me, but he was talking to Bambi opposite and looked as if he would be some time as he had only got as far as telling her about dried tomatoes and his pasta machine. And Patrick was engrossed in the Thumper lookalike's story about how she had once eaten so many blackberries she had come out in spots – all over. Two fingers returned slightly above my kneecap. After mothers the only subject to discuss with leches is religion.

'Being a Catholic, are you going to Midnight Mass or do you just go to the service on Christmas morning? And do you go to confession or can you not go to confession over Christmas?' Off came the fingers. Yes, he did go to Midnight Mass and no, he did not go to confession, and with that he turned to the woman on his other side and I chewed on the blackberries until Rosanna's father made a speech.

It was a perfect speech, funny, very short and looking forward to seeing us all again at the wedding which was going to be the most expensive day of his life – at which everyone laughed – because, he continued, he was going to be losing his only daughter.

Then Xavier said a few words. Although his command of

English grammar and idioms was flawless he still spoke with an unmistakable French accent as if to say that having mastered our language so well, to have spoken with a BBC accent would have been too much like the cherry on the cake. Besides, as he knew full well, it would have detracted from his charm.

Then Xavier's father got up, but although his accent was no more French than Brian Redhead's, his style was blazingly Gallic. He said the same thing – that Rosanna and Xavier were in love – as many times as possible in as many ways as possible.

'What does "love" mean?' he asked. 'It can mean I love strawberries, 'ello luv and, of course, I love you. What sort of love exists between Rosanna and Xavier? It is a love like a rock as it is eternal; it is a love like cement as it binds them together; it is a love like fire as it is passionate.'

It sounded like something our of *Look and Learn*, with hearty helpings of Jackie Collins. It was all rather too much for his phlegmatic audience and after fifteen minutes of further flammable and geological similes, Rosanna politely interrupted to have her say, speaking her English with a faint but clearly distinguishable French accent.

During the dinner a five-strong band had set themselves up in the drawing room. The Aubusson rugs and forest of Louis XV furniture had been cleared away and Carlos, who is the son of an old friend of Rosanna's father, asked me to dance. He is Brazilian and owns four gold mines in Mexico and comes to London about four times a year when he stays down the road in his penthouse in Kensington. I have met him before but this was the first time we had spoken cheek to cheek.

He danced very well. South Americans often do. It has something to do with their hips. On the first dance we talked about the weather, how cold it was, how it looked as if we would have a white Christmas, how I loathed it and how he loved it after the heat of the Mexican sun. On the second he explained the political situation in Mexico. On the third he told me how he had lost his virginity at fifteen with a friend of his mother's in a Brazilian coffee plantation during a picnic. On the fourth he asked me how I lost mine at which point I said I had to sit down.

I sat in the direct firing line of Rosanna's flamboyant, parrot-like aunt telling the canary aunt about her and her husband Piers's recent visit to Hong Kong.

'I bought this silk out there,' she said of her sapphire-and-cornflake-yellow print evening dress, 'and had Clarice's daughter who's doing fashion design at St. Martin's, and terribly clever at this sort of thing, run it up for me. It's a copy of a Jasper Conran – though you would never guess – and I'm in the throes of sorting out all my Jasper silks as next month Piers is off out there again – I can't go this time as I've got that NSPCC ball – and I'll get him to have them copied for me. The Hongkers are hopeless at designing themselves, or fitting you properly, but if you give them something to copy they do it beautifully.

'What I'd like him to do, and what Roberta gets her husband to have made for her out there, is some underwear. I've got those adorable French knickers from Chantal Thomas. You know, that gem of a shop in St. Germain. I always stock up when I go to Paris. But Piers says he'd rather pay for me to go to Paris and get what I want at a hundred times the price rather than him having to go over to Hongkers with a suitcase full of my lingerie. That silk Lucinda is wearing is material we brought back as well.'

Lucinda, bearing an unmistakable likeness to the parrot, was obviously one of Piers's and the parrot's chicks. She was wearing a black silk T-shirt and harem pants made of about six metres of khaki-coloured crêpe de Chine which billowed like a loose groundsheet in a high wind as she cavorted around on the dance floor.

'And she wore those harem pants for the first time last week on Piers's sixty-second birthday night. Thirty of us – we kept it small and just family – went to L'Escargot and then on to a new nightclub in Greek Street. But they wouldn't let Lucinda in because she was in trousers. Those very ones. Quite ridiculous in this day and age. Women, they said, had to wear skirts or dresses. Piers thinks it was all a publicity stunt. There was no need for them to make such a fuss as we were all terribly dressed up and it was not as if she was in jeans. So Lucinda – and I must say I felt terribly proud of her – just stood there in the hall and took them off, right there and then, and walked straight past the desk in her shirt which was so short it barely touched her thighs. She looked lovely, of course. She has such beautiful legs, she modelled tights for Pretty Polly, you know, before going up to Oxford. And she's going to work for them again in the summer vac – just a bit of photographic work to pay for a trip to Thailand. It's so easy for her, being so tall and slim.'

'Especially as her spots have cleared up so beautifully,' said the canary, piping up at last. I turned round. Parrot and canary stared at each other stonily – expensive stones naturally. Before either could put down the other, Rosanna's mother, in the commanding voice of the Highland chieftain she is descended from, interrupted and told her sisters that she needed one of them to become chairman of a new nursery school in Chelsea and, catching my eye, told me to meet Duff.

Duff bounded over like a puppy that never grew up. He was about forty, about three times my weight, with sweat on his brow, a curly beard and hair flopping over his forehead. He steered me purposefully onto the dance floor, bumping me into the rump of a much-acclaimed politician's wife, and asked nervously, 'Can you put your toe in your mouth?'

'No,' I said. 'Well, I've never tried. I doubt it.'

'Thank God for that. A normal person. Everyone here can.'

'Really?'

'Yes,' he said and started dancing, stopped talking and began humming. With the supreme confidence only a public school can confer he danced with total disregard for the music's rhythm and generally accepted movements. Round and round and push-me pull-you movements and his *pièce de résistance*, a sudden spin, all featured in his routine. The band was playing something Sixties-ish. Duff was still humming. I didn't know what it was. Duff obviously didn't either but that didn't put him off humming. He was getting sweatier and sweatier. So too, probably, was I. The fourth time he mopped his forehead, I suggested we might stop and he agreed as, he said, I had taken more out of him than a good chase cross-country on Julius, his new horse.

'It's such thirsty work dancing,' he said, downing some Mumms. 'It's all right for women, they trip along with no clothes on virtually. But what would I give to take off . . . Oh God.'

'Duff darling,' said a woman dressed in a vaporous cloud of rose-pink chiffon. 'Have you made your mind up yet?' Slowly, she ran her fingers through her sleepy, thunder-black storm of hair.

'Er, no. I don't think so, not another one, not yet, thank you.'

'But Duff darling, I thought you liked the other one.'

'Er, yes, I did, but . . .'

'Well then. You shouldn't be so hard to persuade.' If she had had a fan she would have hit him with it. 'I won't let you off so easily, you know. I'll be back.' And she laughed prettily and fiddled with her hair again. 'I'm determined to get my way.'

And she will too, whatever it is she wants. She can only have been about twenty-two but women with iron wills disguised in such an embrace of femininity always get their way.

'What does she want?' I asked Duff, whose sweat had gone cold.

'To do my portrait. Well, that's what she says. Huh.' He was drinking more champagne than was good for him. 'All last Christmas she was bothering me – her parents live in the next village – asking if she could paint my picture. I said no – categorically, I thought. But there's no holding a girl like that back so I thought all right, have it done, get it over and done with and that will throw her off for good. So I let her paint me on Titan, my best hunter. At least I thought I might as well have a picture of him. I asked if she would just do a portrait of

151

the horse. But no, it was me she wanted, she said. Anyway I had it done and hung it in the stables but she's been at me ever since to do another one. Going on how she'd love to come round and see me over Christmas and paint me on Flopsy. Bloody stupid name for a horse. Should have been a rabbit. But I bought it from a woman who had a thing about Beatrix Potter. More champagne?'

'No thanks.'

'The thing is, she doesn't want to do my picture. Of course she doesn't. You wouldn't want to paint my portrait, would you?'

'Well I can't paint so I wouldn't be able to.' Looking as he did just then however, like a puce blob, I might have managed it.

'Of course you wouldn't want to. She doesn't either. But she wants to be a portrait painter. Well, who can be a portrait painter these days? It's not as if she's a Gainsborough. And she is certainly not a Stubbs. Good God no. But her father has this idea that his estate has always gone to the eldest son since sixteen hundred and something and no amount of women's lib and his wife pestering him will make him change his mind so old Poppy here won't get anything and won't be able to paint pictures all day and wear pink floaty things unless she marries a rich man.' He was beginning to slur his words. 'Years ago I was at L.S.E. Only for six months. 1969. I couldn't stick having to speak like a yokel, saying my father worked on the land when he owned half of Wiltshire. But now it's all the other way round. They like my money.' The poor (metaphorically speaking) man put his head in his hands.

'Are you all right?' I asked.

He looked carefully at his watch. 'Yes. I think I'd better be off now. There's something about London that always gives me a headache.'

'You're not going back tonight?'

'Yes, I've got to be home. I've got a meeting tomorrow morning, first thing, which I can't miss, about breeding pheasants more efficiently.'

'Are you driving?'

'No. Train. The last train from Paddington. I can walk from here, can't I?'

'Yes. But I'd take a taxi if I were you.'

'Hmm. Do you ride?'

'No.'

'Pity. You're missing out. You look as if you'd be a good hunter. Goodbye,' he mumbled, hauling himself to his feet.

'Goodbye,' I said. The portrait painter reappeared magically by his side.

'Duff,' she whispered. 'I'm having a dinner party for my hundred most intimate friends at Mummy and Daddy's on New Year's Day, and you really must come.'

'I'm shooting, er, thank you, on, er, the first of January,' he said.

'But not at night?'

'No.'

'Well then, you've got no excuse. I shall expect you at eight o'clock. I'll ride over to see you sometime over Christmas just to make sure you don't forget.' A woman in search of a mate is a formidable sight. 'And I'll be seeing you at Midnight Mass anyway.'

'Oh yes,' said Duff. 'Yes, yes, but I must be off,' and he exited with his tail between his legs.

'Isn't Duff adorable?' said the portrait painter, looking down her nose at me.

'Oh absolutely,' I said. 'Quite adorable.'

'I fall in love with him every time I see him.' And she filled me in on a few personal details about how she had known him since she was thirteen; how her parents and Duff's family were old friends of Xavier's family on his mother's side; how she had done a year's art foundation course in Paris as there is no better place to learn art; how she had learnt French *sur place* as they say in France; how she now spoke the language *courrament* and knew Paris *comme sa poche*. Then she suddenly screeched. 'Sophie.'

'Poppy,' screeched back Sophie, and Poppy shot off with the chiffon billowing about her, as ephemeral and Poppy-like as a

153

prize pink thistle with a stranglehold on an entire Scottish crag.

I went and joined Rosanna's schoolfriends Tara and Yasmin, whom I have met before at Rosanna's parties. 'Some people just have the most extraordinary ability to make money,' Yasmin was saying in connection with a mutual friend whose cooking and catering business was now so successful she was going to open a restaurant in Kensington. 'But *Amelia* of all people. She isn't even very bright.'

'She's very pretty,' said Tara.

'Not that pretty,' said Yasmin.

'Well, very flirtatious.'

'Oh yes. And she'd have to have been an idiot if she'd gone wrong after doing that tea party for Prince Charles.'

'Except I heard he never pays much.'

'No, of course he doesn't. But that doesn't matter as it gets your name around. Also, Lady Lamb adopted her. So with Lady Lamb and the tea party, everyone started wanting those domino biscuits she does.'

'I know, everyone serves them. "Amaretti" biscuits are completely out now. I mean anyone can buy a box of "Amaretti", but dominoes are different. Though it must take her ages, doing all the piping of little dots.'

'But it's worth it with the whole world wanting them because you can't buy them in a box like everyone else, and Prince Charles thinking they're wonderful.'

'And she's had the most amazing holidays out of it all. Some Americans flew her there and back to cook a meal in Kentucky. On Concorde. And I heard she does the Queen Mother's chocolate cake too.'

'You should have a word with Lady Lamb yourself if that's where it gets you,' advised Yasmin. 'Get her to adopt some of your flower arrangements. She's here, I've heard her. Over there. You too, Eliza. You must meet her.'

Lady Lamb, a woman of no discernible shape or age but strikingly loud voice, was talking to a gentleman who said he had spotted her getting into a cab in Cheapside.

'I was seeing my accountant,' she bellowed.

'Oh dear.'

'Yes, but fortunately he's an old friend of mine.'

'Good news, I hope.'

'Yes. Very good.'

'And the family?'

Lady Lamb did not answer but cried out, 'Tara and Yasmin! How sweet to see you both. Come and join us. I hoped you'd both be here tonight as last week I got a letter from Emily, my niece,' she elaborated for my benefit, 'with a large bright-red flower stamp. She's in Africa before she goes to secretarial college, working in a safari park on the horse farm. What that girl doesn't know about horses isn't worth knowing. The same goes for her sister. But she says she's put on two stone.'

'Two stone?' asked Yasmin.

'Yes, it's a lot in one month.'

'What's she doing? Living on cream?'

'I think they work her very hard so she has to eat a lot. She's up at six and works right through the day. But she wrote to say, this will surprise you, that she met, quite by chance, the Rockfaults. Isn't that extraordinary? It's such a small world. But, Tara, I've heard such good news about your sister, something about her training to be an interior designer.'

'No, she's training to be a social worker,' said Tara.

'Much the same thing really, except on a different level. Making sure you don't precipitate divorces, painting the bathroom pink when the wife tells you she likes pink but the husband can't abide the colour.' Tara and Yasmin laughed politely. 'I can't say I much like pink myself but is she still in Chelsea?'

'No. Wigmore Square.'

'Oh no. Not another Chelsea deserter. Perhaps there's not much social work in Chelsea, though Wigmore Square can't be that much better off for social work. But everyone's leaving me. I'm sure it's only because there are none of those shops which are open all hours around Chelsea. Not that I ever go to them. They're far too expensive for one thing. But you've not left Yeoman's Row have you?' (Yeoman's Row, a mere Sloane's throw from Cadogan Square, belies its name.)

'No,' said Tara.

'Well you must come round and do some more of those lovely little posies you're so good at arranging.'

'Oh yes,' said Tara eagerly. 'Whenever you want. When would . . .?'

'Jem,' interrupted Lady Lamb, bawling to a man ten feet away who was in the middle of saying, 'No. Quite honestly, I do not think going to Harrow made much difference to how my life turned out.'

'That was such a lovely letter I read about you in *The Times* on Friday.'

Jem smiled at Lady Lamb and strolled over, surrounded by a penumbra of admiring females. The son of one of the more prominent members of the House of Lords, he has husky good looks which are always being photographed in women's magazines. He was a very successful actor in BBC Sunday evening serials until five years ago when he turned, equally successfully, to politics. Thanks to his theatrical training he can speak even louder than Lady Lamb. She therefore had to keep quiet and listen. Jem explained that he was performing in a charity gala performance on Bank Holiday Monday which would be televised live on BBC 1, and he made considerable comic use of the fact that he was performing for free.

I looked at the Meissen clock, which was sucking in time as slowly as if it was relishing an interminable string of spaghetti. Jem was as unctuous as jelly which has not set properly, only more boring. He continued. On the Bank Holiday Tuesday, he was going skiing in Verbier. He would rather be going to Klosters as he thought the skiing there was better but friends of his had rung from Verbier that morning and said the snow was fine. Had any of us heard news of the skiing this winter in Verbier? He caught my eye. Occasionally catching a member of your audience's eye is a public-speaking technique.

'Don't look at me,' I said amicably. 'I've no idea. I've never been skiing.'

'Oh no,' said Jem. 'How dreadful. You don't know what you're missing.'

Thank God, is all I wanted to say to that. Thank God. Thank God. Not much could be worse than all that cold wet snow, that interminable hiking up and sliding down of all those confounded mountains.

'Oh no,' echoed his penumbra, taking his cue to pipe up with a chorus on how much I was missing.

But it was only a short chorus as Jem, with adoration eddying about him like steam off a bouillabaisse, wanted to continue explaining the plans for the rest of his life: when he came back from Verbier he was going to open a day centre for the elderly in the Isle of Dogs, give a lecture at the English Speaking Union on inner-city deprivation, take part in a debate at the Oxford Union and write a series of articles for a national newspaper. He was a great shooting pal of the paper's editor, a charming man who had just given Jem's youngest brother, only two months out of Oxford, a job in the newsroom.

Jem's plans for February were interrupted because Poppy came screeching up to talk to her dear, dear Lady Lamb. Oh, I thought, to be born with those vocal cords which command the rest of the world to stop and listen. That's where I am missing out. Forget hunting and Klosters skiing. I simply don't have the voice.

Poppy was anxious to announce that her picture was in the National Portrait Gallery. I was impressed. I thought I had underestimated her and that Duff most certainly had.

'That's a great achievement,' I interrupted, 'having a picture there.'

'It is, isn't it? A friend of mine did it,' she said.

'It's not painted by you?'

'Oh no. The picture is *of* me.'

'I'll go and look at it,' I lied. 'I've never met anyone with their picture in there.'

'Really? I'm always finding pictures of people I know there. An old friend or someone who's cropped up from school. You know.'

No. I didn't know. When I was at Hounslow High I was taught that everyone was equal. I believed it too. At school I thought Poppys, Lady Lambs, Lord Mungos and Jems had become extinct. But no. They are alive and kicking more than ever. They have never been misled about equality. Quite the reverse. With lordships for fathers they know from the start that they are not equal to anyone. No one would persuade great prize cockatoos like Jem or Lord Mungo that they would be just as equal if they had been born common budgies. No way. Especially as now budgies have to be so nice to cockatoos. Make any sort of comment on social inequality these days and you'll be dropped right away. You certainly won't be invited to dinner and into their network again. With that fish shop full of chips on your shoulders, you're liable to upset the tone of the party.

'Where are you going for Christmas?' Poppy asked me.

'Oh, um,' I murmured. Yasmin had just been saying that her father was taking the whole family to Italy for Christmas. Poppy was going to be in Wiltshire. Lady Lamb was off to San Francisco. Jem of course was going to Verbier. Tara's parents had closed their home in Derbyshire to the public for the Christmas holiday and had twenty guests arriving on Christmas Eve.

If I had been born at the same time as Duff, Hounslow would have rated fairly high on the social scale. Not as high as the East End of course or, even better, the Gorbals, but it would have represented social heights quite untouchable to someone whose home was so stately it was open to the public. Tara would have been trying to persuade me that her mansion was nothing more than a worthless pile of rubble. Not now, however. Now inherited wealth is back 'in'. Inherited guilt is 'out'.

'I'm staying in London,' I said, cowardly. And with that, as the clock had managed to struggle to one, I went home.

18

Heartburn

Loud cries were coming from next door's flat when I got home. She would be out of business if virtually everyone in this block of flats were not deaf or mad. The cat was stalking about in the hall. It growled at me. I never knew cats could growl until I met this one.

There were no messages except for one from Cassandra asking me to ring her, no matter what time I got in.

'Hello,' she answered as brightly as if it was lunchtime, not half-past one in the morning.

'What's the matter?' I asked. I was exhausted.

'Nothing. I'm making a list of all the men whom I could ask to be father of my children – or child rather, as I wouldn't want more than one on my own. I know lots of men who would be more than happy to sleep with me.'

'That's reassuring,' I said drily.

'Yes. But I don't know whether I should include Nick. He's got the physique. He used to play rugby, still does, in fact. And he's got the looks but I don't know if he's really got enough brains.'

'Cassandra,' I interrupted.

'But I'm not sure if brains are really that important. It would be far better to be beautiful, wouldn't it? Especially as, being a child of mine, it wouldn't be very rich.'

'Cassandra, what's the matter? It's the middle of the night. I thought you were seeing John tonight.'

'He's left.'

'Left?'

'Right.'

'How do you mean "left"?'

159

'He's left, right? Hey, Eliza. There's something in that. Left, right, left right. It's the basis for a pun. You can have it if you like. Use it for the heading on a shoe article or something.'

'Left for good?'

'Not for good. For his wife. To have another go at making a go of it with her.'

'Oh, you poor thing. Are you all right? Do you want me to come over and see you? I'll get straight in a cab. I'll come right away. I can be with you in no time.'

'No. I'm fine, really. Hold on a minute.' She was gone about five minutes and returned eating something.

'What's that?'

'Mashed potatoes. I made them – proper ones with cream and butter. John had this meeting in Paris all day and he said he didn't know what time he would be back so he said he'd come straight round to me. So I had all this food ready. And I did creme caramel. You like creme caramel, don't you?'

'Yes.'

'It's amazing stuff. I think it's the texture. You know. The way it slips down. I've eaten it otherwise I'd have saved you some. I'm going to write about it.'

'About John, you mean?'

'Yes. Parthian shots. He was hunting around for some tie he thinks he left here and while he was doing that I found his passport and under the section for distinguishing characteristics I wrote "no penis".'

'That's brilliant. I'm really impressed,' I laughed. 'Well done. That is good. Very good.'

'Isn't it? You can't imagine what a difference it makes, doing something like that. None of that moping like usual. It cured me instantly. Normally, you know I can't eat – though I could have done with losing my appetite now for a bit. Now I'm perfectly all right. Not emotional. He'll have to pretend he's lost his passport and get another one, won't he?'

'Yes, but hopefully he won't spot it until he's actually having to show it at passport control. But you should have written "huge penis".'

There was silence on the other end of the phone and then Cassandra started to cry, loudly.

'Oh God, yes. Why couldn't I have thought of that? That would have been more embarrassing, wouldn't it? Much better. Oh God. Why can't I think of these things?'

'You do. You did,' I said hurriedly. 'And now I think about it I don't think "huge" would be any more embarrassing. Anyway, yours was the original idea.' Cassandra said nothing. 'And it was a brilliant one. Cassandra?'

She sniffed. 'Perhaps I'll advise using "huge" in the article. Wait a moment.'

'Are you eating again?' I asked when she got back.

'Yes. I hate eating on my own. And I had this question I'd written down to ask you.'

'Oh yes.'

'Did you actually consummate matters with The Bostonian?'

'You wrote that down on a piece of paper to ask me?'

'Yes. I only thought of it about an hour ago and I had to discuss it with you. Because Claudia – you know that American friend of mine who used to work on the *Herald Tribune*?'

'Vaguely.'

'I spoke to her this morning, and you know how she spent all that time pining for that L.S.E. professor?'

'Yes.'

'Yesterday afternoon, after three years and two months exactly, they actually consummated things, and you know what? She's gone off him now. After all that time thinking she wanted nothing more from life than him. So I thought I could do an article on it. So, did you and The Bostonian?'

'You know I did. I told you.'

'I know, but I wondered if you could pretend you didn't so I could interview you on how you go over your every meeting with him, looking for missed opportunities, and all that, you know, just in case I get desperate and can't find anyone else.'

'Why can't you interview your friend Claudia?'

'That's the problem. She's halfway to Australia.'

'Because this man wasn't what she thought he was?'

'No, of course not. She was going anyway for Christmas to stay with her sister who is out there. And I wanted to discuss the idea with you. The danger of fantasy. The climax of obsession. How when you actually consummate things with the keystone of your universe, the whole edifice can suddenly come tumbling down. How you can waste years longing for a single moment and when – or if – it transpires, it is so different from what you had imagined.'

'I've got the idea,' I interrupted.

'But what I'm most stuck on is advice and I thought you might have a few ideas. First of all, how do you stop being obsessed?'

'How should I know?'

'Well,' she said hesitantly. 'I thought you might have a few ideas. What with all that time it took you getting over Jack. And now look at you with Sam.'

'I was not obsessed with Jack. I loved him. And I'm not obsessed with Sam. Why do you have to reduce everything down to one of your wretched magazine articles?' I snapped. 'Anyway, I've no idea how you cure obsession. Especially not at this time. Why do you have to give advice anyway? Why can't you just say this is what can happen if you do turn a man into an unfillable fantasy, and leave it at that?'

'I write an advice column, Eliza. People look to me for answers. I'm supposed to give counsel,' she sniffed pathetically.

'Well I'll think about it for you,' I said more kindly. 'I promise. Oh wait.'

'What?'

'Tell people to think of someone who has been obsessed with them,' I said, thinking of St. George, 'and look at how far it got them.'

'Thank you. That's perfect. I really owe you one now. Can I see you soon? What about tomorrow?'

'It's the editor's Christmas party.'

'Could you come round afterwards? I'm really miserable right now so I must talk to you,' she said, starting to sob again.

'All right.'

'Don't forget, will you? I'll cook something.'

'Of course I won't forget.'

'Good night then, and thanks again for the obsession tip.'

'My pleasure,' I said and went to bed and slept badly, thinking that when you are in love with someone, or think you are, the imagination never works so well or so incessantly. It is forever perfecting the loved one's image, remembering meetings, rehearsing conversations. It makes you see the whole world in relation to the object of desire: a smelly old battered number 16 double-decker bus reminds you of the rapturous day you spent in Greenwich together; mention of Arsenal recalls the hours you sat happily – happily, note – watching football, aching with cold in a sleety ice-chapped Wembley stadium. It lifts you high out of the crowd and wastes hours of your time.

19

How the Rich Give

As I walked into the office next morning Tron thundered up.
'Lize, you know you're off to Bestes, don't you?'

I did know.

Bestes is a china and glass shop, the sort of place where
colonials bought their suites of glass and dinner services for
ruling the empire. It has not changed much. Bestes had invited
four famous interior designers to lay their ideal Christmas
table, and we were going to photograph the final results for the
'Who's Who' page.

To be featured on the 'Who's Who' page you have to be at least
one of the following: titled, outrageously rich, sickeningly
beautiful or a friend of some significant member of the
magazine's staff. (Tron's best friend's husband is a director of
Bestes and Tron gets all her china there at half price. With this
sort of publicity in the magazine she should now get it for free.)

'I want you to make sure you understand what J's table
design is all about,' she said as if telling a two-year-old not to
eat with its fingers.

'Of course,' I said politely.

J is an interior designer who calls himself by the letter J. In
magazine speak J is 'an austere man, *un philosophe* who
incorporates symbols and hidden meanings into his designs'.
In other words, his designs have a tendency to be mind-
blowingly obscure. To my mind they are art with a capital 'P'
for pretension.

Tron continued. 'He is sure to have an original conception of
a Christmas table, and I don't want you to miss the point.'

'No, Tron,' I said not quite so politely, and went and found
Basil the photographer.

The two of us walked to Bestes as what would take fifteen minutes on foot would take forty driving through the Christmas traffic in Basil's van. But as Basil wanted to take shots looking down on the tables, we had to carry his ladder between us, me holding one end, him the other. We mowed down the trumpet players and the Salvation Army I had heard yesterday. A policeman stopped Basil to ask where we were going with a ladder. A woman with a double pushchair for twins shouted that we shouldn't be allowed on the street. And my end knocked two baubles off a street trader's stand and as I refused to pay for them – street trading like that is illegal according to Rosanna's mother – we got held up even longer.

Bestes' publicity director, Cecilia, a former Junior Olympic butterfly champion, trotted over as soon as we had negotiated the swing doors. She was all dressed up as if she had just done a raid on Hermès – horsey scarf tied up in a lamb cutlet frill round her neck, leather belt with stirrup-style buckle, khaki suede hairband.

'Eliza! How lovely to see you again. I haven't seen you since our china grizzly bear exhibition. You are looking wonderful. And you're always so sickeningly slim. Oh how do you do it? I wish you would tell me. None of the designers have arrived yet but they said they'd be here by eleven. It's the traffic I suppose and parking is impossible. They should be here any minute. They've done most of the tables, but they're not quite finished and they have all specifically asked me not to let you take any photographs until they have had a final check. But you might as well go along now and take a look so I can start telling you which china, glass and so on they have chosen. Everything from the cutlery to the dinner plates had to come from the shop, you see, just to go and show what a simply superb range we at Bestes have, how many different looks we cater for and of what high quality it all is. You will put that in your article, won't you? That everything wonderful is available in the shop?'

'I'll do what I can,' I said and went and looked at the tables. J arrived first. He had laid his table with marigold yellow plates, green glasses and a royal blue table cloth. The overall effect was of a child's paint box. There were no crackers or holly, nothing Christmassy in sight.

'I've only two minutes,' he said. 'I've got my fencing lesson at eleven-thirty and what with the traffic I don't have time to stay around and chat. And no, I don't want a coffee and in actual fact I don't believe in Christmas lunch anyway. And this table is the sort of table I lay when breakfasting in Provence in a glorious Mediterranean sun. Not a traditional Christmas table at all. Not at all.'

'Why?' I asked, having been ordered by Tron to find hidden meanings and not miss the point.

'I hate making gravy,' he explained. 'With eight children, and all the friends I invite to spend Christmas Day with us, I end up seating at least thirty, so I find it much easier to forego Chrismas dinner altogether and just give everyone kedgeree instead of the usual goose, gravy and pudding palava. So I did this sunny breakfast kedgeree table, and if you want you can ring my office for the kedgeree recipe – everyone is always asking for it – but I can't give it to you as I have to fly.'

'Thank you,' I said as he flew off, and Cecilia called out, 'How interesting, and thank you for coming,' when she was interrupted by her assistant who had just taken a phone call from the designer Gordon Twister (a man said to have 'a passion for the decorative and outrageous') who would not be able to make it to the photographic session as he had a headache. Also, the other designers, Petrushka ('a romantic revolutionary') and Lord Brand ('a classicist with the imagination to outwit conventionality') had arrived and Lord Brand was demanding to know where the calligrapher was as he needed someone to write out place names for his dinner table – immediately.

Galloping through Lord Brand's hordes of courtiers, all doing creative things with holly, Cecilia explained that the calligrapher was not here just yet, but was on her way and should be here any minute now.

'It's just too much,' cried Lord Brand, obviously in great

distress. 'Petrushka's table is so much better than mine. And that needs more berries. No, not those – not orange. Orange is ghastly. The black ones. Look – more, like this. Cecilia, where is the girl? I thought those place names would have been done by now.'

'I'm so sorry, I really am. She's probably been held up in the traffic.' Interior designers are like kings – or queens. At least they think they are, and they expect to be treated like royalty. 'I'll go and ring her office, immediately, to check she's on her way. But let me just introduce Eliza.'

Lord Brand knew exactly who I was and he looked at me as he had at his ghastly orange berries – as if he wanted to squash me too under his foot.

'Oh there's Petrushka,' he cried, turning his rude back on me. 'Petrushka, poppet. Your table is simply wonderful. Just perfect. You always do it so beautifully.'

Petrushka too looked wonderful, perfect and beautiful. She is six foot tall, a former model, and has had silicone breast implants. 'It's just so much better than mine,' continued Lord Brand.

Between all these top designers, there is as much jealousy, spite, competition, wounded vanity and dislike as between warring cats. Lord Brand does not dislike just me but everybody from *Circe*, because in the summer he was interviewed for a piece on how British interior designers decorated their own bathrooms and, as we were short of space, the piece had to be cut down to just five designers and his was the bathroom that got left out.

'Don't be silly, John. Yours is lovely . . . It's so jolly.'

'Jolly?' Lord Brand blanched. 'Jolly?'

Petrushka smiled down on him. She could have pummelled him into the ground. 'Hello sweetie,' she said to me. She could have stamped on me too, but didn't as she had been given top billing in the bathroom piece. 'You want to talk to me, don't you? Just wait, can you, as . . .' Two of her pages walked in carrying colossal mirrored screens and four Russian storm lanterns from a van parked outside. They had evidently come from her own dining room. 'Just there, please,' she ordered.

'She's not supposed to do that,' Cecilia whispered to me.

'That's just not fair,' said Lord Brand to Cecilia.

'She's only allowed to use what you can buy from the shop,' said Cecilia. 'She's not supposed to bring things from home. Can you ask Basil to keep all her own stuff out of the photos?'

'Why is she allowed to bring her own stuff?' carped Lord Brand. 'I thought the rules were that we only used what you could buy in Bestes. It's too, too much. Timmy,' he called out to a man who would make Tarzan look effete. 'Timmy, there are twelve of my books in the boot. Go and get the lot of them. It she can use her own designs I don't see why I can't put my book on the table.'

Timmy lugged in twelve copies of *The Inside World of Lord Brand*. It was Lord Brand's latest book and consisted of photographs of rooms he had decorated and was the size of a coffee table. Timmy moved a soup tureen heaped high with neatly tiered apples and stood all the books in a pile in the centre of the table. This meant any pictures of his table would be dominated by this tower of self-publicity and the editor would not want to print them.

'It's a lovely book and I think Tron is planning to review it in the interior pages,' I lied. 'If we take a picture of them all on the table like this it might overlap with the other article.'

'Of course it won't. Besides, it's part of the decoration – all the Christmas presents standing there, full of promise, in the centre of the table.

'Haven't you got more of those black berries,' he said, turning his Jean-Paul Gaultier back. 'And where's all that crystallised ginger?'

I went to find Petrushka.

'Are they the cherries?' she demanded of one of her lackeys who had just hustled in with a Fortnum & Mason box.

'Petrushka, I'm sorry, they didn't have any cherries. Well they did, but they were only those small ones which are almost white.'

'What are those?'

'Grapes.'

168

'Red ones?'

'Yes, yes, red,' he mumbled, fumbling open the grey cardboard box to produce two bunches of grapes. They were black.

Petrushka removed the grapes from the box and attempted to stage them reverently in four little bowls, shaped like pudding basins and inlaid with deep-blue lapis lazuli. But whichever way she placed the grapes their stalks kept hanging over the edges.

'They don't fit,' she said. 'You'll have to go back.'

'But Petrushka, they didn't have any cherries.'

'Someone must have some cherries. I told you to go to Harrods, anyway. These are from Fortnum's. Or try Selfridges.'

'But they all buy their fruit from the same place. If Fortnum's haven't got any, Harrods won't either.'

'Tell Jane to ring round everywhere for cherries – red ones. She'll find some. And these grapes aren't red. They're black. I need red to match the tablecloth.'

'But Petrushka –'

'No, no, no. You see, sweetie,' she was addressing me now, 'grapes are wrong. I need cherries – red, red, red. Everything is red, blue and glitzy. The table has to be busy, busy, busy. Just like a Russian Christmas. It's to show you what you can do with nothing. The storm lanterns are mine and so are the plates but the Baccarat came from the shop, so did the cutlery. It's not really dark enough. My own – much golder – would have been better. A Christmas table should be all about surprise: gold bees hidden at the bottom of the salt and pepper pots, a gold frog peeping out behind a napkin. And look –' she pointed to bows on the backs of all the chairs – 'these are silk ties, tied onto the chairs. They're an extra present. A touch of the unexpected. All the plates are antique. The tiny ones are for the beluga. You can do anything with a bit of imagination. Even if you're poor. Just make it warm and cosy and exciting. I've brought those mirrors along – I don't think I was supposed to bring my own and Cecilia seems terribly upset about it – but

I wanted to add romance. Romance is all too easily forgotten at Christmas, don't you agree?'

'Yes,' I agreed.

'And you must light everything well. Put candles under vases of flowers, make use of everything you've got. Change that crystal, will you? No, it's quite wrong. The one with the *thick* gold rim.'

Cecilia interrupted us because she wanted Basil and me to get a move on and photograph Gordon Twister's arrangement. It was going to have to be dismantled as it constituted a fire hazard and it would be a shame if we couldn't capture it on film before it was taken down or burnt down.

The general effect of Twister's table was of a forest. Little Christmas trees were fastened to the backs of all the chairs and there were great candelabras made out of branches tied together with old rope. With all the decorative bits of holly and pine needles covered in highly inflammable hairspray – hairspray stops pine needles falling off – and carefully arranged pine cones near great candles blazing away, it was hideously spectacular and highly likely to combust spontaneously.

'It's so irresponsible of Twister to do something like this,' moaned Cecilia. 'It really isn't fair of him. He must know we can't have something like this. No wonder he has a headache and wouldn't tell me what he was doing. He said it would spoil the surprise. It's a surprise all right. I mean, look at all those candles . . . Stop, you can't go.'

Twister's team were packing up to go off for lunch.

'You can't leave it in that state. As soon as Eliza and Basil have finished you'll have to do something about all those candles.' So, hurriedly, Basil went up his ladder and took pictures while I took notes before the candles were put out.

20

Passion Cake

Once Basil and I had negotiated his ladder back to the office, I charged off to meet Rosanna in a self-service health food restaurant – her choice not mine. I can't be doing with all that chewing and eating out of flowerpots and feeling weighed down with roughage for the rest of the day, but Rosanna is vegetarian although I suspect more because of gastronomic preference than principle.

She was already there in a black velvet coat, making corrections on her article about men's shoes with a Cartier fountain pen.

'Will you read it?' she asked. 'I'm not sure if it makes sense.' I would rather have heard about Xavier than read about men's shoes. 'Please. Read it while I get you lunch. What do you want?'

'Cheesecake, please.'

This absurd idea – an intellectual look at the concept of men's shoes – was archetypal *Circe* material. Rosanna had interviewed a number of well-known men on their passion for their shoes. A Shadow Cabinet Minister had explained how he thought you could judge a man by the shoes he wore and how he cleaned his with a velvet duster. A backbencher had told her how he perceived the life of a shoe. A Booker Prize winner had dictated a few lines as if he were the shoe in question. An artist had elaborated on the beauty of glossy conker-brown and spotless black shoes, solemnly staged in men's shoe shops. And a marquess had said that since the age of twelve he had worn nothing but a Lobb's brogue with a particular number and arrangement of holes.

'After the piece on the marquess's brogues,' I suggested

when Rosanna returned, 'perhaps you should explain that brogues were originally coarse Celtic shoes made out of raw hide and that all those little holes, whose positioning he is so particular about, were once just punctures to let the bog water drain out.'

'Really?' she laughed.

'Yes.'

'Bogwater and marquess in the same sentence might upset Tron. Otherwise is it all right?'

'Yes it's fine.'

'Thanks Eliza.'

'This isn't cheesecake,' I said, looking at something like a forest in a bowl.

'No, I know.'

'What is it?'

'Spinach bake.'

'Oh God.'

'Sorry, they'd run out. So . . .'

'So tell me about Xavier.'

'Xavier, hmm.' She grinned. 'He's different.'

I nodded.

'Don't nod like that. I've never said that about anyone before.'

It is true, she has not.

'Well he's different', explained Rosanna, 'from the men I've ever gone out with before. They were all, you know, oh I don't know, terribly nice, maddeningly polite and so damned cool and collected about everything. But Xavier is less correct, not so disciplined, madder, more fun, more impulsive, less obviously perfect somehow.' Rosanna's men have always struck me as bland as boil-in-the-bags, not that she ever sees them long enough for me to get to know them any better. 'Hugh, you remember Hugh?'

'Which Hugh?'

'Hunting Hugh, though Hugh with the Aston Martin was not much better. But before Hunting Hugh went to bed, he had to make sure he had his socks out for the morning and his wretched shoes were standing neatly side by side ready for when he got up. And William, whenever he stayed at my house he always used to have to faff around for ages, winding his watch, re-setting my alarm and phoning the operator to get her to wake him at five-thirty. They never got worked up about anything – I don't just mean sex. I don't mean I want virtuoso performances in bed – ' the man on the table next to us looked up – 'but that they just couldn't get worked up about anything at all. Nothing. And it wasn't because they were so worn out careering ahead. I thought it might be because I always went out with the busiest man in the world, but James – you know, who set up his own freshly squeezed fruit juice business – he used to work out in the gym three times a week. He had the energy for that. William used to ride – very well too. I used to envy you. At least you had that time with The Natterjack.'

'But look where that left me,' I said miserably. 'I make Pollyanna look promiscuous.'

'That's not true at all, but that's by the way. At least you were in love with Jack. Now you hardly ever hear of people falling in love. People have relationships, not love affairs. Marriage is a matter of mutual convenience and interest. We sensible, intelligent men and women of the world do not have naïve illusions about love. Love is something for the young and immature. Love is a fling we had in our foolish student days. Love is too much of a dreamy abstraction for us now. Love isn't real in the same way as our mortgage. Love isn't real like cooking supper – over which we have a rational, liberal, harmonious agreement in which she does it one night, he the other. Love is too intangible for us prodigies of reason.

'Instead, we think with our heads, not our hearts, so we can plug ourselves into relationships which operate with the smooth sophistication of brilliantly refined electrical circuits, never sparking dangerously or blowing a fuse. Hearts are something silly and childish, what you carve on your desk at school, find in the offal freezer at Sainsbury's or things which give you cardiac arrests. Passion is embarrassing, discomforting, too steamy or in poor taste.'

'What's in poor taste? Can I join you?' It was Melindi. 'Rosanna, whose is that coat? Valentino's? Did you get it in Rome? I've always wanted a velvet coat. That's a beautiful one. Can I try it on? It's lovely. So soft. But I didn't think you were coming back into the office. Or are you just coming in for Lady Cutlet's show? I met Lady Cutlet at a party last week with *mon petit ami*. Their families know each other, you see. I told her I was going this afternoon. But what's in poor taste, Rosanna?'

'Oh, we were talking about this stuff,' I said, pushing the bowl of spinach bake away. 'Do you both want coffee?'

'Yes, please,' they replied in unison. 'But decaffeinated,' added Melindi. 'And black.'

'Anything else to eat?'

They looked at me. It was a silly question.

I joined in the queue. Perhaps Rosanna is right, I thought miserably. Perhaps we are too engrossed in ourselves to fall prey to the oblivion and abandonment of love. Perhaps we are starving our souls in a desire to avoid its madness and confusion.

But there is also more romance in the world than I can possibly swallow. 'Heartbeat' was playing on the restaurant's radio; the girl queuing behind me was describing her bead-encrusted wedding dress and Caribbean honeymoon; a woman in the corner was reading *Real Life Romances*. An idealised vision of impossibly passionate romance coats everything with a sweet stickiness. I'm stuck with it, singing from Capital Radio, selling instant coffee, cavorting in the cinema, walking in cooing couples in Regent's Park. I long to throw it off but I can't. It's like a drug, the cheapest, most readily available narcotic around. We're hooked on finding someone to fall in love with. It is an ideology to take our minds off the ordinariness and disappointment in our lives. It makes us demand the impossible from another human being. It makes us cowards dependent on Mr or Miss Right to banish our isolation and inadequacy, give us fulfilment and purpose. It is no wonder people rush into marriages which fail against such tidal waves of high hopes.

'Jack was asking after you this morning,' said Melindi, as I sat down again.

'Oh?' I said, as if she had told me it was cold outside.

Rosanna glanced at me.

'Oh?' I repeated with a bit more emphasis.

'You're so lucky being able to eat things like that and stay so sickeningly slim,' said Melindi, toying with her salad. 'I can't remember the last time I ate passion cake.' She looked at it lustfully.

'Do you want a bit?'

'Oh yes please. Just a small bit.' Melindi dug in.

'So what did Jack say?' I finally asked.

'Nothing much. He just asked how you were. Out of politeness really. This is terribly good.'

'Finish it off,' I said, pushing the plate over. I didn't like it anyway. Whoever thought such a great, stodgy, weighty mass, which sits so heavily on your stomach, should be called 'passion cake' must have had a particularly bad time of it all.

21

Catwalking

'You didn't tell me you'd seen Jack,' Rosanna whispered once we had disposed of Melindi back at the office and were waiting for the cars to take us to Lady Cutlet's fashion show.

'There's nothing to tell,' I said.

'Really?'

'Yes, really.'

'He didn't come on to you, did he?'

'Rosanna,' I moaned. 'Please. He's taken for. Married. God, I should know it.'

'But with all this business of her possibly going back to America to do that film, with her rather overshadowing him now,' she said carefully, 'things could be, well, a bit rocky.'

'But he loves her. Adores her. Believe me. I know all about it. Gazing into her magic eyes is like a benediction. In her presence he experiences fineness, nobility, truth. He feels replenished with nectar and honey. She radiates such beauty and kindness . . .'

'Stop it, Eliza. You're being ridiculous. She radiates such beauty and kindness she was able to make Jack fall in love with himself. Not with her. Anyone could have seen that.'

'No. He does love her – to the point of vertigo, her legs are so darned long. He told me.'

'Nonsense.'

'He said he loved her more than me.'

'What? He said that yesterday?'

'Of course not. Three years, two days ago he said it.' And eight hours ago, for it was seven in the morning when he rang to say he was going to marry Grace. He had told me he was in Edinburgh photographing a book on eighteenth-century architecture. And I had believed him. It had not occurred to me not to believe him. But of course he was not in Edinburgh. There can only be about two hours daylight in Edinburgh in December. It would be too dark to photograph anything. Coming up with such a weak excuse, especially with me being so knowledgeable about weather conditions and hours of sunlight, I thought he must be out of his mind with love for this woman.

'Yesterday we didn't really say anything.'

'You'd better take care or – '

'There's nothing to take care about,' I said sourly. 'I've amputated him.' And with that we crushed into the back of an old Mercedes with the three junior fashion editors.

We set off in convoy with the fashion chicks crammed into two ordinary black cabs in the lead. We followed. And the editor, Persephone and Ingrid brought up the rear in a black limousine with splodgy pudding seats. Like a bride, the editor likes to arrive late and last at fashion shows.

The first junior fashion editor next to me, with her hip bones jutting into mine, had spent the morning with Lord Rainedon, shooting the March cover of Britain's Undiscovered Beauty.

'We were so relieved,' she told me. 'Persephone had given the girl her prune and black coffee diet and I must say it works amazingly. It was like watching the tide going out, seeing her ribs and her cheekbones once more as the pounds ebbed away.'

The second was telling Rosanna that she could not decide which model to use for a fashion story called 'A Month in the Country'. 'I thought about Poppoea,' she said, 'because she's got that farm fresh smile. And I know she can ride but it's a real action story, so the point is, can she jump?'

The third had seen a black dress that morning which, she said, was so beautiful it brought such a lot of tears to her eyes the press officer has lent it to her for the editor's Christmas party.

I ignored the three of them as they all went on about what they would wear to Madam's Christmas do tonight and I wondered what life would be like if I could afford to wear clothes by Lady Cutlet. For the past ten years Lady Cutlet has designed some of the most expensive fashions, furniture, fabrics and restaurants in the country and two months ago she branched out into the creation of designer chocolates.

What makes her clothes so special is not that you can buy them to match your plates and chocolates but that they are only available, and by appointment only, from Lady Cutlet's conservatory. (Calling it a shop would be too banel.) The theory goes that all anyone needs is a Cutlet in their wardrobe, for 'Is that a Cutlet?' is *le dernier cri* in dress compliments. No matter that buying a Cutlet would make it pretty difficult to afford much else. That is part of their appeal.

Moreover, Lady Cutlet isn't like Chanel, who has been ripped off by every store from Woolworths upwards. You can't copy her designs because they are generally so simple their effect depends on incomputably expensive fabrics. In a polyester mix, her £700-shift, for instance, looks like a bit of black polyester with a seam up each side, but Lady Cutlet's Italian crêpe silk, at £50 a metre, could make a hippo shapely. Besides, she only makes cocktail, evening and balldresses and one-off wedding dresses, which are not mass market.

Unlike other designers she does not feel the need to compete in the great commercial shindig at the conventional spring and autumn collections. Instead, just before Christmas, she holds an exclusive little show in the conservatory. This is, Lady Cutlet hopes, more of a pleasurable party than a fashion show, a delightful way of spending an afternoon at Christmas time in the company of friends.

On arrival we were offered champagne cocktails with loganberries floating on top, and were shown to genuine Chippendale chairs. There is a natural order in the fashion world, akin to that of the Middle Ages. This hierarchy reaches its apotheosis in the seating plans at fashion shows. My editor has to have the best seat, dead centre in the front row. Persephone sits on her right, and Ingrid and Tron on her left. Behind them, in the second row, sit the junior fashion editors,

Rosanna and me. The fashion chicks sit behind us. Glossy, glamorous magazine editors hold the other front row but less central positions. Their minions sit at the back. Newspaper fashion editors sit in front rows round the sides.

Melindi had managed to seat herself in the second row beside me, rather than in her rightful position in the third. The girl will go far. I pulled my coat around me. The conservatory is modelled on the draughty Orangery at Kensington Palace and Lady Cutlet had the thermostat turned down low.

It was three thirty-five. Since the show started at three and we had not left the office till five past, everyone else had been waiting a good thirty minutes. We had been waiting five. The editor hates waiting.

'We're here, they can start now,' she said in the voice from which she expects and gets instant results. Sure enough, the lights dimmed in seconds, Benjamin Britten boomed forth and four models swanned on in black chiffon. Models don't walk like the rest of us. They get taught to walk. Their bottom – or what they have of one – leads. Movement comes from the hips and their legs are thrown forwards. All looked as gloomy as I feel at cocktail parties.

Melindi opened a large blank notebook and began making great flourishing marks with a Rotring pen in an attempt to record the look of the sweetheart neckline and swathes of silk. Rosanna started pushing back her cuticles. I hunted for a handkerchief in all my coat pockets but couldn't find one. Three six-foot-two goddesses in grey silk columns walked up and down, looking as miserable as if they had put on seven ounces and were going to have to restrict themselves to one rather than two lettuce leaves a day for the next week. I assessed Melindi's sketching skills. They were hopeless. That was a relief.

The next model came on in a skimpy wisp of chiffon weighing about two ounces, making the dress about £500 an ounce. She had no clothes on underneath and was revealing most of the bosom she had. She must have been cold. I was freezing with my coat on. I really needed to sniff.

The next half-hour was a long one as I twitched my nose discreetly and watched skinny teenagers parade around in so much silk the worms must have been working overtime. With lips curled down and noses turned up, some girls looked peeved, others glanced at you with contempt. Flat-chested, with endless twiggy legs, they all looked as if they had not eaten for weeks. You would find more curves in a Rubik cube than in all these girls put together.

Women do not look like these girls. But they want to. I do not know whether they want to because of some masochistic streak, and because thinking their naturally curvy bottom is too big is just another thing they like to give themselves a hard time about; or because they cannot face growing up; or because magazine editors employ a minority of misogynist homosexual photographers who only like photographing women shaped like boys; or because women feel they need to be as lean and perpendicular as men so they too can take over multi-national corporations.

Even women whose bodies would not know cellulite till you pinched them blue, are quite indifferent to the delights of chocolate mousse and are often compared favourably with a beanpole, think they are too fat. Today's highest earning model, for instance, refuses to have pictures taken from the back because she thinks her bottom is too big.

Meanwhile, Melindi flourished away and Rosanna contemplated her hands until the finale which, as in all fashion shows, was a bride. There was six foot of this one, poured into a sheath of white velvet fastened with countless pearl buttons and with her hair hanging three feet down her back in a great Rapunzel plait intertwined with bits of jasmine and stephanotis.

We all clapped and murmured politely about the beauty and brilliance of the clothes. Lady Cutlet walked on in her inimitable black shift so we all clapped and murmured some more. The bride stayed on the catwalk, looking as if she had arrived at the wrong occasion, for everyone in the audience was dressed in black as if they were at a funeral. Once, a taxi driver picking me up from a fashion show asked me if I

180

belonged to a weird women's religion as he had never seen so many women dressed in black before. Yes, I had said, I did.

Lady Cutlet then thanked us all for coming, especially as it was so near Christmas when we must all be so busy. But as it was Christmas time, she had something for us all. Everyone tried not to look excited for something from Lady Cutlet is really not to be scorned. Even a Cutlet's rosette for putting on your shoe or in your hair would set you back £25. And something like a Cutlet scarf with a Cutlet label would be extremely nice to go home with.

To everyone's not-very-well-disguised disappointment, our going home present turned out to be a miniature box of her new chocolates: five white truffles. No one eats chocolate except for me, and I too would have far preferred a Cutlet scarf. I ate them on the way back to the office where Ingrid and Persephone and Melindi gave me theirs as well before they all rushed home early to embellish themselves for the editor's Christmas party.

22

Getting On Famously

If you have seen one little black dress you have not seen them all. Not a single woman at the editor's party was in colour. They were all in black. Ingrid's little black dress was a Cutlet shift adorned with half a hundred-weight of pearls. Tron's was off the shoulder with a slit up the side, looking more foghorn than siren. Persephone's was a 'Come-Spank-Me' pinafore worn with nothing underneath. The junior fashion editors' and the young fashion chicks' were demure sweetheart neckline and calf-length numbers. The editor's was velvet, fitting as tight as the skin on a plum. Bella's – she had come out of hospital that afternoon – was a long, languorous pre-Raphaelite affair and her left foot was in a velvet slipper with a big gold bee on top, and her right in plaster. My dress was chiffon.

Some days I do not mind how I look. But tonight I did. The editor's bone-white drawing room was unfurnished except for one piece of contorted metal which I took to be a table and a wall-sized mirror at which I was looking face-on. I was staring at myself with unmitigated horror. I looked awful.

My face is inadequate. There is no getting away from it. It tries to reach a standard imposed by men, magazines, me, but it fails. On goes shell bisque foundation, dewy glow pearl powder, magnolia lipstick, oriental rose blusher. But in vain. They do not make my skin look as lovely as a sun-kissed flower on a summer's morning. The Persian violet eyeliner, French navy mascara, break their breathy pledges to make my eyes exotic, rampant, and utterly irresistible. Not even access to every new gizmo in make-up can make my face sufficiently pleasing. Not even my uncommonly extensive knowledge of the beauty business. Not even my weekend at a health farm.

Not even intimate knowledge of the fifty most beautiful women's beauty tips.

I was talking with the photographer, Basil, and two of his friends, Cole and Guy, and we were all staring into the mirror assessing Cole's new hairdo. Although Cole designs some of the most coveted jewellery in Britain and New York, he is a few sandwiches short of a picnic when it comes to his own personal style. His colossal crown of hair, blossoming around his black face, had been freshly dyed red to match his Morgan, and he was dressed in a suit in a fabric similar to but more flamboyant than the one I had sat upon on Lady Chewton's chintz sofa. He looked like a poppy in a field of flowers, but was admiring himself with unqualified delight. Guy was also looking very pleased with himself. Being tall, tan and lean, he is such a cliché of a good-looking man, he had renewed his exclusive multi-pound modelling contract with Jaeger Man that very morning.

'Good God,' he and Basil suddenly cried out, catching sight in the mirror of Max's elderly aunt. 'Look at what Lady Rose has turned up in.' Her dress was in the terracotta colour-way of her nephew's wallpaper print. Not wearing pure black, she stood out like a baked bean in a jar of beluga.

'What gets into them? Dressing like that. Really. Isn't she a lady-in-waiting to the Queen or somebody?'

'I wouldn't know, Basil,' answered Cole.

'But they're all doing it,' Basil spluttered. 'Dressing up like that. Haven't you noticed older women's fashions lately?'

'God knows I have,' interrupted Guy. 'My mother has taken an excessive interest in them. She goes to Harrods, tries all the clothes on and spends all afternoon in there, driving me and the assistants bonkeroso and then says she's not spending five or six hundred pounds on a dress and that they're all outrageously overpriced.'

'Well they are,' said Basil. 'I mean I spent £30 on a shirt in a sale – a pre-Christmas sell off. Come on! £30!'

'£30 is all right,' said Guy.

'But in a sale? And last week I bought a pair of pyjamas for

£50 in Hilditch & Key. And that was a sale too. Outrageous. I'll be back to M & S.'

'Who wants pyjamas?' asked Cole. 'Why wear them at all?'

'For the past couple of years I have done. Ever since I had to go to Leeds – it's so cold up there. Don't you bother then?'

'No,' said Cole.

'I suppose your duvet has a higher tog rating.'

'I don't have a duvet but one of those goose feather quilts as well as three blankets and I wear a T-shirt,' explained Cole.

'That has much the same function as pyjamas.'

'Well, it keeps the shoulders warm.'

'They can get a bit exposed, especially in your flat. It's a bit "chillesque", your flat. Oh Max, well done.'

Max joined us with five glasses of champagne.

'Eliza, sweetie. I saw you there and know how you can't resist bubbles.'

'Thank you, Max.' I said.

'And you're looking such a poppet in that dear dress.'

I always feel like a doll in the company of gay men and somewhat taken aback by their exceptional good looks. Cassandra once – very many years ago now – went to bed with a gay man and told me it was deeply unsatisfying as after a bit of perfunctory nuzzling he just fell asleep on top of her so it was as much fun as sleeping with a lump of bricks.

'And it was so dear of you to let me know about poor Bella's accident,' he continued. 'Dressing a woman like that is such a joy. And it's quite a stroke of luck her breaking her right ankle because I always make my samples up in the left foot first and I've got more than I know what to do with. Even though they're rejects they are still a part of me and I can't bear to leave them to the mercy of the dustmen, but she came round this afternoon and bought five left feet. You see the shoe she's wearing now? When I created it I didn't think it quite worked but now I see it on her it looks quite lovely.

'But you know who's here?' he said, addressing Basil, Guy and Cole as well. 'Thomas Milton, that *Observer* man. I thought, who's that ugly little man, but then I heard someone call him The Epic.'

'Funny-looking, isn't he?' said Basil.

'Funny?' said Guy, smoothing back his blonde curls which he has insured for £10,000 against baldness. 'I don't think it would be funny looking like that. Severe disability, I'd call it.'

'Why doesn't he do something about it?' suggested Cole.

'It'd be very easy. All he needs is a bit of cartilage injected in his nose.'

'He wasn't born like that then?' asked Cole.

'I think it was an accident,' said Guy. 'When he was very young.'

I couldn't see The Epic's nose properly as he was standing behind the editor who was much taller than him. I scanned the hundred-odd people revolving about her. Standing in the centre of the room, she was swapping compliments delightedly. I was hungry again. A waiter was proffering a midnight-blue platter on which was arranged a shoal of untouched vegetable fish. Their bodies were carved out of carrots, their fins were the underside of mushrooms, their eyes tiny dollops of caviar and they swam through seaweed depicted in mangetouts and matchsticks of cucumber. Along the bottom of the plate was the ocean bed dip.

I gave the waiter my appealing smile though I cannot always guarantee it doing the trick. But he walked over. Everyone else had either showed dietary or aesthetic restraint, for as yet no one had destroyed the composition of the vegetable picture. I ate a mangetout and as much dip as you can get on a two-inch stick of cucumber.

I had been at the party eight minutes. I took a second mangetout which used up another five seconds. I ought to go and make the effort to talk to somebody. Guy was talking about a good plastic surgeon he knows.

I looked around me. I wanted to go home. The fashion chicks were in a huddle in the hallway, like a flock of anxious black swans. Tron was talking to a Duke and having an orgasm over his title. Persephone was cutting dead everyone she did not like. I could not see Hermione in the dining room but I could hear her talking about the rising incidence of gangrene and amputations as a result of the freezing weather. Melindi was doggedly set upon some serious networking. Tossing her hair in front of men, switching off the huskiness in her voice with women, she moved from one useful contact to the next, telling them how much she loved their latest fashion collection/book/magazine article. Rosanna had not bothered to turn up.

It was at a party like this that I met Sam. But no one would notice me tonight. Tonight I had put on my black chiffon dress in order to look irresistibly ephemeral. But I had obviously overdone it. I was looking so ephemeral no one knew I was there. I turned back to Max and co.

Guy, Cole and Basil were trying to decide where Max should go on holiday in January. All Max knew was that it had to be somewhere warm enough for him to get up and just pootle around in his pyjamas outside. (What is this thing about pyjamas?) I made an effort. Lord Rainedon, the photographer, was standing within eighteen inches of me, not talking to anyone and looking as glum as I felt. Perhaps he wished he was back in Positano.

'Hello,' I said.

He said nothing.

'I liked your pictures for the most beautiful women in Britain feature. I had to write the captions so I spent a lot of time looking at them.'

Still he said nothing.

I persevered. 'I have already had people ringing me up asking if they will be able to have copies. They're really in demand.' Thinking of all the stupid things I have said just for the sake of saying something can make me feel quite ill. I gave up. We stood sipping our champagne. It was the company's best, the vintage they use for engagement celebrations and sackings. Then Lord Rainedon looked at me.

'I am afraid,' he began.

'Yes,' I said encouragingly. My God, I thought, the man is going to make an effort.

'I am afraid I am most terribly bored. I'm going home now.' And with that he left the room.

What a wonderful way I have. I looked about. Who else would like to be bored by me? The waiter was hovering by me again as none of the other razor-thin guests would eat his wretched vegetable fish.

'A hearty appetite I see, Eliza,' said a voice behind me. It was the Chairman.

'Yes,' I said, somewhat embarrassed.

And he began to tell me about the amazing success he was having from sending his 'advertising girls' on assertiveness training courses. 'Amazing you know. Positively amazing what a difference it makes to their selling performance. You should go on one, Eliza. It would be worth investing some of your own money. It's not just about selling more advertising space but how to deal more successfully with people. It affects all areas of your life, you see. They teach you to believe in yourself and once you believe in yourself you can sell yourself.'

There are many more ways of selling yourself than opening your legs like my neighbour.

'They sound really worthwhile,' said Melindi huskily, spiriting herself to his side. I introduced them. I thought they would like each other.

'Can anyone go on them?' she asked eagerly.

'Oh yes,' the Chairman began to explain. I tried to look interested but Melindi is just so much better at looking interested than me. I left her to it.

Apart from the Chairman who, rolling around in his wide pin-striped suit, was like a jellyfish out of water, the editor had invited no one from the business side of the magazine. Hers was a Christmas party representing creative, not commercial interests, but she was obliged to invite the Chairman as he paid her substantial salary – even if it was from the profits of magazines like *Right Royal* and *Racing Now*.

Most of the guests were women who had featured in the magazine during the year. These included a fair proportion of actresses who were famous because they were starring in a Hollywood blockbuster or a new production of Henry V; a

187

small proportion who had been the first to navigate an impossible stretch of the Amazon or had written eye-witness reports from warzones or had made a breakthrough in the treatment of cancer; and a huge proportion of women who were famous for being famous.

About ten minutes later I gave up completely and went round to Cassandra's.

23

Consuming Passions

Cassandra had prepared an uncharacteristically colossal supper. Two melons, parma ham, a loaf of bread, best buffalo mozzarella, avocados, cashew nuts, bakewell tarts, chocolates were on the table like a harvest festival arrangement.

'There's more in the fridge,' she said, pouring her fourth vodka and tonic. Normally she only drinks neat tonics – slimlines – but her emotional condition has clearly affected her appetite. I wondered if she was pregnant though it was unlikely given her cheeriness and the carefree manner with which she was slapping butter onto her third slice of bread. I cannot remember the last time butter featured in her life. I hope she stops eating soon for after she next steps on the scales she will be dieting for weeks and she gets infectiously depressed when she is single and dieting at the same time.

'It's amazing what a liberation leaving John has been,' she said. 'I don't know why I didn't do it sooner. I have had enough ideas since last night to last me weeks. I think it could be lack of sex.'

'That's giving you all this creative energy?'

'Yes.'

'It's only been twenty-four hours, Cassandra.'

'Yes but not having to be consumed by one thing gives you more room for the other.'

'Not always,' I said grimly. 'Most people think it works the other way round. Yeats said that verse-making was not possible without love-making. And George Eliot did not start writing until she met a man in her thirties, as if only that sort of happiness and fulfilment could unleash her spirit and imagination.'

189

'But the Brontës weren't repressed by any virginal restraint. Quite the reverse, it fuelled their fantasies.'

'I wouldn't liken your experience to the Brontës'.''

'No, but they knock down your theory. So does Jane Austen.'

'But think what they might have written if they had found someone. Creative powers might have been freed – '

'They'd have become household drudges,' she interrupted, 'if they did not die in childbirth – as Charlotte Brontë did – and wouldn't have written a word. God knows what other novels she had up her sleeve.'

'Maybe she wanted to have a baby more than a book,' I said feebly.

'Would you have wanted a baby in the nineteenth century with the thought of all those iron tongs they used to use on you?'

'No.'

'Too right you wouldn't.'

'Is this the basis of one of your articles?'

'Sort of. Something on the greater toll nature exacts on women and how little society does to alleviate it.'

'Hmm,' I said dubiously.

'What do you mean "hmm"?'

'It's not one of your more original ideas, is it? I mean it's been done before.'

'Good God, Eliza. "It's been done before," ' she mimicked. 'We are not talking about beehive hairdos here, or bell-bottom trousers. This is truth. Because a grim reality has, at last, been recognised, you can't just give it fifteen seconds of fame because people like you always have to write about something new.'

'I'm simply saying that I don't need to be reminded what the disadvantages of being a woman are. And things are improving.'

'Oh yes. Some bright managing director builds himself a crèche because he knows it will earn him good publicity in the papers, a big fat article on how his precious company is setting

190

an example in the provision of childcare – that's how much and the reason why things are improving.'

'You're wrong . . .'

'All right. Say I am wrong,' she said, agreeing uncharacteristically quickly. 'Suppose women actually do get all the maternity leave, childcare facilities, all the opportunities they want. They may still end up worse off. If women prove themselves capable of doing everything independently, men will be absolved of all responsibilities and pressure to look after children. Women will have given men a bullet-proof excuse for not getting involved. So, women who want babies will have to do it all on their own. Men can just turn round and say, "You liberated yourself from me, darling. Thanks very much. It's all yours." So while we have the baby we also have to go and get jobs as airline pilots, and I can't think of anything worse than being an airline pilot. All men will ever have to do is stir themselves to one burst of effort in bed and after that they are not obliged to help us anymore. We'll be just as badly off as before, only in a different way.'

'Some men might help.'

'Would The Natterjack have helped, for instance? And what would have happened if, after your torrid night of passion in that spaceship in NASA – '

'Hotel near NASA.'

'Well, wherever. What would he have done?'

'I just think,' I said, ignoring her question, 'that although an article on those lines would be quite brilliant, if you write it just now it could deteriorate into polemical prejudice, given your current mood.'

'Women need men more than men need women.'

'But – '

'And whichever way you look at it and whatever your "mood", women certainly need men *before* men need them. No prejudice deludes me from the fact that however many changes feminism may bring, women have to have reproduced by the time they are forty at their latest. Last week I read in the *Telegraph* about a man who became a father at sixty-five.'

'That's showing off. No child wants a sixty-five-year-old picking them up from school. Besides, he'll probably do his back in picking it up.'

'Very funny. Look, give me one advantage of being a woman.'

'Over being a man?'

'Of course. God, Eliza. What do you think I meant? Oh yes. Of course I'd rather be a woman than a dog or a pig or a cat or a cow . . .'

'All right,' I said. 'I've got the message.'

'See, you can't,' said Cassandra after about ten minutes.

'I can. Women don't have to have erections.'

Cassandra stopped wolfing cashew nuts. 'I take it all back. That's brilliant. That really is. That's a huge advantage, isn't it?'

'It's not always huge.'

'No, but you see what I mean. Women can always have sex whenever they want. Women are never impotent whereas men can be. Men can't even fake it. And now, because women are more experienced, any fears men might have about their, er, performance, are compounded because we can compare them with their predecessors. In the past they could boldly go where no man had been before, thinking what a wonderful time they were giving you. Now, they are thinking that you are lying there criticising them for not being as good as John or Harry or whoever.'

'They can't actually think much at the time. All the blood rushes down there.'

'No, but in the run-up they can. And do – that's their problem. Well, it is sometimes. Thank you, Eliza. That's great. I can do an article on that. But I am right about women needing men more than women. Think what you were like after The Natterjack. And now with The Bostonian. Has he lost his job yet?'

'He's not going to lose his job. Let me get this straight. He might resign on a matter of principle.'

'Principle? Oh my God, Eliza. Principle. That makes you all the more smitten, I know. The idea of this great crazy bear of a

192

man giving up his job on a matter of principle, as well as bailing out his sister and doing all these good things while you think the rest of the world is prostituting principles all over the place, is just making you wild. Knowing you in this mood is like being personally acquainted with a sunflower. Whatever he does you beam upon it, turning the full force of your approval upon his every move. Hang on, that's really good,' she said, leaping up, 'I must make a note of it.'

'Wait. You're not having him for your column.'

'I'm just writing down the sunflower analogy, and that was mine not yours. So when's he due to ring again?'

'I ring him on Sunday – Boxing Day.'

'At his sister's?'

'Hmm,' I said doubtfully.

'Has he given you her number?'

'No.'

'So how are you going to ring him?'

'Well I won't.'

'What do you mean?'

'I can't, can I? If I don't have his number.'

'Well ring him and ask for it.'

'No.'

'Whyever not?'

'I don't know. Maybe I don't want to rush him.'

'Rush him? You'll be forty before you're holding hands with him at this rate, let alone kissing him.'

'Yes, but . . . Oh I don't know. Anyway have you talked with John?' I asked, to change the subject. 'Has he seen his passport yet?'

'Not as far as I know. We haven't spoken but I had this amazing dream about him.'

And what was left of the evening was taken up with Cassandra's dream for her dreams are always epics with continually changing locations and casts of thousands.

24

The Price of Vanity

Something terrible was happening to my head when I woke up next morning. Somehow, someone had got inside and was running around in there in a pair of stiletos, then someone else joined them in tap shoes, then someone in wooden mules, then beetle crushers, then reinforced gumboots, then platforms, then spiked rugby boots. It was like being a floor. I opened my eyes, then closed them.

I must not wake up yet, I thought. Not yet. Not yet with this crashing, splitting mind-blowing pain in the head. Think about something else, I thought. Something else. I thought about my toes. My toes did not hurt. Nor did my legs. I padded to the bathroom. I looked horrible. Really horrible. I thought I'd never looked quite so horrible before. Think about something else, I thought. I thought how horrible it would be if I looked this horrible every day, and took a double dose of aspirin. I put on the radio. It was the coldest day of the year again, with a record-breaking chill factor, and the forecast was no change.

Oh God. Why is it always so cold? Why do you always give us such cold weather? Look at it out there. Oh God. I ate some cereal. I ate more cereal. That was better. All those people had stopped stomping and clomping around in my head. A doctor was talking on the radio about the seasonal depressional syndrome which I have severely. Certain human beings suffer acutely from lack of sunlight and need to hibernate during winter.

I listened but my concentration was suddenly disturbed by this great banging noise. I put my head in my hands. A whole army of Trons was running around in Doc Martens. And the banging got louder and then there was a shout and the wall shook. It was the colonel next door banging for help.

'It's all right,' I shouted through my kitchen wall. He had fallen over again. 'I've heard you.' And I called the police and they broke in and took him off to hospital. But before I could go to work they wanted to know whether I would be going away for Christmas. I said I would be at my parents until Tuesday and would be back that night as I had to work on Wednesday.

'All right,' said one of the policemen whom I now seem to be meeting under these circumstances on a weekly basis. 'We'll suggest they keep him in till you're back.'

How I have ended up responsible for a man who loathes me I have no idea. He's not even a real colonel. It's just a name he acquired from somewhere. I went to work.

Normally on the last day before Christmas everyone is sitting around wrapping up presents waiting for the twelve noon champagne so they can then get going home or to Klosters or the Maldives or wherever they are spending Christmas. But the office was like an aviary full of blackbirds. Everyone was flapping about, squawking down the phone with disgust, and crowing, 'Outrageous.'

'What's outrageous?' I asked Ingrid as I got in. She handed me a memo sent to all members of staff from the Chairman: *I would like to thank you all for your excellent hard work during the year.* Circe *has been a credit to you and I am very pleased to be able to offer you a standard pay increase of 5% with some further rewards for exceptional merit.*

'Five per cent,' I spluttered like everyone else. 'We should get more than that.'

'Outrageous,' echoed Ingrid.

I read on. *Indeed I would have liked to have rewarded you more substantially, but as you know, we have spent generous amounts on redesigning the offices and installing showers on the fourth floor.* 'I didn't know there were showers on the fourth floor,' I said.

'None of us did. Apparently they're used by . . .' Ingrid paused with disgust, '*Royalty Now.*'

Finally, concluded the memo, *I would like to wish everyone a very Merry Christmas and I look forward to seeing you again in the New Year.*

I read it again. It made my head hurt all the more.

'Eliza,' called out Naomi, pointing in to the editor's greenhouse. 'You're wanted.'

'Maybe you're being rewarded for your merit,' suggested Ingrid.

'Sit down,' said the editor immediately, not making me wait one moment. This was an excellent start. 'Did you enjoy last night?'

'Last night?' I asked blankly. She said nothing. What with my headache, the colonel, and the thought that my annual pay rise had been spent on wooden floors and reaping the benefit of a Harvard graduate's interior design experiments on rats, I could not think what I was doing last night.

'My party,' she said peevishly.

Oh God. Oh God. 'Oh yes,' I said. 'Yes. It was a lovely party, thank you. Sorry, I had a difficult morning.' My head hurt. 'I, er . . .' This was not going as I had hoped. 'I had to – '

'Anyway, Eliza,' she said. 'I have some good news for you. I'm sure you've been worrying about Rosanna's replacement as the two of you will be working in close conjunction.'

I nodded. I had not given Rosanna's replacement a moment's thought.

'And you will be pleased to hear that we have already found someone whom I feel is extremely good news and who will be starting January 4th, right away. Petronella Plunkett-King.'

'Petronella Plunkett-King?' I repeated, not because the name was such a mouthful but because she is the sweet, twenty-one-year-old daughter of a high-profile marriage and has no journalistic experience whatsoever other than for editing *Isis* and I have yet to meet someone who has not edited *Isis*. She also has no knowledge of fashion which, although in the great scheme of things is of no relevance whatsoever, is a serious drawback when you have to do nothing but write about fashion. Petronella worked here for six weeks this summer before going on a grand tour of South America. She is terribly nice and very pleasant to chat with but not a substitute for Rosanna who has been on the magazine five years, can think of two puns in the time it takes her to file her nails, knows all the designers and how to spell their names, has an eclectic but good knowledge of fashion history and can write a thousand print-worthy words in a day, even when she has a headache. Petronella's greatest gifts are her father, Tom Plunkett, who is the creative genius behind the government's advertising campaigns, and her mother, Elizabeth King, who has twice been a runner-up for the Booker Prize.

'But she's got no experience,' I blurted.

'I know, Eliza. But although I don't believe in nepotism, I do believe talent breeds talent. Of course she's going to need help, and we appreciate much of the burden in helping her through the first six months will fall on you, but your pay rise will reflect the extra work you will have and I must say it is a particularly generous rise when you look at what everyone else is having.'

'Yes,' I said, more hopefully. I will do a great deal for money.

'Yes. Yours will not be five per cent like the others but six per cent.'

'But six per cent is nothing as well,' I cried, my head cleaving under the blow. 'It'll enable me to buy – what? One more McDonalds a week than the others. What sort of . . .' I stopped short. Oh God, I thought for the millionth time that morning. Why did I say that? You don't speak to the editor like that. You certainly don't bring hamburgers into the conversation. My poor, poor head.

The editor pursed her lips. She has good lips – a double Cupid's bow – and cannot resist showing off their remarkable shape whenever an opportunity presents itself. I had thrown one in her lap but her Cupid's bow was wasted on me.

'I'm sorry you feel like that, Eliza, but that's the way it is,' she said. And with that I had to leave the room.

I went snapping off to Ingrid. 'Did you know about Petronella Plunkett-King?' I said furiously.

'Well I knew it was a possibility, darling, as Madam had lunch with Elizabeth King yesterday. I'm sorry, darling. I thought it would make you fed up. And it's going to land you with a lot of extra work, isn't it?'

'Yes. I told Madam so as well.'

'Oh darling, you didn't, did you? That was quite stupid of you.'

'I know.' I put my aching head in my hands. 'Oh God.'

'Petronella will probably have the hang of it by the summer,' said Ingrid. 'And if she hasn't they'll have got rid of her by then.'

'I know. It's just the thought of spending January and February having to work so hard, staying late doing most of Rosanna's work as well. January is bad enough as it is. But the thought of all those hellish, black-night days doing nothing but write about spring clothes . . .'

'At least you like the spring clothes, don't you?'

'Yes, but I'm not going to be able to afford any, am I? Not on six per cent. And when am I going to have time to go anywhere in them?'

'Petronella will probably be thrusting and keen and will catch on quite quickly. Another Melindi, perhaps.'

No, I thought, not another Melindi, please. Oh please.

At that moment Melindi, working her way through all the men in European capitals, was on the phone to either her boyfriend in Paris, or Ashley, and enthusing about all the important people she had met at the editor's party and how they were going to help her in her burgeoning career. Ingrid interrupted her while she was explaining how the creative director of Kiss and Make-Up, the cosmetic company, had already rung her to ask her to do some freelance styling for the launch of their new cream for getting rid of cellulite in the upper arm.

'Melindi, will you fetch my sharp knife, please?' interrupted Ingrid.

'Are you pineappling today?' I asked.

'Do you want some?'

'Please. Perhaps,' I said, perking up, 'Petronella's father will be able to help her. And her mother. But her father especially. He did that campaign for sliced white bread before he took over the government's account, you know. He made his name on string vests. That was why the government switched to him. They thought anyone who can make people buy sliced white bread and string vests must be brilliant with lost causes.'

'He did string vests?' said Ingrid.

I nodded. (I know all this thanks to Ashley.)

'But that string vest campaign was brilliant, Eliza. No wonder Petronella's got the job. Persephone even did a whole fashion story on string vests as a result of it. Just suggest to Petronella that she asks her father for advice. We're sure not to be paying her much, and Madam thinks this is a cheap way of having Tom Plunkett on the payroll. Darling, stop worrying that you'll be overworked. If I were you I'd start worrying that she and her father between them will be so good they'll be able to do your job as well.'

I blanched. 'Thanks, Ingrid. That's really cheered me up.'

'I didn't mean it, darling. I was joking. And frowning like that does dreadful things to your skin. Look, have this.' She delved into the beauty cupboard. 'It will do you good.'

'Thanks,' I said. It was a pot of Bio-Performance, Extra-Firm, Skin-Vitality cream. 'Isn't this what the Princess of Wales uses?'

'Even more expensive,' said Ingrid. 'But you look as if you need it today. You really ought to save yourself better, Eliza.'

'I know,' I said. Although I don't know what I am saving myself for.

I went and asked Hermione for some aspirins as she has a medicine chest in her desk. But because of her impending baby she was not taking aspirins so she gave me a homeopathic alternative and showed me her latest scans which made me feel sick. Naomi then produced some aspirins so I wolfed down those on top of Hermione's pills. Neither got rid of the pain in my head. But they left me feeling as if I was on a higher plane to everyone else – not that this was difficult as everybody was so flat after hearing about their paltry pay rise.

Despite being Christmas Eve, we sat around gloomily, trying to think of viable economy measures to enable us to survive the next financial year. None of us thought we could buy fewer clothes. We certainly could not eat any less. One of the new recruits to the fashion department suggested that we get the company to pay for our dry-cleaning by sending our clothes along with those used in the fashion shoots so our bills would go on the company account. But most of us do that already. Persephone said she would introduce a proper lending system to enable us to borrow clothes more frequently from the fashion cupboard and so save buying them ourselves. And that was it. Ingrid could not think of a single beauty treatment we could do without. And none of us could think of any other economies so we opened another crate of company champagne and spent the rest of the morning reiterating how unfairly the company was behaving.

The crux of the matter was that we were expected to be model women but we were not being given the means with which to live up to our name. We were supposed to set standards which we would not be able to meet – for being a model woman does not come cheaply. Dieting – now and then – and the odd bit of exercise in the living room are not enough. Who, everyone asked each other, can be a model woman in both boardroom and bedroom with nails gnawed into nothing and hair that looks like a sheep on a bad day? Who can afford to grow old gracefully when the competition is so fierce? Who can ignore the importance of good personal packaging? Who does not need to look young, fit, attractive and in control? The answer is no one. You have to look good – at any cost. And the cost is high. You can't just pull in your stomach. You must also pull out your purse.

Firstly, there is the cost of exercise for ensuring a top-class cardiovascular system and thighs as free from cellulite as a puma's. Unflagging members of the sweat set must pay for membership of a health club and at least two classes a week – any less and it's a waste of time. Some top model women posses their own personal trainers who will run them through their paces in their own home but this private tuition triples your exercise bill, although it does save you both time and money on taxi fares to and from the gym. A dress code, too, must be observed. The old tracksuit in which you walk the dog is absolutely *verboten* in the fiendishly fashionable health clubs. You must sweat instead in lycra-and-cotton-mix designer label leotards.

Exercise, of course, makes your hair horribly messy and, ugh, sweaty. A good haircut every six weeks which shakes easily into place during the fifteen minutes it takes you to buy some fresh basil for that night's dinner party, feed the baby and discover an ecological alternative to nuclear energy, is therefore essential. But however high your visible expenditure, grey hair will come to you all too soon and for the best highlights in town you're talking £100 plus. Also, that essential salmon protein hair conditioner that your cat loves to eat works out at about £2 an ounce.

If you are already becoming anxious about costs, calm down right away as you have barely begun and anxiety will only make those grey hairs sprout faster. And, indeed, make your hair fall out. Yes. Baldness in women is a growing problem – something to do with all the new stresses you're under – but thankfully new products are being developed to stop the fallout.

Next there's the cost of skin care. Hmm. Skin care is a problem. You could save money by using baby oil as a cleanser; witch hazel for toning; lanolin and Vaseline for moisturising. But unless you are beautiful enough to look your face in the mirror and say you can afford to cut costs, can honestly see no room for improvement, need nothing more than an old teabag or a slice of cucumber to get rid of those dustbin bags under your eyes and do not look your age, initial investment in a skin care regime is high, particularly as model women need at least triplicates of everything. You need one set for the bathroom, one for the office, one for your travel bag which stands ready packed by the front door for when you suddenly have to fly to New York on business or rush into hospital to have another baby. Ideally you should have a fourth set for when you run out – every three months or so.

Also, for a well-polished image you must not flinch on the regular servicing charges – weekly manicures and pedicures and, ouch, waxing. The very thought of waxing may bring you out in a cold sweat but there is no way of avoiding it unless you want to wear thick tights all summer and long dresses on the beach. Most salons perform waxing operations but if you would rather cry with agony in your own bedroom you can find beauticians with portable waxing kits who will do it at your home. Since a friend of Hermione's recently went to a public salon and departed with a follicle infection – horror of horrors – a personal beautician seems an increasingly sensible investment. After waxing, massage is much nicer for damsels in de-stress. If you are a busy woman – and of course we all are – you should try to have one every week.

Next, consider the cost of the contents of a make-up bag. Be easy on yourself. Do not count the blue lipstick that you bought in a sale thinking it might come in handy if you ever wanted to dress up as a ghost; the foundation which seemed all right when you tried it on the back of your hand in the shop but now makes you look like death cooled down. Just add up the essentials, your mascara, eyebrow pencil, blusher, lip liner, lipstick . . . Broken your calculator trying to work it out? You've gone broke yourself? Depressing, isn't it? Yes, especially as your lipstick wears down every three months and your powder runs out every six as you are the sort of person who, on opening a powder compact, showers it all over the bathroom.

And so we went on and on working ourselves into a great slough of despond.

'Just don't worry,' Ingrid concluded as we all trooped off for our Christmas holidays. 'Nothing ruins your looks more quickly than worry. Oh, and too much sunbathing, of course.'

25

In the Family Way

No amount of visible expenditure could have made me look better, for by the time I arrived at my parents' I was genuinely ill. At least that put paid to any ideas of my spending the night in a sleeping bag. Instead of heading for the fridge I went straight for whisky and bed. According to my sisters and brothers-in-law who arrived shortly after, I had flu. I didn't argue. They should know.

'How are you?' they asked me at about one in the morning after I had submitted myself to the heavy artillery of their care and swallowed heaven knows what they prescribed. All night they had been preparing what stank like gallons of turkey giblet gravy and what with that ghastly, stomach-wrenching smell on top of their medicines, all the alcohol, and flu itself, I felt I had almost snuffed myself out.

'Not dead yet,' I croaked.

The four of them took this as a professional insult. Their faces registered the same annoyance I experienced when they look disparagingly at a pile of my magazines over which I have spent weeks dredging up the words as if to say: 'Keeping the dustmen busy, aren't you? Making them lug that lot away.'

'Well you look much better,' said Susan.

'And you certainly sound it,' said Jane.

'No,' I moaned. 'You can't imagine how ill I feel.'

'It can't be flu, only a twenty-four-hour bug,' they said, relishing their last word before letting me rest in peace.

They were right. By the time I woke up fifteen hours later I did not ache and I was not hot. It was four o'clock in the afternoon. I had missed most of Christmas Day asleep in bed and the phone was ringing. I perked up. A slave of the phone again, I had to be better. Whoever it was did not want to speak to me.

I fell back into bed. I thought about getting up but did not do anything about it. When it is black as night at four in the afternoon, when you have to have the lights on, the curtains drawn, fires burning, shut up with all the snug conveniences of the underworld, it is no wonder people get ill. I lay there and stared into the black for three more hours.

I couldn't be bothered to move. It is always an effort to move when I'm at my parents'. Being in the same room in which I did my homework induces an insuperable lassitude in me. The sight of my china tortoise, a complete set of *Mallory Towers* on the bookshelf, a picture I was given on my thirteenth birthday, weigh heavy on my head. All my mechanisms for making myself face whatever I have woken up to, fail totally.

Christmas makes it even harder. I lose any sense of being an individual or separate identity and feel like any other chick in a hen coop. Independence goes right down the shoot. Christmas does this to people. However many multi-national corporations you take over during the year or however often you win the Booker Prize, you still have to go back home to the coop where the other chicks couldn't give a straw for what you do the rest of the year and will jump on you because you ate the chocolate they wanted or nag you to shift yourself from their favourite chair. You become just another little unit in this rather odd collection of people. Even my editor, who is spending Christmas with her family on their Cornish estate, has something as commonplace as parents and brothers and sisters lurking in the background. Even she has to retreat back into being just a member of the family. I doubt, however, that her family is like mine.

I could hear them all talking downstairs. Anyone meeting them for the first time could rightly think that the only people we knew were those who had just been committed to hospital or who had some congenital deficiency when it came to parking cars. Talk of clamps, poor old Mrs Watkins, only leaving it there five minutes, St. Mary's ward, broken meters, replaceable hips and single yellow lines went on for three hours.

By seven I had mustered the energy to pad downstairs to contribute by telling them about my colonel next door.

'Are you all right, dear?' asked my mother. 'Would you like something to eat.' She has this primitive compulsion to keep her children fed, though the twins could do with a bit less feeding.

'Yes, that would be – ' I began.

'You must be better if you want to eat,' interrupted Susan.

'She shouldn't eat, though. She should give her stomach a rest,' piped up Jane.

'Let her eat if she wants to,' said Jane's husband James, my favourite of the four.

'Yes, she certainly looks as if she could do with something,' said Jonathon, Susan's husband. 'She always looks hungry.' My family hand round insults the way other families hand round chocolates.

'But she eats all the time,' said Susan. 'If she was Isaac Newton she would have eaten the apple.' She's been making this joke since the day she learnt about gravity.

'If we could discover the secret of Eliza's metabolism we could all retire,' said Jane. Neither of the twins can even look at a Mars Bar without gaining two pounds.

'That's a thought, Eliza,' said Jonathon. 'Could we use you as a guinea pig? Conduct a few experiments on you and see why you don't put on weight? If we find out we'll make a fortune and you can have twenty per cent. Or is there some secret you have that the rest of us don't?'

'Living dangerously,' I said.

'Huh,' spluttered Jane.

'Looking like that, my love,' said Susan, 'you do not ring true.'

'It's so funny to think you work for *Circe*,' said Jonathon. 'I always thought,' he persisted, determined to make a joke, 'that women who worked for magazines like yours were glamorous.' I really can't abide this man.

'My love – ' began Susan.

'Stop calling me "my love".'

'All right, all right. Don't get so upset. But it's bad for you being so thin. Isn't it bad for her, Jane?'

'When you're forty-five, your metabolism will probably change, and one morning you'll wake up fat.'

'What, like you?'

'Please,' interrupted my father looking up from his book, *The Authorised Biography of John Stuart Mill*. 'Stop squabbling.'

Going home makes us all revert to being five-year-olds again. We fall back into ways we should have left behind with the Ladybird books. I went in to the kitchen to talk to my mother who was making sandwiches.

'There's a note there for you, darling,' she said. 'Someone rang you.'

'Who?' I said.

'Ask Jane. She took it.'

'Jane, who rang me?'

'Sam. Well that's who he said he was. He had a really weird voice.'

'Why didn't you tell me?'

'You were asleep.'

'But you could have woken me.'

'I didn't like to. Not after all the fuss you were making last night saying you were so ill you thought you might die.'

'I didn't . . .'

'You did. Didn't she, Susan?'

Susan said, 'Yes.'

'You were delirious so you don't remember,' continued Jane. 'But we were all very worried about you. We thought you might die as well.'

'Did Sam leave a message?' I said.

'Only Happy Christmas.'

'Did you tell him I was ill?'

'Not exactly.'

'What did you say?'

'That you had taken to your bed until further notice.'

'What?'

'That you had taken to your bed until further notice – they were my very words, if I remember rightly.'

'What did you say that for? He'll think I don't want to speak to him.'

'My God, Eliza,' interrupted Susan. 'Hear this, Jane. This is a real turn-up for the books. It's about time we saw some interest in someone new.'

'I'm only teasing,' said Jane. 'I told him the truth, that you were dying and that there was no point in him rushing round to your death bed.'

'As you were already past the point of no return,' explained Susan. 'But we'd let him know about funeral arrangements.'

'Did he leave a number?' (I had never rung Sam for his sister's number in Vermont and I didn't know her married name.)

'No. I'm afraid not. There wouldn't have been any point.'

'Stop winding her up,' interceded my father again, as if I were an old alarm clock.

'But think how she was behaving last night, as if she was Camille. She's always thinking she's dying or going mad. I've yet to meet a hypochondriac to beat her.'

'I'm not a hypochondriac.'

'Do you know what a hypochondriac is?' asked Jon. I ignored him. 'It's someone,' he went on patronisingly, 'with an irrational fear of disease.'

'There's nothing irrational in fearing disease,' I said. 'People die of them all the time. You should know.'

All four suddenly looked grave, as if to say: 'Don't even try to imagine what we know,' and I returned to the kitchen where my mother told me how she had met the mothers of three of my old schoolfriends and that between them they had five grandchildren and two more on the way.

Later that night I gave the Twin Sets the bird tables, which sweetened them up enormously as they thought bird tables were a wonderful present. I wish I could have said the same about what they had given me: a walnut barometer. It read

207

'foggy', so at least it worked but it was a joint Christmas and birthday present, they said, as it was so large. I got that old feeling of being fobbed off, that the twins were, as usual, capitalising on my birthday being so close to Christmas.

'I mean really, a barometer,' I said to my mother next morning when the others had gone off for their constitutional Boxing Day march across Osterley Park.

'What do you mean?'

'Well what do I want a barometer for?'

'I thought what a good idea, actually.'

'But it's hideous.'

'It's all right.'

'And it's so big.'

'Well, it's a sophisticated piece of equipment.'

'But where am I going to put it?'

'In your flat, of course.'

'But I haven't got any room.'

'What about over your bed?'

'I'm not going to bed with a barometer on top of me. What if it falls off the wall? They're really thin, my walls. It'd kill me. It's typical of those twins. They go out of their way to choose a present that will annoy me. It's not fair, four against one.'

'Don't be ridiculous.'

'Well why give it to me?'

'No doubt they thought you'd like it.'

'Why would I like something like this?'

'Because, darling, no one, simply no one is as obsessed with the weather as you, that's why.'

'But it doesn't even work.' It still registered foggy and the fog had cleared. Some hateful, mucky snow had been slurping down for at least half an hour.

'Really, Eliza, you should be grateful you have got anything.'

I left her and lay down on the sofa with a box of chocolates to watch a Lassie adventure film.

'That box was virtually full last night,' was the first thing Jane cried out as she got back from her walk.

'What box?' asked Susan.

'The pralines. She's eaten them all.'

I looked in the box. I had too.

'Honestly, Eliza.'

'Sorry,' I said, a bit late.

'Can't you turn that television off,' said my father. 'Madge and Michael and Kate and her fiancée are coming round for a drink in a minute. What's his name again, Eliza?'

'Robert.'

'We met them in the park and Kate told us you're going to be her bridesmaid,' said Jane. 'Why didn't you tell us?'

'And why will you be a bridesmaid for Kate when you wouldn't be one for us?' asked Susan.

'Because she's older than me,' I said.

'Only by a few weeks.'

'Look, can you just leave me alone and let me watch the end of this. It'll be over in five minutes.'

'And then can you get dressed, please,' said my mother. 'You're making us all feel ill mooching around looking like that.'

'Yes,' said Susan. 'It's like living with a haddock with you flopping around all over the place.'

'And with all your clothes I don't know how you manage to look so awful,' added Jane.

'I'd have thought they'd teach you a few things about clothes at *Circe*,' said Jonathon.

'It's pronounced "Sir-See", not "Sir-Kay",' I corrected him, 'after the goddess.'

'What goddess?'

'Circe. Now please will you let me watch this?'

'No. What goddess? Have you ever heard of Circe, Susan?'

'Never.'

'Circe', I explained sadly, 'was an enchantress, as modern women are supposed to be – miracle workers with their lives, paragons in boardrooms, bed and with babies. And she used to turn men into swine.'

'Don't believe her, Jonathon,' said Susan.

'It's true. Men were so spellbound by her she liked to turn them into horrible honking pigs.'

'I think pigs are rather sweet,' said Jane.

'I'd rather have a man myself,' I said, 'but she preferred them as pigs. Though she left Ulysses as a human as she was rather taken by him and he wasn't as stupid as all the other men she met.'

'You're making this up.'

'I'm not.'

'She is,' said Susan.

'She's getting worse and worse,' said Jane as if I was someone whom they would soon be discussing along with all the other people they knew who had just been committed to hospital. And with that they had to stop arguing as the doorbell rang and Kate and her family sardined themselves into the sitting room.

'And this is for you,' said Kate later, handing me a truly beautifully wrapped present which I had been eyeing all the time Robert was introduced to my family, while the Twin Sets tried to find enough chairs for everyone, my father poured the drinks, my mother opened the packets of crisps and while Kate opened my present to her of pearl earrings which were so pretty I had almost kept them for myself.

'This is wonderful,' I said. I was actually rather excited, for my present was three foot long and wrapped up in yards of tissue paper and looked as if it was going to contain some exquisite piece of silk lingerie and Kate always gives me such beautiful things. I tore off the paper and came to a large black box. In it was a fish.

'Oh,' I said. 'Er, wow. Er, thanks, Kate.'

'It was Robert's idea, actually. He knows how much you like smoked salmon and his uncle farms them up in Scotland and he always get hundreds sent down for Christmas.'

'Well it's lovely, Robert. Thank you. Such a big fish too.'

'Robert thought you'd like a whole one, didn't you, Robert?'

(Engaged a whole twelve days and they are already talking in marital stereo.)

'Yes,' smiled Robert.

'Well, thank you, Robert. I might have guessed this was your idea.'

'Why don't you all stay for lunch then?' suggested my mother. 'And we can eat the salmon.'

At first Madge and Michael were not sure whether to accept because they had a cold turkey and ham salad all prepared next door but they soon decided they would rather like some fish and that they could have meat this evening. So the Twin Sets went off to the kitchen to set about cutting up my salmon as cutting things up is something they are very good at; my father, Kate's father and Robert all went out to the garden to bring in the extra fold-up table from the shed; Madge and my mother set about buttering bread and laying tables and those sorts of things. I stayed put with Kate.

'Listen,' she said quietly, moving up to me on the sofa.

'Yes?'

She hesitated. 'It's about Tim.'

'Kate,' I said firmly. 'I don't give a toss about Tim.'

'That's all right then but I thought I ought to let you know that he spoke to Robert on Friday and apparently next week he's going off to Paris with a seventeen-year-old from Benenden called Topsy.'

'I thought he was in love with me,' I cried.

'Not any more. Apparently he's irrevocably devoted to her.'

'But just forty-eight hours beforehand he was asking me to Paris.'

'But you didn't want to go.'

'But you can't fall in and out of love with people in forty-eight hours,' I said furiously. 'Though I suspected it all along. There he was, pretending he was as sweet as a milkshake and as cute as pie, coming on all sensitive and fascinated in my brain, when what he really wanted was some Flopsy who hadn't got two A-levels to her name.'

'Oh Eliza, she said. 'Calm down. I'm sorry. I wouldn't have told you if I thought you'd be so upset.'

211

'I'm not upset. Not one bit. But don't you see, one minute he wants to take me and the next a brainless bunny.'

'I think she's quite bright, actually. She's just heard she's got into Oxford.'

'Then what's she call herself Flopsy for?'

'It's Topsy, not Flopsy.'

'Even better. Topsy and Tim. Why do people like that always have such nursery names? Is she a Lady Topsy?'

'Her aunt is Lady Chewton.'

'I know. And they're cousins and love blossomed up in her feudal castle in Wales. And they're destined to have perfect spotless children together.'

'Are you upset about something?'

'No. Why?'

'You seem to be taking this rather badly so I thought maybe you were. Has Sam rung?'

'Yesterday. But I was asleep and Jane didn't take his number and he's at his sister's.'

'I thought his sister was mad.'

'Not this one. Anyway the other one's not mad, just got a lot of problems right now.'

'Has Sam lost his job yet?'

'As far as I know he's not resigned, if that's what you mean.'

'Oh dear, Eliza. I'm going to make it my mission next year to find you somebody. And I'll rope Robert in on it because he knows you so well now too. He must know somebody whom you'd like. It would be lovely if we both had children at the same time.'

'What?' I spluttered.

'Well they could be best friends too.'

I can't believe I am hearing this.

'Sorry,' she said, seeing the horror register on my face. Kate has been engaged less than a fortnight and she is already on the border of the other side of femaleness. My other old schoolfriends crossed from seduction into reproduction long ago. From worrying about that extra two pounds on their bums and the way their new mascara runs, they now think of nothing but the children in the pushchairs before them, on their backs and inside them. 'I'm just getting a bit sentimental right now.'

'Well, don't, Kate. Don't you dare. If you start flaunting that smug complacency of the woman who thinks she's got everything just because she's got a baby and hubby to look after, I won't be able to stand you.'

'All I meant was that I liked the idea of us both having a baby at the same time.'

'Well I don't. Not unless I marry some millionaire of a knight in shining armour who will employ me a whole army of nannies to get up for it in the middle of the night, buy me a huge house so I could leave it in a far off wing when it cries, and promise me a limitless expenditure on dry cleaning so I wouldn't have to worry about it being sick on me.'

'Eliza,' shouted my mother. 'When did I tell you Tracy's third baby was due?'

'I have simply no idea, Mother.'

'And Kate,' called out Madge, 'how much did little Holly weigh?'

'Seven pounds two ounces,' replied Kate, going into the kitchen where Madge was saying that Wendy, the 'girl' down the road, produced her second baby girl yesterday, on Christmas Day. (Females are 'girls' all their life – little girls, girlies, thirty-year-old women are girls and eighty-year-olds are old girls.)

'A baby girl,' continued Madge.

'A girl. How lovely,' exclaimed my sisters, looking up from their washing up and drying up. They have got this gushing madonna act down to a much better art than me and can gaze admiringly at a baby as if they have never seen anything quite like it before. It is because their hips are so huge.

'Yes, a girl. And they're calling her Holly because of Christmas which I think is a lovely idea.'

'Oh yes,' chorussed everyone but me.

'Eliza, it'll be you next,' said Madge.

'Dear God I hope not,' I said, slapping my hand on my flat stomach.

213

'I mean to get married,' explained Madge. 'Not to have a baby.'

'It'll be ages before Eliza has a baby,' said Susan.

'She shouldn't leave it too late though,' said Jane.

'Well it's not a problem as I don't like babies,' I said because sometimes I just cannot be doing with this great caring and sharing act of my sisters. There was silence.

I am the one said to be obsessed with fashion but it is these women with their glamorisation and sanctification of motherhood who are in fashion, not me. And I hope it is a fashion which does not catch on. If women like Kate and my sisters start thinking that giving up careers for crèches is the only way to be a whole woman, we'll all be clamped to the sink again before we can say the earth moved. 'Or rather,' I continued, 'I don't positively dislike babies. Though some days I do. Some days I don't. I feel the same about kippers.'

'Eliza, please,' said my mother. 'Stop talking such nonsense and give me a hand making this coleslaw.' And she handed me a cabbage to chop.

26

Problem Pages

On the Wednesday morning, the first day back in the office after Christmas, I had literally just plodded in when Ingrid phoned.

'Oh Eliza. I feel quite awful,' she groaned. 'Just awful. I'd fancied some smoked salmon – as one does – and it must have been that because I haven't eaten anything else. It's made me so, so ill. It hadn't been in the fridge long but you never know these days and it must have been off.'

'You poor thing,' I said unsympathetically. (If Ingrid had eaten as much 'off' smoked salmon over the past few years as she claims, she would be dead.)

'It's such a nuisance. I'm sorry to leave you there on your own but Melindi will be around. It doesn't seem to be getting any better. I thought I might eat some dry toast but, oh dear, perhaps not. I certainly won't be able to come in the next few days. So, darling, I'll see you next week.'

'The week after next.'

'Oh you've got next week off, haven't you? Where are you going?'

'I haven't decided yet. Maybe Paris. I'm not sure.'

'Paris. How lovely. Is it snowing there?'

'Probably.'

'Have you ever seen Paris in the snow?'

'No, thankfully.'

'I've always longed to. Will you stay with that beautiful friend of yours working for Karl at Chanel?'

'If I go, yes.'

'Perhaps she can get you a discount on a Chanel suit.' (Colette can, but even with twenty-five per cent off I still can't

215

afford one.) 'Well have a lovely time. Oh dear. I'd better get back to bed.'

'Yes, you do that,' I said grimly.

'Goodbye then.'

'Bye.'

Ingrid was undoubtedly at her friend's house in Yorkshire and about to sit down to breakfast and read the papers. I took off my coat, scarf, hat, top two sweaters, boots and socks. It was a real bruiser of a day and the chill factor was as bad as ever. I couldn't think what to do. I sat down. The major investigation into the history of the bra was still lying on my desk. I can't remember a time when it wasn't. A fashion article called 'Black is Blue' which I was supposed to have checked for the February issue had also found its way on top of the piles of old magazines and unanswered letters. I reread the newspaper headlines. Negotiations between the management and electricity union had broken down and power cuts would start in selected areas as of midday. Melindi was on the phone to one of her boyfriends in Paris. I didn't know where to start. I rang Paris too.

'It would be wonderful if you could come over,' said Colette. 'I could really do with your company right now.'

Colette did not strike me as in need of company. As well as adopting Coco Chanel's clothes, jewellery, perfumes and make-up, Colette had also embraced Chanel's dictum, 'A woman is nothing if she is not loved.' On this criterion, she was ranking a great deal as she was in the throes of seeing three men.

'They all complement each other,' she explained. 'One is no good without the other two but between the three I've got the perfect combination.'

'Do they know about each other?'

'Of course not. Please come, Eliza. Then you can meet them before I do something about it.'

'Are you going to end it?'

'Yes. I don't think it's fair on them. And the logistics are impossible.'

216

'So how many are you going to leave. Just the one? Or two? Or all three?'

'All three. None of them is quite right. I only like bits of them so between the three of them I have the perfect man. But with just the one I'd only have a third. And that's no good. So will you come?'

'Can I let you know tomorrow,' I said. Paris was losing its attraction for me. 'I won't know till then if I can get the time off,' I lied. 'It all depends on the situation in the office. We've got phenomenally behind so those of us who haven't got anything definite booked . . .' I wittered on. I have already spent more than enough hours listening to her boyfriends tell me how she is the most beautiful woman they have ever known. The thought of going through it all again with three rejected Frenchmen was too much. Besides, I looked at the weather report. It was 2°C colder in Paris than in London.

I attacked the bras again. I had got as far as deciding not to leave the office until I had finished them when Cassandra rang, saying she would buy me lunch at Le Caprice as she had just had some 'brilliant news'.

'But I'm not dressed for Le Caprice,' I said. If you are not dressed in black at Le Caprice you have to wear designer label clothes otherwise you upset the décor.

'It doesn't matter,' said Cassandra. 'You can hide behind me as I'm looking amazing.'

It was true. Cassandra was looking amazing, twirling about at Le Caprice's entrance in a coat I had not seen before in ankle-length scarlet cashmere with a fake leopard-fur lining.

'It's the perfect coat,' I said. 'I mean red and fur in one. You couldn't ask for more.'

'I know,' said Cassandra delightedly, spinning around twice more in case anyone had missed its full glory.

'Whose is it?' I asked, emerald with envy.

'Sonia Rykiel's.' It would take Cassandra six weeks' worth of emotional problem articles to earn enough for a Sonia Rykiel coat. 'They had a pre-Christmas sale,' she said guiltily. (Perhaps five weeks' worth if it was reduced.) 'And I put on half a stone in two days last week as I couldn't stop eating. I'm suffering from so much sensory deprivation right now that eating and spending money is all I have left. And I'd rather be broke than fat. Hence the coat.'

'Is this why we're having lunch here? To celebrate the coat?'

'No.' She searched around in a battered old briefcase.

'You'll need a new bag with a coat like that.'

'I know. I want you to help me choose one afterwards. But here we are.' She produced a letter.

'Do you want me to read it?'

'Yes, yes.'

It was a letter from a publisher saying how much he respected her articles in *Woman's Mail* and that he thought they could be compiled into a book.

'Isn't it brilliant?' she said.

'Yes,' I agreed, 'brilliant,' though I don't know what else I could have said. 'Quite brilliant. Well done. So exciting. Have you discussed it yet?'

'I spoke to them on Friday – only briefly as they were all about to go off for Christmas. I'm going in next week but they said they thought there was a real market for a book like this. You know, for a book which covered all aspects of modern relationships, for a thorough investigation, a definitive study, like an encyclopedia, they said.'

'Like an encyclopedia?' I repeated incredulously.

'Something like that. A sort of A to Z of relationships.'

'Would you like to order?' interrupted the waiter.

'Another five minutes, please. And they think they will be able to get masses of coverage for it – other women's magazines, breakfast TV, *Woman's Hour*, you know, discussing and advising on the state of modern relationships. They think there's a real need for a new voice. The current state of affairs between men and women is totally new in the history of humankind. We have managed to destroy the old concept of man providing for and protecting the woman and children, and of woman nurturing both man and children. The principles behind marriage have changed but we have not really worked out a viable alternative. Should women put career or children first? Should men sacrifice their career prospects to wash the nappies so women can fulfil themselves in the workplace? Are women finding that taking over multi-national corporations every other day is as fulfilling as they thought it would be or do they sometimes hanker to spend their time at home teaching the children to read? Should men stop trying to provide for a woman and children and just worry about providing for themselves?

'We've got all these new questions and so much more confusion. We have not got any role models. Madame Bovary's problem was not whether she should put her child or her job first. Cathy and Heathcliff were not squabbling over whether Cathy was fulfilled staying at home. Vronsky did not think that if he made a pass at Anna Karenina she might regard him as horribly wolfish and sexist. None of them were in our predicament. So now we've got no one to turn to.

'Sexual problems used to be moral ones. People had to deal with the immorality of having sex before marriage, committing adultery. Now we can do all that with a pretty clear conscience. We sanction most things. Now our problems are practical. And no one has had to deal with them before. Plato, Socrates and er, all those other philosophers didn't. Flaubert, the Brontës, Tolstoy didn't. There is no one in the past to whom we can look for advice and we have so few sages in our society today. That's why they want this book – a sort of practical guide.'

Cassandra is right in that although we have advice galore on the physical ideal – I spend five days a week telling people what they should look like on the outside – now we all have to battle alone in deciding what we should look like inside. But the idea of Cassandra setting herself up as the twentieth-century Tolstoy or Plato, especially after all that twirling around in her beautiful new red coat, irked me a little.

'Are your intended publishers aware of your own degree of practical success in the field of human relationships?' I asked, like the cat who has not got the cream.

She didn't hear me, fortunately, as the waiter was remarking on her wonderful coat and asking again whether we were ready to order.

'Oh thank you,' she beamed at him. 'Sorry, what were you saying, Eliza?'

'Never mind. What are you going to eat?'

'I don't know. What are you having?'

'I don't know what I want.'

'Actually I don't feel too well,' she said. I didn't either. 'Perhaps I should just have a starter.'

'Oh no,' I said. 'I need more than that.'

'I've eaten hardly anything today.'

'Perhaps that's why you're not feeling well.'

'Maybe.'

'I haven't eaten much either. Perhaps we would feel better if we ate,' I suggested.

'I don't know. I'm not sure if I'm feeling ill because I have eaten too much or because my stomach is empty.'

'Might I suggest,' interrupted the waiter (these sort of conversations must go on all the time in Le Caprice), 'the quail's egg soufflé is very light, or the hot salad with cold vegetables,' he began.

'I'll have that,' said Cassandra. I plumped for scrambled eggs with smoked salmon, thinking that with any luck the smoked salmon would give me food poisoning so I could have the rest of the week off like Ingrid.

'So what exactly are you going to call this A to Z?'

'I don't know. They suggested *Safe Sex*.'

'*Safe Sex*? You can't call it that.'

'Why not?'

'Because there's no such thing. Sex is never safe. Unless you've been married millions of years and have blind faith you'll never be ditched, laying yourself open to getting hurt is a risky business, regardless of how many rubber trees you plunder.'

'You seem to have managed it pretty safely since The Natterjack – deliberately only seeing men with whom you knew you'd be the one to do the ditching.'

'That's ridiculous.'

'Off the cuff, I could name you – '

'What about Sam?' I interrupted before she could start the naming of names.

'You're safe with him three thousand miles away.'

'And St. George?'

'The man's devoted to you. Anyone can see that.'

'Wrong. On Friday he told Robert he was blissfully in love with his seventeen-year-old cousin called Bunny or something like that and was already planning on whisking her off to Paris just two days – no, even less than that, about forty hours – after asking me.'

'Really? That's brilliant,' she said delightedly. 'Now I can interview you. What do I always say about new men? They're worse than old men for at least you know where you are with old men and can play them at their own game. But with their sensitive scions who knows? Is all that New Manism just a front? Is what they really want a pretty chick? Underneath, are all men just the same? Of course they are.

'Great. That's N for "New Men" sorted out. And what you were just saying about safeness is a really good idea too,' she said, getting out her notebook.

'Oh Cassandra, please. Don't start making notes.'

'But this is excellent stuff. I could have S for "Safeness". Although I've already got so many Ss: S for "St. Georges", S for "Stood Up", though I could make that G for "Getting Stood Up". The grammar is not ideal but I'd really like to do a major piece on safeness,' she went on, starting to scribble. 'With holes in the ozone layer, cancer in everything we eat, the possibility of push-a-button nuclear wars, we desperately search for safeness. Even sex must be safe. Abandonment, surrender, oblivion, are too dangerous. Passion is not important. What is important is practicality, whether our separate careers are compatible, whether it makes economic sense to have a marriage contract, whether we both like opera, want holidays in France.

'Cocooned in nice homes with indulgent parents, not

having to go off to war, never wanting for food or material comforts, any daring in our characters has been knocked out. All we want is another nice home, a BMW, a good job which enables us to go to the theatre whenever we want and which pays for three weeks' safe excitement on a supervised canoe trip down the Amazon. Our lives consist of leaving home to spend three years closeted in some educational establishment and then retreating into safe relationships and safe houses and shutting the door securely, having never dared set a toe outside.

'It's as if we are already sixty, as if at thirty we have got all life has to offer, as if we have nothing more to learn, nothing more into which we want to be initiated. There is nothing we long for, be it material, spiritual, or another human being. There is never any suggestion that there might be something which transcends the practicalities; no thought that, although very nice, the security of companionship, a beautiful house, and a job might not be the answer to human fulfilment; no suspicion that being in love can give you a sense – albeit a fleeting one – of being in tune with the rest of the world and that for a few moments it enables you to say, "I know why I'm here." ' She put her pen down. 'It does, doesn't it?'

'What?'

'Being in love makes you closer to understanding.'

'I can't remember.'

'Nor can I, exactly. It's sad, isn't it?'

'What is?'

'My life – that I can't remember any more. It's so, so sad,' she went on muttering, miserably, manipulating a cold mange-tout. 'The way my life's a tragedy.'

'Oh be quiet. You've just bought yourself the best coat in London in which you'll never again have to fall over on Paddington station for men in their swarms to queue up to give you their cards. And you're going to be the Socrates of the twenty-first century.'

'But look what happened to Socrates. Anyway,' she said, perking up with suspiciously business-like brusqueness, 'tell me all about Sam.' And she picked up her pen again.

'One of the reasons I like Sam,' I said, eyeing Cassandra poised to take notes, 'is that he can't be simplified into a thousand-word advice column. Because he's three thousand miles away I don't have to go through all that pantomime of going out to dinner, worrying whether phoning him the next morning looks too keen, deciding if it's his place or mine, spending a torrid time in bed – not that I'm underestimating the appeal of that – but then stumbling through post-coital etiquette: should you stay the night but leave before breakfast? Quit right away? It's totally divorced from that old game so it seems more honest. It's not the stuff of your practical guide.' I paused.

'Don't stop,' said Cassandra, writing furiously.

'That's all.'

'Oh. Well, that'll do to get me started. I'll have O for ''Overseas Boyfriends'' or maybe O for ''One Night Stands'': do soulmates manifest themselves overnight? I could interview you arguing for, and talk to myself arguing against.' And she spent the rest of the lunch taking notes on herself by which time it was as dark as night outside.

We went sale shopping for a new briefcase for Cassandra. After seeing all that black in Le Caprice I thought I might buy a black sweater. Eventually, Cassandra chose a tiny beaded bag, the sort of thing Titania might have carried. And I bought a sweater in a crimson which would outshine a fire engine. I also splashed out on four mugs – special purchase seconds – for the Twins Sets' birthday presents.

'I've got something for you,' said Melindi when I arrived back in the office.

'Oh yes?' I said, as she produced a twenty-four-pack of light bulbs.

'I met Ashley for lunch, at L'Escargot, and he told me to give you these as they emit special rays like the sun to stop you getting depressed in the winter when there's no sunshine. For he says he doesn't know anyone who is as much of a misery as you in winter.'

'How nice of him,' I said, inspecting the light bulbs. 'I presume he's doing the advertising for these.'

'That's right,' she said, squeezing into her coat. 'He thought maybe you could do a piece on them. And now you're here I'm going home as I've been working solidly all day.'

With that she left me alone and in a great burst of feverish activity I sat in the empty office polishing off the bras. I would do 'Black is Blue' at home for I get scared when the place is deserted and there is no one in there but me.

27

Out of the Blues

I rang Sam when I got home but there was no answer. Some days, days like today, are cold and bare and there is nothing in them at all. So I replaced all my old light bulbs with Ashley's and then didn't know what to do with the lampshades – the instructions told you to remove the lampshades as they undermined the bulbs' efficiency. I thought about reorganising my wardrobe of unwearable clothes and fitting them in there, but dumped the lot in the hall and had a bath instead and then went to bed to correct the 'Black is Blue' fashion article. The argument ran that blue had developed new powers as *the* basic colour.

'If your wardrobe is unremittingly steeped in black, think again about blue. Plain, pure, primary blue is the same as black. Blue too is classic, sophisticated. Blue too slips from day into night. Blue too represents unimpeachable chic. Blue is black.

'Look at the collections showing how blue works for day and night: city suits livid in Prussian blue, raincoats in un-adulterated French navy, ethereal chiffon shifts as dreamy a blue as a winter's sky, indigo silks . . .'

I had to keep ploughing through 'blue' in the Thesaurus and it took me till midnight to finish, by which time I was feeling pretty blue myself. I rang Sam again. This time he answered. He had just got back from Vermont where it was bitterly cold outside, too cold to ski.

'I'm so cold too,' I said. 'And here it's cold inside as well,' I went on, when he interrupted and, changing the tone of the joking, singing music hall act he had been conducting since we met, said that he wasn't going to be leaving his job, that he

225

really missed me and wanted to see me again. To which I, instead of saying that he had crossed my mind too, just laughed, put up one false front after another and bowled right back into our usual comedy of self-concealment.

These days my cowardice has got the better of me. When I was young I thought I would have hundreds of love affairs. But I haven't. I met The Natterjack and since him I haven't had the strength to take the plunge again. There was Ashley I suppose, and a couple of others. Or maybe it was three or four or however many, I didn't give a toss for one of them. I didn't want to take on the baggage of someone else's life again. I didn't want to get embroiled in asking: Was it a night of love? Of delight? Of triumph? The latest grand slam in the crutch of his vanity? I didn't want the bitterness of turning over and finding him not there. Loving The Natterjack exposed a pit of vulnerability and I didn't want to dig into it again. So much of myself had been subsumed in Jack that on the morning he rang to say he loved Grace I was faced with a void. In the seconds it took me to fully comprehend what he was saying, the focus had changed. Something had been drained from the world I was used to. I lay in a steaming bath with hot tears pouring into the water, so stoned with misery, I thought I could only sober myself up by getting so drunk I could forget him.

And I just went on lying there until all the hot water ran out and then I went back to bed and lay there with a pain in my heart until the phone rang again and it was Tron wanting to know where I was and where was my article on non-crumple linens?

I got up, got dressed, went to work, thought of something to say about non-crumple linen clothes, went home, got up again and continued to imitate a normal person otherwise I would have just lain there until I was farmed out with all the nutcases in my street.

When I was busy I felt as if I was ill with terminal inertia. I functioned. I ploughed through the day. I dredged up the words at work. But the nights, when I was on my own in my flat, away from friends who were always ringing me up and inviting me to dinner and telling me I was too good for The Toad and that I would get better with time and saying all the things you say, were much much worse. Then I lost my concentration and the dull ache would turn into an almost unbearable despair and it was just the despair and me fighting each other. And the despair frightened me as it made me so helpless for there was nowhere I could ask for help as I only wanted his help.

I kept bumping against his memory. I would speak to one of the photographers at work and notice that he had the same camera or I would see a man rub his eyes in the same way or a stranger with his grin and he would be before me again and all the pain and bitterness would return. And I would think how he would put on his tie, kick me in the middle of the night as he was always dreaming he was scoring goals, how he never felt the cold. And I began to hate him for leaving me and I thought that if I could continue hating him my hatred would free me of him. But it didn't as the only thing I hated about him was that he no longer loved me and I kept giving in to a hideous longing to see him again and think how we had spent nearly all our time together and how I felt so at ease with him and my spirits so alive and that I could not bear to learn to live with the emptiness.

Pity and my mountain of self-pity fed on each other. I only had to hear a maudlin song on the radio, see a child in a wheelchair, or have someone say a kind word to me, and I wanted to cry. I became obsessed with suffering. Life and happiness seemed such fragile commodities that I thought it a miracle we possessed either of them. I kept thinking of all the thousands of people in the world who were dying from cancer, from Aids, from starvation, and I would spend hours quantifying how much everyone was suffering and after a while all this suffering became a mission in itself. Misery made me feel alive again and I thought how ironic that I should feel as alive when I am deeply unhappy as when I am deeply happy. And then, thank God, thank God, as my friends were all ready to shoot me in the kneecaps they were so sick of me talking about illness all the time and walking round with a face as long as a mile, I thought that if I continued in this vein, irony was all I would ever be mistress of.

I had got The Natterjack out of all proportion. Defining what a man is, or should be, by him was absurd. Kissing his lips, lying in his arms was not the only way of relieving my pain. So I had the affair with Ashley & Co., and the less said about all of them the better. Meeting Sam was therefore such a relief. After writing off one half of the species I actually liked someone again.

But I'm not sure that love is worth the bother any more. We believe, with such trusting eagerness, that in love and sex we find the answers, but even if you have nothing more important to do with your time than say 'black is blue' a hundred different ways, love can so make you suffer I don't know if it's worth suffering anyone again.

So I didn't tell Sam I missed him too and after we put the phone down I couldn't sleep. I twisted the sheets into a noose and outside it sounded as if World War Three had started. The roof on the workman's hut had fought loose again and was clanging in the wind. The cat next door was warring with some other mad Tom. The dustmen had not been over Christmas and all the plastic bags had split open so bottles and cans were rattling in the gutter. And the snow had thawed into a heavy, pounding rain, which all night flushed down my window.

Hours later, doors began to slam and radios blared and water pipes rumbled and people began running down the stairs and more doors crashed and cars started. And at about half-past eight when I was staring out my window at a sky like iron, someone banged on my door. It was Jack.

'How did you get into the block of flats?' I asked as he walked right in.

'The front door was open. Anyone could walk in off the streets. It's very dangerous, you know.'

'I know. Careful,' I shouted as he went to put his foot through one of my lampshades piled up in the hall.

'What are all these doing here?'

'I've got these special light bulbs to stop me getting depressed in the dark. And to get the full benefit you shouldn't cover them up.'

'Do they work?'

'I don't know yet.'

'What are you depressed about?'

'Nothing.'

'So what do you need them for?'

'I don't know. Just in case. Anyway what do you want? You look as if you've been up all night.'

'I have. You look as if you haven't slept either.'

'No, I couldn't.'

'You don't actually have to sleep with these glaring lights on, do you?'

'Of course not.'

'They look like frozen teardrops,' he said, staring at me with a most awesome tenderness.

'Jack, what are you talking about?' I asked nervously. 'What are you doing here?'

'I had to speak to you,' he said, moving towards me and curling my hair through his fingers. 'Marrying Grace,' he whispered, stroking my cheek, 'was madness. Without you I was nothing.' And with that speech – he could always be concise – he kissed me.

I had spent so long longing for him to kiss me again that I let him, most willingly. I used to think that our lovemaking was the tenderest expression of the purest, most loving feelings you could have towards another human being, and pressed against his skin I thought nothing in the world could ever come between us. And curved into him now, in this long, slow kiss, deliciously recognising the ecstasy escalating through me, I thought I could lie exchanging embraces with him for ever.

'I never want to give you up,' he said, holding me so tight my ribs hurt.

I turned my head from him. 'But you already did,' I said. 'You did,' I cried, getting out from his grip. 'You did. You did

Jack,' I shouted. 'You did give me up. I'm not one of your photographs that you can suddenly focus in on again and assume I'll still be there.'

'Eliza, I love you. I've always loved you.'

'No, Jack, you haven't. You left me.'

'I didn't know what I was doing. I was mad.'

'You knew just what you were doing,' I said furiously. 'Don't give me all that madness, blinded by love stuff. You held my happiness in your hands. No one has wronged me as you did and – '

'Eliza, please. You're the most loving woman who ever existed, you can't . . .' He stopped short for a great cry for help suddenly reverberated from next door. 'You can't say you don't love me, not after . . .'

'My love for you has been so overworked that if any still exists it is so faded and exhausted it's worthless. So go,' I said as there was another cry for help. 'I've got to ring the police.'

'Leave her,' he said impatiently, gesturing next door.

'It's not the girl, it's the colonel. He needs help.'

'Colonel? Oh God, Eliza. You don't have to stay here. Come with me,' he pleaded. 'The place is Bedlam.'

'Well spotted,' I said with disgust. 'You think that with your camera you can see things the rest of us can't but you're just as blind as the rest of us, seeing just what you want to see.' I dialled the police. 'Now get out otherwise I'll ask the police to get rid of you too while they're at it. Get out.'

'Eliza, please.'

'No,' I repeated and repeated until he left me alone.

His going felt like suddenly being given a quite delicious box of chocolates, right out of the blue.

'Mind the lampshades,' I chuckled to myself as he closed the door. It was a most miraculous release. The lights were back on. The clamps had been taken off. Perhaps, I thought, remembering how I had just been basking in the heavenly delight of his kiss, it was never his heart that I loved, just his body. I picked up the phone and, watching the day at last wake up, rang Melindi at the office and told her that I wouldn't be in for the rest of the week as I had the most appalling food poisoning from smoked salmon.

'Like Ingrid?' she asked suspiciously.

'Yes,' I said. 'Just like Ingrid.'

The same may also be true of Sam. Maybe it isn't his heart that I love, but his body. Whichever, I thought wickedly, as I rang British Airways to book the next flight to Boston, we would now have a delightful time finding out.

Also available from
Mandarin Paperbacks

SUSAN LEWIS

Stolen Beginnings

Marian seems to have a charmed life – not only does a sudden windfall make her rich but she is also happily in love with her handsome boyfriend Paul. Then, horribly, everything changes – Paul leaves her for her glamorous model cousin, Magdalene, and she loses all her money overnight. In the struggle to make a new life for herself she joins a film company. On a film set in rural Tuscany, one of the actresses disappears mysteriously. In the ensuing panic, Marian beings to learn that the dangers involve her personally, as she begins to discover love once more . . .

ZOË FAIRBAIRNS

Daddy's Girls

Three decades of great change . . .

Three daughters in a crucible of family
ferment . . .

'This is an impressive novel – profound, funny and
disturbing by turns . . . without doubt, establishes
Zoë Fairbairns as one of our leading novelists'
OPTIONS

'Such a pleasure . . . Zoë Fairbairns tackles head-
on the awkward question of sisters and sisterhood'
NEW STATESMAN AND SOCIETY

'A far, fierce yet compassionate cry from the usual
saccharine sisterly saga, this book exposes how
mothers and daughters had to suffer for love, just
because they were born a generation too soon'
COMPANY

'Fairbairns writes with zest and wit. The
cumulative drama is fascinating, as lies spawn
more lies, and the women show themselves
increasingly handicapped by their failure to
register reality'
SUNDAY TIMES

A Selected List of Fiction Available from Mandarin

While every effort is made to keep prices low, it is sometimes necessary to increase prices at short notice. Mandarin Paperbacks reserves the right to show new retail prices on covers which may differ from those previously advertised in the text or elsewhere.

The prices shown below were correct at the time of going to press.

☐	7493 0576 2	**Tandia**	Bryce Courtenay	£4.99
☐	7493 0122 8	**Power of One**	Bryce Courtenay	£4.99
☐	7493 0581 9	**Daddy's Girls**	Zoe Fairbairns	£4.99
☐	7493 0942 3	**Silence of the Lambs**	Thomas Harris	£4.99
☐	7493 0530 4	**Armalite Maiden**	Jonathan Kebbe	£4.99
☐	7493 0134 1	**To Kill a Mockingbird**	Harper Lee	£3.99
☐	7493 1017 0	**War in 2020**	Ralph Peters	£4.99
☐	7493 0946 6	**Godfather**	Mario Puzo	£4.99
☐	7493 0381 6	**Loves & Journeys of Revolving Jones**	Leslie Thomas	£4.99
☐	7493 0381 6	**Rush**	Kim Wozencraft	£4.99

All these books are available at your bookshop or newsagent, or can be ordered direct from the publisher. Just tick the titles you want and fill in the form below.

Mandarin Paperbacks, Cash Sales Department, PO Box 11, Falmouth, Cornwall TR10 9EN.

Please send cheque or postal order, no currency, for purchase price quoted and allow the following for postage and packing:

UK including BFPO	£1.00 for the first book, 50p for the second and 30p for each additional book ordered to a maximum charge of £3.00.
Overseas including Eire	£2 for the first book, £1.00 for the second and 50p for each additional book thereafter.

NAME (Block letters) ....

ADDRESS..

....

☐ I enclose my remittance for ....

☐ I wish to pay by Access/Visa Card Number

Expiry Date